Readers love
SUSAN LAINE

Kissing Lessons

"I really, really enjoyed this and recommend it highly."

—The Blogger Girls

"I loved this novella. LOVED it. The well-developed characters, their friendship, the actual lessons. Completely full of smiles and sweet happiness…"

—Jessie G Books

After the Romance Novel

"…*After the Romance Novel* is a solid read with a cute cast."

—Alpha Book Club

"This was a wonderful short story about two young men coming into their own."

—Gay Book Reviews

The Disciple

"Love murder mysteries? How about romance too? Here's a whole series to gobble up! Start at the beginning and work your way through until you reach *The Disciple*. I highly recommend them all."

—Scattered Thoughts and Rogue Words

By SUSAN LAINE

Falling for Rain
Flushed
Haunted Heart
An Island in the Stars
Sage Advice
Sauna Lover
The Sensualist & the Untouched
The Witching Hour

BEFORE... AND AFTER
After the Romance Novel
Kissing Lessons

HEROES AT HEART
Yellowbelly Hero
Yellow Streak
Code Yellow
Good as Gold

ISLESHIRE CHRONICLES
Lofty Dreams of Earthbound Men
Wishing Wings

LIFTING THE VEIL
The Wolfing Way
Genie's Wish
Hunter's Moon
Monsters Under the Bed
Love of the Wild
Stealing Dragon's Heart

SECOND CHANCES
Accidental Chemistry
Twice by Chance

SENSES AND SENSATIONS
Love in Plain Sight
A Luminous Touch
Sensible Commitments
Sounds of Love
The Sweetest Scent

THE WHEEL MYSTERIES
Sparks & Drops
Devil's Own
Fireworks & Wild Cards
The Disciple
The Wheel Mysteries:
Books 1 & 2
(Print Only Anthology)

Published by DREAMSPINNER PRESS
www.dreamspinnerpress.com

An Island in the Stars

SUSAN LAINE

DREAMSPINNER
PRESS

Published by
DREAMSPINNER PRESS

5032 Capital Circle SW, Suite 2, PMB# 279, Tallahassee, FL 32305-7886 USA
www.dreamspinnerpress.com

ISBN: 978-1-63533-632-0
Digital ISBN: 978-1-63533-639-9
Library of Congress Control Number: 2017900362
Published June 2017
v. 1.0

Printed in the United States of America
∞
This paper meets the requirements of
ANSI/NISO Z39.48-1992 (Permanence of Paper).

CHAPTER 1

"HEY, YOU dropped something!"

Sam stopped trying to run from the rapid-paced footsteps behind him and skittered to a halt as he recognized the voice. He turned around and found Marcus jogging leisurely, as if he was in no hurry to catch up with Sam, down the twisting footpath that led through the woods from the bus stop.

Naturally the jock wasn't even winded or sweaty from the exertion. Not that any perspiration would have been visible beneath the winter attire anyway. It was snowing—thick, heavy flakes that floated about gently in a soft breeze. Snow gathered in Marcus's hair, giving him a dreamy halo.

Grinning, Marcus slowed to a walk. "Hey, Sam."

His breath puffed in front of him in the chilly January weather of the Rockies, and his cheeks held a rosy glow. Compared to Marcus, who managed to look hot, figuratively speaking, even in the middle of winter, Sam had clammy skin, a runny nose, and a mild cough. At least he'd done away with his glasses and sported contacts now.

"Hi, Marcus," Sam replied warily.

Being of the geek variety, he had no expectation of any mutual interest from his secret crush—who also happened to be his big brother's best friend.

You scared me, you... you jock. Sam kept that piece of unwarranted chagrin to himself.

But Marcus always seemed to have his number. "Sorry. I didn't meant to scare you—"

"You didn't. I wasn't," Sam cut in, vexed but mostly at himself.

"Here." Smiling that endearing lopsided grin of his, Marcus offered Sam the light wooly cap Sam had dropped while running from a perceived threat. When you were a freshman, gay, and a geek in college—and still seventeen 'cause you'd skipped a grade for being so smart—and you saw a jock twice your size coming toward you fast, you ran the other way. Basic common sense and an enlightened sense of self-preservation, to be precise.

Grudgingly Sam snatched the hat from Marcus and crammed it back onto his head. "Thanks," he mumbled, looking away. He whipped around and hurried down the snow-covered path through the woods on his way home from another busy day at college. Anything to get away from the guy behind him.

But Marcus walked alongside him, matching his speed. "Something wrong? Did you get an A-minus on a test? Or is your favorite library section closed for repairs?"

Sam gnawed the inside of his cheek. He was the nerdy little brother of Marcus's best friend, the invisible boy who faded into the background. Why was Marcus giving him the time of day?

"Don't you have any *other* people to pester?" Whoa, that was super mean; Sam acknowledged that to himself and cringed in instant shame and regret.

Marcus chuckled. "Ouch. Point taken. Sorry."

His apology made everything worse. Despite the bad rep of jocks in general—at least with respect to their treatment of smaller smart kids and overall bullying—Marcus was a nice guy. He always had been. He'd never bullied Sam in his life. Sam pressed his lips together, vowing not to speak. He increased his speed to get rid of his annoying shadow and the unnerving emotions trailing along with him.

To no avail. Marcus was in better shape, being an athlete and all, so Sam had zero chance of outrunning him. "You trying to ditch me, Sammy?"

"My name is Sam. Not Sammy. And to answer your question, yes, yes I am." He hated sounding so cantankerous, but if he actually talked to the guy, he feared his attraction would come through clear as day. He wasn't sure which of the possible bad outcomes would be the worst: hate, disgust, or pity.

"Well, someone's sure grouchy on this lovely, sunny winter's afternoon." Marcus's high spirits seemed unaffected. He bumped Sam's arm with his shoulder, almost toppling him over.

"Geesh, cut it out. Why are you always picking on me?" Sam didn't mean to sound all whiny, but somehow he always did in Marcus's company. Why couldn't the superhot jock leave him alone so Sam could die of embarrassment all by his lonesome in some hole in the ground?

Marcus shook his head, appearing bemused. "Why do you always treat me like you expect me to be a dick around you?"

People surprise you when they learn you have smutty thoughts about them.

Sam held back a sigh. Rationally he knew Marcus wouldn't hurt him. Marcus wasn't violent—a bully or a homophobic asshole. But fear wasn't logical. And crushes on straight guys you saw every day were even less so.

On the best of days, Sam's poor teenage head was a mass of contradictions. He did like Marcus, but he was scared of him too, mostly of Marcus's reaction should he learn how Sam felt about him. So Sam loved the guy from afar, all the while hating that he felt so strongly about someone he couldn't be with. He steered clear as best he could, though that was sometimes difficult since they went to the same college, Whitefish Lake College, which was close to their homes.

"Seriously, don't you have football practice or something?"

"It's winter, so we practice swimming and wrestling. But not today. Wrestling was cancelled. Coach is out sick." Marcus snorted. "Well, a hangover is what he's got." Then he turned to look at Sam at the exact same moment Sam chose to glance at him.

Sam quickly turned away, his cheeks on fire. It was hard not staring at Marcus. Tall, fit, and muscular in just the right proportions, Marcus was at his physical prime at the age of twenty. His black faux hawk seemed to have been designed for him especially, his blue eyes had the audacity to shine like priceless jewels at every opportunity, and his masculine, rugged good looks had a tendency to shift from grown-up raw sex appeal to sweet boyish charm, complete with dimples, with no warning.

In short, Marcus was perfect. So fucking unfair.

"Where are you off to in such a hurry?" Marcus asked in a curious tone.

Sam stopped dead in his tracks and started to say something cheeky when his wooly hat flew off and blew into the woods in the grips of a strong gust of wind. "Shit!" he cursed and ran after the damn thing.

A few yards from the path, amid tall, thick snow banks, rose a mound of what looked like dirt, rocks, and maybe a tree stump, half covered in snow and ice. On the top of the mound was a hole. And naturally, the wind threw Sam's cap right into it.

"No!" Sam cursed some more, knelt down over the hole, and peered inside.

The opening was larger than a rabbit hole. A person could have fit through. Not a very big-boned or robust person, but a regular one.

"Don't even think it." Marcus's warning came from right behind him.

"Go away! This is all your fault."

"How exactly is this my fault?"

Sam bit his tongue so hard it bled and blinked back sudden tears. Of course it wasn't Marcus's fault. He was just a nice guy who always had a smile and a kind word for Sam. He wasn't responsible for the quirks of wind or Sam's rotten luck. Nor was it Marcus's doing that Sam was hopelessly in love with his brother's best friend, the straight jock.

"I'm sorry, Marcus. It's not your fault." The confession was tough but necessary.

"It's okay, Sammy. I'm not offended." Marcus's eyes softened.

Shoving his awkward thoughts away, Sam peered down into the hole again. It was too dark to see, so he fished his tiny blue flashlight from his pocket. (It wasn't geeky to carry a flashlight, was it? You never knew when you might need one.) He aimed the light into the hole, and there, not ten feet beneath him, lay the dark green wooly hat his grandmother had knitted for him last Christmas, caught on some dead roots.

He started to lean into the hole and reach for the hat, only to be yanked back, hard.

"What the hell do you think you're doing?" Marcus asked, sounding both worried and miffed. "Don't go sticking your hand into dark holes in the ground. Are you an idiot?"

Sam pulled away. "Shut up. I'm getting my hat." He felt more than saw Marcus go stony behind him, and he lowered his voice. "I'm sorry, Marcus. I didn't mean to snap at you." He didn't want to confess any more, but his mouth did the talking for him. "The cap's a Christmas present from Grandma, and I really want it back."

Marcus knelt down next to him, smiling gently. "I get it." His big palm came to rest on Sam's shoulder, giving him chills down his spine—and heat waves in his groin. Sam resisted the urge to jerk free. Then Marcus ditched his backpack on the snowbank next to him and scanned the hole, frowning. "I think I can get it if I reach…."

His voice faded as he shoved his hand and arm down the hole. Sam instinctively put his hands on the small of Marcus's back, to hold on to him just in case. Then he drew back fast, his face flaming with embarrassment.

That's when Sam heard the crack, a dry sound of wood breaking.

And then Marcus disappeared down the hole, face-first.

"*Marcus*!" Sam screamed, scared out of his mind. He kept peering down into the dark and yelling Marcus's name until he remembered his flashlight, which he'd dropped when Marcus grabbed him. He spotted it quickly as it was still lit, and he fumbled in the snow with his mitten-covered hands, grateful it hadn't broken in the fall.

"Sam" came a distant voice from the darkness.

"Marcus? Oh my God, Marcus, are you okay?" He may have sobbed some of those words, but he didn't care as long as Marcus was all right.

"Yeah. Fine. No worse for wear. I didn't fall far." Judging from his flat tone, Marcus sounded as calm and composed as ever.

Sam was anything but. "Can you climb up? Do you need a light? Should I call 9-1-1?"

"Easy there, little chipmunk. I'm okay." Marcus's tone had gone back to amused and teasing, so he could not have been hurt, not badly anyway.

Sam hated that nickname. To him it sounded derogatory, but apparently Marcus thought it was funny. "Can you get out of there on your own?"

"Aren't you gonna ask me about your wooly cap?"

"Fuck the cap! Can you climb out or not?"

A moment of silence dragged on until… "Yeah, I think I can. As long as these roots don't break under my weight."

"You should become a vegetarian."

Marcus chuckled from down below. "Rabbit food's gonna suddenly make me sprout wings and take twenty pounds off me? Pass."

"You're a jerk, you know that?" Sam worried his lower lip to the point of bleeding so as not to cry out in panic. "If you're not out of there in two minutes flat, I'm calling the cops or firemen or somebody, dammit."

The wind rustled the trees, and snow blew on Sam. Only silence came from below. Goddammit, that guy was gonna be the death of him.

"Warm."

"What?" Sam asked, confused.

"It's warm down here."

"You want to argue the benefits of geology now? Get out of there!"

"There's a larger cavern down here—"

"Don't even think about it! Marcus?" He wasn't above begging. "Please, come up."

"Okay, okay. Hold your horses, chipmunk." Marcus's voice came closer. The sound of dry twigs breaking followed, and then a larger thud and an "Ouch."

"Marcus? What happened?"

"I… I may have accidentally broken one of the roots."

"So?" Sam was getting alarmed.

Marcus sounded at least somewhat embarrassed when he said, "And… it may have accidentally rolled on top of my leg. And it's coincidentally kinda heavy."

"Oh. My. God." Sam shook his hands in front of him, trying to calm himself. "So can you move?"

Scratching and a few thumps came, then nothing. "Nope. It's too heavy for me lift on my own, with me on my back."

"You're on your back?" Sam didn't wait for a response. "I'm coming down. Is there enough room?"

"Yeah, past the hole there's room for, like, six people. But I don't think you should."

"I can't very well leave you down there, now can I?"

Without waiting for a smartass response, Sam flipped around to sit on the edge. He turned off the flashlight and shoved it in his pocket to leave both hands free. Then he wiggled and slithered his way down the hole, feet first, cautious of his backpack, which he had forgotten to take off. He grabbed ahold of the lip while searching blindly for anything to rest his booted feet on. Desiccated roots, rocks, and dirt were enough to keep him balanced until he was able to lower himself farther and drop down fully, Finally he felt solid ground under his winter boots—and something softer against his foot.

"That's my leg, Sammy. Don't step on it." Marcus's murmur echoed in the confined space, half-amused, half-strained.

Sam took out his flashlight again and turned it on. Barren, frozen tree roots were sticking out of the hard dirt ceiling, piles of fallen autumn leaves covered much of the ground, and the space smelled of rotting leaves, chilly air, and decomposing earth, surrounding him with pungent odors.

Once his eyes had adjusted, Sam saw Marcus lying on his back in a small cavern with a big, moss-covered, heavy-looking tree trunk on top of him, almost as long as he was.

"Marcus? You okay?"

Snorting, Marcus replied, "Yeah, sure, why the hell not? Give me a hand, would you?"

Nodding frantically, Sam placed his flashlight at the branch of a nearby root so that the beam of light illuminated their efforts. Together, with Sam lifting and Marcus pushing, they got the piece of wood high enough for Marcus to roll to the side. With a loud crack, the wood landed on the rocky ground again as they let it fall.

Marcus got up, checking his limbs and torso for damage.

"Anything broken or seriously hurt?" Sam asked, very worried.

Marcus shook his head. "Scrapes and bruises. The ankle's not broken, just strained, I think. Nothing that won't heal by tomorrow."

Sam took his flashlight back, turned it off, and then stared at Marcus, steaming. "How could you be so stupid as to—"

"Hey, you're the one who wanted the hat back," Marcus retorted, bringing his hands up in a surrendering gesture.

Remorse and guilt swamped Sam. His jaw quivered as numerous conflicting feelings pushed to the surface. "I'm so sorry. I shouldn't have said anything. You could've been killed—"

"Light."

"Huh?"

"There's a light down here." Marcus sounded surprised.

Sam peered around Marcus and saw the tiny pinpoint of light in the distance. "What on earth is that?"

Marcus shrugged, but even in the low light Sam saw the curiosity in his expression. "I don't know. Fireflies? Fungus? Minerals?"

Though skeptical, Sam said, "Maybe." Then he recalled that the situation they were in, while not dire, was bad nonetheless. "Ignore it. We have to get out of here."

But Marcus was already moving toward the distant luminance, though with a slight limp. "Like I said, there is a bigger cave in here. Look, the floor's collapsed into it. The light's coming from down there somewhere."

Sam hurried to his side. "Marcus, I forbid you to even consider it."

Smiling so widely the whites of his teeth gleamed, Marcus chuckled. "Chicken?"

Sam bristled. "I am *not* chicken. But if you think for a second I'm going down there, let alone letting *you* go down there, you are certifiably insane."

"Who are you, my mother?" Marcus scoffed with an irreverent grin, stepping closer to the ragged, rubble-covered edge. "It's only a few feet down."

Sam wanted to shout. "Marcus, please. Let's go back up."

Hesitating, Marcus turned to face Sam. "Come on, Sam. I just wanna see what's down there. Could be pirate treasure." He winked mischievously. To him life was evidently an endless party full of constant surprises. Marcus was fearless. And in Sam's eyes that made him at once sexy *and* stupid.

Sam scoffed. "This is Whitefish, Montana, in 2017, not the Caribbean in the 17th century. We're smack in the middle of woods and mountains, it's midwinter, and there's snow everywhere. Plus the ocean's over six hundred miles away in the wrong direction."

"Come on, Sammy. Where's your sense of adventure?" Marcus cajoled.

"That part of me ran away the moment you fell in here headfirst, you moron. And it's Sam!"

Marcus chuckled. "God, you're cute when you're sulking."

He thinks I'm cute? Sam's heart jumped, thrilled at the outrageously impossible chance that his secret daydream might come to life. But his mouth ran the show, and he scowled. "I'm not sulking!"

Marcus's amusement grew, and he belly laughed. "If you say so."

"I do say so." Sam tried not to steam. "Now come *on*!" He almost grabbed Marcus by the arm to drag him out with him, but at the last second pulled his hand back. Touching his crush was far too dangerous.

"I'll be with you in just a sec, okay? Just wanna see what's down there." Marcus never backed down from a challenge, Sam knew, and he must see this as his own personal quest.

"And if you fall farther down somewhere—"

"Like where? The pit of hell?" Marcus snorted and rolled his eyes.

Sam was ready to scratch those same eyes out. "Stop it. That's not funny. You have no idea what's down there. You could…." He almost said it out loud. Marcus could die. But that felt like painting devils on the wall and inviting disaster to strike. Was that superstitious or just common sense? Sam couldn't decide.

"I'll be fine," Marcus said with an annoyingly smug and confident tone of voice that seemed to suggest he was fate's favorite plushy toy and no harm could ever befall him.

Before Sam could utter more refusals, Marcus had slipped over the edge and vanished from sight. Sam could still hear him moving about, rasping sounds echoing as his booted feet shifted the loose pebbles, rocks, and dirt. The beam of light through the opening they had fallen into provided the only illumination where Sam waited, and it was a gray dimness at best.

"Marcus?" Sam called out softly. A part of him worried that if he raised his voice too much, the whole mountain would come crashing down on his neck. And his slender shoulders could not handle the entire weight of the Rocky Mountains. "Marcus?" There was no answer. "*Marcus!*"

"Quit hollering, chipmunk." Marcus appeared at the drop-off and hoisted himself up to stand at the edge again. "You'll bring the whole mountain down on top of us."

Sam damn near swallowed his tongue. Great minds think alike? Or was Marcus also a mind reader now? Considering Sam's thoughts about him, he sure hoped not. "You've had a look, so now can we go?"

"Stop being such a baby," Marcus replied, quirking an eyebrow.

"Then stop being such a douchebag." To Sam's quip, Marcus responded with a louder laugh. "Take a freaking selfie already, to prove you were down here so we can—"

The ground quaked and tilted in the middle of Sam's speech. The floor slanted sharply like in an amusement park fun house. Marcus let out a yelp and fell backward, disappearing into the cavern he'd just climbed out of.

Shocked at the horrid sight, Sam flailed uselessly and comically before slipping, losing his footing, and falling face-first on the earthen floor. Unable to control his swift descent, he spun down the incline after Marcus like a bouncing ball and plummeted over the edge, falling…

CHAPTER 2

...UNTIL HE landed on something soft that grunted in pain.

"Get off me." At last Marcus sounded grumpy and pissed off.

Sam was too shocked to be vexed, even though he probably had the right at the moment. He rolled off Marcus, hoping he wouldn't continue falling. When he discovered he lay on solid ground again, his ire returned with a vengeance.

"I hate you so much right now," Sam muttered through gritted teeth.

Marcus let out an awkward chuckle. But Sam heard the underlying embarrassment and ache. "Why? I'm so lovable. A fucking lovable rogue."

"You're a royal pain in my ass, is what."

Sam stumbled onto his feet carefully to see if the roof was low enough to touch but felt nothing but air above him. The light that had enticed Marcus was too faint to pierce the dark reaches of the large cavern, like a star too distant to illuminate the vastness of the night sky. Thankfully Sam's flashlight had made the journey intact, along with his backpack.

Marcus had also gotten up. He rustled in the dark, probably swiping dirt and leaves off his clothing. Then he sighed. "Where are we?"

"In search of your fabled pirate treasure, of course." Sam snorted, but he was neither angry nor amused anymore. He was scared, and he wanted to go home. But he knew better than to confess his feelings to Marcus, who knew no fear.

"Sam? I'm sorry I got us in this mess." Marcus sounded small, alone, and almost fragile in the dark where Sam couldn't see his expression. "I'll get us out of here somehow. I promise."

Sam wanted to believe him, so he relented. "Okay."

Marcus cleared his throat. Collecting his courage, Sam surmised, so he gave Marcus a moment of peace. Then Marcus let out a long breath.

"We should probably head toward the light source we saw from above. I can see it more clearly now."

Though Sam couldn't tell if Marcus had gestured in any particular direction, he also saw the faint, cold illumination up ahead. The light was bleak and bluish. Though it wasn't inviting, Sam was well aware that direction was their best bet. His wild imagination envisioned everything from a clandestine lair of hardened criminals to a hidden underground domicile of secret government labs to dormant zombie hordes or warrens of cybernetic mole people.

"Take the lead." Sam waved at Marcus to go first.

Marcus's boots crunched on the loose stones as he proceeded toward the light at a slow but steady pace. Less certain, Sam followed on his heels, partly to stay within reach of his only available protector and partly to feel close to the guy he'd been fantasizing about for too many years now.

While Marcus focused on what lay ahead, Sam brooded about a means of escape. Screaming their heads off wouldn't help since their houses were in the mountains, several miles away from the center of town. And the footpath they'd taken wasn't in regular use by anyone other than denizens of the area. Of which there were few. Besides, who knew how far underground they were now?

"What do you see?" Sam asked in a whisper.

Marcus glanced at him over his shoulder, his face all weirded out. "Dude, why are you whispering?"

Sam flushed in embarrassment. "I don't know. Monsters?" To end the awkwardness, he shoved Marcus hard to push him back into motion. "Shut up."

Marcus rolled his eyes but thankfully stayed quiet. He continued forward.

As they slowly approached the source of the light, the dirt and rock walls of the cavern morphed into roughhewn stone and finally into what was clearly a manmade structure, smooth and flawless. A crack with no jagged edges appeared in the wall. It rose before them like a sliver of silver cut into the rock with a blade. The light spilled from the crack.

"No glowing mushrooms, then," Sam murmured, fisting the back of Marcus's coat like it was his only lifeline. "You hear anything?"

Marcus shook his head. "Nope. Just you. Shush."

For once Sam felt it was quite appropriate to follow orders, and he obeyed without question.

As they came to the opening, they realized what they were looking at was a set of automatic sliding doors jammed slightly open. Marcus waved his hand through the crack lightning-fast. Nothing happened.

"I think it's stuck."

Sam nodded, though Marcus had his back turned. "Can you wedge it open?"

Marcus faced him, shock written all over his handsome features. Sam understood. He'd even surprised himself uttering those brave words. But whatever lay ahead was manmade from the look of things, so there had to be tools, supplies, or best of all, an alternative exit. Sam blushed but said nothing.

Shrugging, Marcus turned to the doorway again and shifted from side to side, trying to discern what was beyond. "Check it out. What do you see?"

Marcus stepped aside, and Sam moved into position to peer through the crack as best he could without putting himself in harm's way.

The space appeared to be circular, a chamber of some sort. A metallic construction rose in the center, but Sam couldn't tell what it was as a dusty sheet covered it. Oval alcoves lined the walls at regular intervals, but they were shadowy, so he couldn't detect what, if anything, was in them.

Sam huffed with frustration. "I can't see. The light doesn't provide much illumination."

Marcus snorted. "Only you would use a word like illumination at a time like this." He continued, however, before Sam could retort. "I think we can squeeze through the aperture."

"Oh, so aperture is not a big word?" Sam stepped back. "I wouldn't normally agree with such a stupid plan, but it's not like we've got a lot of options here." Then he narrowed his eyes. "You go first."

Marcus grinned. "By your command, my liege."

Sam gritted his teeth, biting his tongue not to snap at the smartass remark. Marcus was, after all, doing his best to save them both. Regardless of the fact that his actions and curiosity had landed them in this underground facility to begin with.

After waving his hand in the opening a few more times, Marcus shrugged and wiggled his way through it. He could barely fit, his winter coat probably chafing and perhaps even getting a bit torn. But he managed to cram his muscular body through the crack, so Sam figured he could do the same.

Once Marcus got inside, he stood looking around without moving.

"What does it look like?" Sam asked, hoping for more information before he ventured through himself. "Does it look like someone's living there or been there in a while? See a blinking sign for an exit?"

"Hang on, chipmunk." Marcus moved off into the dim. Sam heard his boots scuffle on the stone floor, their steps cautious, but he couldn't see Marcus anymore. It took him a good while to return to the opening. "No one's here. But there are... lots of doorways. Or openings. Sort of."

Sam frowned in confusion. "What do you mean?"

Marcus gave him a chin lift. "Better see for yourself."

Sam swallowed hard. With no small amount of hesitation, he squeezed through the fissure. He didn't have any difficulties fitting, as he was far more slender than Marcus. Once inside, however, he was no longer sure they should have entered the facility at all.

A wide round light in the domed ceiling gave off a faint blue glow, not enough to show any details, only to give a rough picture of the chamber. Though the entrance had been rough-hewn rock, the walls of the room were metal, their surface gleaming polished and clear. As Sam had seen before, oval alcoves appeared every few feet, pitch-black like open mouths.

One of the recesses, however, showed an automatic door similar to the one they had used to get in. Sam gestured toward it, and Marcus nodded, moving closer. But when he reached the door, nothing happened. Sam joined him. He could see no buttons, handles, levers, or toggles.

"I think it needs power," Marcus suggested, and Sam agreed. The place seemed to be in lockdown mode or powered down. "Could we jimmy it open like the other door? Got a crowbar or two in that useful backpack of yours?" He smirked, nodding toward Sam's backpack.

Sam snorted and rolled his eyes. "Am I habitually carrying breaking-in equipment in my bag? Sorry, I must've missed that memo. I'm in college, not in the CIA."

"Okay, okay. No need to be such a smarty-pants." Marcus turned around and checked out the room, and Sam followed his example. "We could search the room for something to use, but there doesn't seem to be much here," Marcus finally said.

"There's that." Sam pointed at the object covered by a white sheet, only metal struts showing under it. The overall shape, however, suggested to Sam it was a chair.

"Okay. Let's take a look." Marcus strode toward it and yanked the sheet off, sending a dust cloud dancing in the air. Marcus coughed, and Sam waved his hand in front of his face to see what was revealed.

As they had expected, it was a metal chair. A simple hard seat with a backward tilting backrest and two armrests.

"At least there was no skeleton. Not even an alien skeleton." Sam smirked at Marcus's smile.

"Were you waiting for one?" Marcus asked, chuckling.

"I watch a lot of science fiction on TV."

Laughing harder, Marcus inched closer and placed his hand on the seat. Sam imagined it was cold and smooth to the touch. At the moment, though, he was too concerned to think about sensations.

"What the hell do you think you're doing?" Sam asked in alarm. "You better not be thinking of sitting in it."

Marcus quirked an eyebrow and gave Sam a lopsided smile. "Why not?"

Sam huffed in indignation. "Why? 'Cause you could get hurt in it. Prick your finger on a metal shard and get blood poisoning or—"

"Or what? Gangrene?" Marcus laughed, shaking his head in bemusement. "God, you can be such a worrywart."

"You have no idea what that thing is," Sam argued back angrily. "For all you know it could be an alien electric chair, or something." He was afraid. Without Marcus's help, his chances of getting out of this unharmed would be greatly reduced. "Please, Marcus. Let's just find a way out of here. I don't wanna die before I get the full college experience and graduate with honors."

"Why? You got big plans? Gonna be on *College Guys Gone Wild* or something?" His smug smirk only served to infuriate Sam more.

"Or something. And it's none of your business," Sam snapped defensively, feeling his cheeks flame with embarrassment. The mental image of hot guys with flawless six-packs writhing naked while water spouted over them turned Sam on whether he liked the reaction or not.

Marcus merely chuckled in response. Then he sat in the chair.

Nothing happened.

Marcus sported his winning smile. "See? Everything's cool."

Sam had his doubts. Worrying his bottom lip, he cautiously eased closer to see the chair for himself. Maybe nothing bad happened because this facility, or whatever it was, had no power. The doors didn't open, and the chair didn't work. Unless it was just a fancy metal seat for no real purpose.

Then there were the odd alcoves. Sam peered into them from his position in the center of the room. The chair stood on a slightly raised metal dais. Yet the vantage point yielded no answers because the sole source of light, the round lamp above them, didn't cast any beams into the darkness of the niches. Their function and purpose remained a mystery, and Sam didn't feel like exploring.

Marcus cried out suddenly and sharply, and Sam cried out as well in a purely instinctive reaction.

"Jesus Christ, what?" Sam asked, practically yelling.

Grimacing, Marcus rubbed at his palm where a bloody smear formed a circular pattern but spread no farther. "Something nicked me from the armrest."

"Oh my God, I told you to be careful." Sam fisted his hands and prayed for control. No reason to kick a man already down. "What was it? Is the chair broken or twisted or something?"

Marcus studied the armrest closely, squinting and frowning. Then he shook his head. "I don't see anything. It felt fine before. A clean surface. Don't know what happened." He inspected his palm. "Nothing serious. The wound's already closed."

"You got lucky," Sam murmured with disapproval.

Marcus let out a relieved chuckle and gave Sam a sheepish smile. "As long as I don't get gangrene."

His singsong voice was deliberately intended to drive his companion bonkers, Sam deduced, and he resisted the urge to flick his tongue at Marcus. That would have been childish. Still, Sam wanted to glare Marcus into submission so that he would never try or do anything crazy again. But he didn't want to crush the guy's spirit. So he answered with a chuckle of his own, as choked and unhappy as it sounded.

The light above flickered. A slow hum rose in the chamber, and a heavy noise like grinding gears or generators powering up echoed inside the walls and under their feet.

Then a bright flash brought up a slightly upward tilted, panoramically concaved, blue-glowing holographic console in front of Marcus, who still sat in the chair.

"What the fuck?" Marcus called out in surprise, raising his hands at his sides, his eyes wide and his mouth gaping. "What the hell just happened?"

Sam had only ever seen such elegant holographic technology in the science fiction TV shows he loved to watch. But that was fiction; this was fact. "It's a hologram." Marcus stared at him like he'd grown a second head so Sam elaborated, "Remember, like in that movie *Minority Report*? In it the main character used a holographic screen to do his job."

Marcus blinked, frowning. Then his brow cleared and he nodded. "Yeah, vaguely. It's a pretty old movie. It came out, like, fifteen years ago? Seen others since then. Like *Avengers* and *Iron Man*, for example?" He scanned the unmoving screen before him. "But that's what this is? I thought they were, you know, not real."

Sam shook his head. "No, they're real. Works in progress. There's, for example, a virtual holographic DJ console. In the movie, and others since then, they had all kinds of stuff, some already here, some still in the works—like holographic computer interfaces controlled with gestures and words. The movie sucked, but the tech was cool. Xbox Kinect uses those too."

Marcus licked his lips, looking nervous. "So… I control this interface with, like, my hands, or…?"

Sam let out a disbelieving gasp. "What? You'll do no such thing. Get out of that chair this instant. Do *not* fucking touch any of it." He stared at Marcus intently. "I swear, Marcus, if you do anything stupid… I'm leaving you here."

Marcus gave him a warm, amused glance. "No, you wouldn't. 'Cause you're a great guy, Sam." Then he grew serious. "Look, I'd love to oblige you and all, but… how am I supposed to get out of this chair without touching this… holoscreen?"

Sam hadn't thought of that. Would the holoscreen activate if any part of Marcus's body came into contact with it, or would it respond to just his hands? An epiphany hit him like a lightning bolt. He snapped his fingers. "That must be why you got pricked. Your palm. Maybe to make you, I don't know, user-friendly with the technology?"

Marcus glared at his own palm, growling angrily. "Fuck, Sam. You were right. I am fucking stupid. I should never have—"

"It's too late for that," Sam interjected. "And self-recriminations won't help us in this situation. So stop wallowing and think." He cocked his head as he examined Marcus sitting in the chair. "Could you, maybe, I don't know, slide under it?"

Marcus scoped out his position with great care. Finally he shrugged. "I don't know. Maybe." Though he appeared skeptical, he did start to wiggle downward, attempting to slide under the screen without getting caught.

Suddenly he stopped and pointed at the holoscreen. "What's IDX?"

Sam was utterly bewildered. He moved to stand next to the chair and peered at the odd futuristic console. On top of the screen were... squiggles. "Where does it say IDX?"

Marcus pointed toward the weird scribbles. "Right there."

Sam stared with his mouth open, unable to understand what was going on. "No. That's gibberish. Just random, meaningless squiggles."

Marcus looked up in bewilderment. "What? No, look." He gestured at the weird curls that were apparently writing. "See? I-D-X. It's right there."

Sam swallowed, his throat clogged with rising surreal fear. "Marcus? I swear to God, I'm not messing with you. It doesn't say that. It's just... illegible scrawls. If it's a language, it's not any language I've ever seen."

Marcus huffed out a frustrated breath, running a hand through his hair. "Okay. And I'm telling you I can read that. Whatever it is." Then he directed an amused wink at Sam. "So... at first you were sure this was a secret underground government facility testing mutants or zombies, or mutant zombies. But now you're thinking... aliens?"

Sam flushed with embarrassment. That had totally been what he'd been thinking. Alien monsters. "Shut up, and get out of that chair."

Before Marcus could comply, the holographic screen flashed. Then an image appeared on it. Though without colors, the scene looked serene and lovely, portraying a lush meadow in the middle of snow-topped mountains. Flowers bloomed on the field where grass swayed gently in the wind, white billowy clouds floating high in the blue skies above.

"What did you do? What is that?" Sam asked, half-confused, half-alarmed.

Marcus shrugged. "I didn't do anything. Looks nice, though." He let out a little chuckle of surprise. "Above it reads Meadows of Seranis."

Sam had no idea what Marcus meant. Above the image he saw nothing but more of the squiggles that meant nothing to him. Clearly the pinprick from the chair's armrest had made Marcus compatible with the chamber's technology. That absolutely worried Sam to no end.

A second flash of light emerged, and a new image replaced the first. This one depicted a windy desert with tall dunes of ice-blue sands, clouds of the sand flying about on the breeze. Above them, a golden sky shone brilliant and bright.

"What does it say now?" Sam asked, observing the fluid change in the written text.

"Dunes of Domar," Marcus supplied, glancing at Sam with curiosity and concern. "Do those place names mean anything to you? Geography isn't exactly my strong suit."

Sam shook his head fiercely, his worst fears seemingly confirmed. "No. Those words are *not* from this planet."

Marcus regarded him doubtfully. "I find that hard to believe. Come on, Sam. You only speak three languages, same as me: English, French, and teen. You couldn't possibly know every place on earth, let alone be able to recognize someplace as being alien or whatever. Get real."

Sam was ready to continue arguing his point, even though after what Marcus had said he was no longer 100 percent certain of the accuracy of his declaration. But he didn't get the chance.

A blue flash later, another novel image arose on the holographic screen. A lone tropical island rose from a cyan-hued ocean, beautiful sunlight illuminating a green mountaintop, gray rocks, and golden beaches. Palm trees and tall ferns swayed in the wind, and colorful creatures flew about, too fast to make out any details.

"Now it says Isle of Suryan," Marcus said, pointing at the image.

Unexpectedly his hand jolted forward, as though it had a mind of its own, and slapped against the holoscreen image.

A blue oval light lit up above one of the alcoves on the wall.

"Holy shit." Marcus sounded and looked stunned, eyes wide. "I swear I didn't mean to do that. My hand just—"

The holographic screen glowed briefly and then died down and vanished from sight.

Marcus jumped up from the chair as though it were on fire. "Jesus fucking Christ, I'm so glad to be out of that thing." Then he faced the dark recess in the wall, squinting as he tried to make out whatever might be there. "What just happened?" He gestured vaguely toward the oval opening. "Did I do that?"

Sam suppressed the urge to roll his eyes and mutter "Duh."

"Is that the way out?" Marcus asked, sounding hopeful.

Sam hesitated. "I… I don't think so."

But Marcus moved forward, his gaze glued to the niche as though mesmerized by the sight. Sam hurried over to him, caught his arm in a lame attempt to stop him, and pulled back. But Marcus was bigger and stronger.

"Look," Marcus said, his voice odd—hollow and void. "I see... swirls of stars. Can you see them? So beautiful...."

Sam saw nothing but blackness. He yanked on Marcus's arm again but was dragged after him into the recess. "Marcus, I don't know what weirdness has got ahold of you, but please fight it."

"Come on, Sam," Marcus cajoled. "I just wanna see...."

Marcus reached into the darkness of the niche. Blackness swallowed them. Sam couldn't see or hear anything. Dizziness swamped his consciousness, causing him to stumble. Marcus took him in his arms, steadying him.

"Sam, you okay?" Marcus sounded troubled and more like himself again.

A dim beam of light appeared. The chamber looked... different.

The metallic walls were grayish-green from moss and brown from rust, not to mention dirty all over. Long vines and colorful flowers grew within jagged cracks in the walls. The floor was covered in mud, dirt, dead palm leaves, and piles of sand and gravel. An uncovered chair, similar to the one in the other chamber, stood in the center but was twisted to the side, one armrest broken and dangling from a tangle of wires, the whole base bent and releasing an occasional spark shower. Obviously it was damaged beyond repair, but how long had it been that way? Sam had no clue. If this was the same room as before, surely this couldn't have happened in the span of a second or two they'd felt dizzy and confused?

Where the jammed double doors into the chamber had been now rose a stone staircase. The light came from that same direction.

"God, it's hot in here." Marcus speaking out of the blue startled Sam. He smiled softly and added, "I must be half-brained, leading us into trouble again. Sorry."

Sam didn't respond. He'd already observed the significant rise in temperature, the air now practically sweltering and forcing him to open his winter coat. He was listening to a loud cacophony of birds singing, but not any birdsong he'd ever heard.

In the dazzling heat, Sam had to shuck off his winter coat altogether. He tied the thing around his waist, observing out of the corner of his eye that Marcus was doing the same. Then he checked the straps of his backpack; they were fine.

This time it was Sam who began to walk as if in a daze toward the steps, Marcus on his heels.

Immediately he stopped and stared at his feet, flummoxed. "Why do I suddenly feel twenty pounds lighter?"

Marcus came to stand next to him. With a frown, he jumped up and down a few times. His head practically hit the ceiling each time. "Whoa. Trippy."

Sam swallowed. He refused to voice out loud the disturbing thought rattling inside his head. Whatever this place was, gravity was lower here than back home. That was what made them light on their feet, as if they'd lost over a quarter of their weight in an instant. *Where are we?*

They resumed going up the stairs, each step lighter than the last. As a result, the steep ascent was the easiest climb of their lives.

Chips and flakes had broken off the steps, and twisting tree roots spread down along them and pushed through the compact earth-and-stone slabs of the stairs and walls. Flowers and grass had risen from every hole to show how nature won out in the end. As Sam walked up, soil crunched beneath the soles of his boots. The beam of light grew wider and brighter, until he had to shield his eyes from the shine.

He stopped dead on a stone landing as he emerged from the tunnel into the sunlight outside. Sam blinked because his eyes had to be playing tricks on him.

The terrace stood on a steep hillside, covered by a dense tropical jungle. Far below an ocean spread as far as the eye could see. Turquoise waters glittered in the light of the rising sun, and the waves slowly turned to orange and yellow on the distant horizon. Gigantic palm-like trees, ferns, bromeliads, and ginkgos, all of them with blue-and-green leaves, rose from the verdant, tangled thickets of lush vegetation, swinging gently in the warm breeze carrying salty air their way. Small, colorful creatures flew and flitted about, singing and shrieking, and bushes below rustled from the movements of animals they could not see.

Sam had never been outside the Rockies. He'd seen jungles only in books, in movies, and on the internet. The sight would have felt like an incredibly vivid dream or hallucination—if it weren't for the assault on all his senses.

The unending mix of noises coming from creatures all around them. The hot, wet air seeping under his clothes and onto his skin until he wanted to rip all his clothes off. The nauseatingly sweet scents of wild tropical flowers mingling with the salty fresh air blowing in from the ocean and the pungent earthy odors of the jungle. Sam was no longer sure if he wanted to inhale deeply or hold his breath.

"My God, Marcus, where are we?" Sam gasped, on the verge of a panic attack.

When he got no reply, Sam turned to Marcus, only to find him staring high up in the opposite direction, eyes wide with shock. Baffled, Sam followed his gaze—and realized they were in deep trouble.

The flat, large peak of the jungle mountain appeared close, a mere short, steep flight of stairs away. But above the island and the ocean, far beyond the dark night sky, spread a heavenly vision Sam's mind couldn't comprehend.

A massive green gas giant blocked out at least a quarter of the sky, its dust-and-rubble rings expanding the width by another third. A colorful expanse of nebulas and a multitude of bright, blinking stars gave way to four moons orbiting the planet. Beyond them, in the distance, shone an unfamiliar, blue-hued galactic belt in all its glory.

Sam felt dizzy. Then he passed out.

CHAPTER 3

"SAM? SAM, please wake up. Come on now. Speak to me, bae."

As he slowly came to, Sam initially only heard Marcus, whose cracked voice sounded shrill, pleading, and urgent, although his words barely registered. When he finally managed to pry his eyes open and blink to dispel the haze, the first thing he saw was a small furry face of brown and gold.

"Huh?" Sam blinked some more, and the peculiar face became clearer.

The little critter cocked its head side to side like a primate. It had brown fur and orange-colored cheeks, big floppy ears, and a long tail swishing behind it—and gem-hued wings spreading on its back.

"Holy shit," Sam murmured in astonishment. Perhaps the fluttering and dots of colors in the jungle hadn't been from birds but these animals. "Is that a…?"

"A flying monkey? Yeah. Sort of. The jungle seems to be teeming with them." Marcus sounded more levelheaded again, as though he'd regained his cool composure at the sight of Sam's recovery. "I nicknamed them… ozzies."

At that Sam just had to laugh out loud or he'd suffer a hysterical nervous breakdown. References to the *Wizard of Oz* movie seemed like such a gay thing. Then again, even straight guys knew about flying monkeys and green-faced witches. Although in actuality the animal resembled a lemur more than a monkey.

The ozzie started, jumped farther back from the stone steps to a tree branch, and flew away, feathery wings flapping—and sparking with some kind of electric discharge. The jungle, which had been relatively quiet, now echoed with chirping. It sounded like a lively cocktail party, with high-pitched squeaks and hollers that could only be alarms, followed by a concert of roars, shrieks, clicks, yaps, squawks, and even long, elegant melodies like birdsongs.

Whether these animals considered Sam and Marcus to be threats wasn't easy to tell with the indistinct noise. At least they weren't attacked by troops of ozzies.

And knowing what he knew, Sam was glad the creatures didn't appear as huge as he expected them to. Lower gravity meant taller flora and bigger fauna.

"Congratulations," Sam said to Marcus as he rose to his feet with Marcus's aid, chuckling. "Wow, Marcus. You just named your first alien animal species. I think you can officially call yourself an exobiologist now."

Marcus huffed out an indignant breath. "Very funny. I was fucking worried about you. Stop joking." He still held on to Sam's arm and the small of his back, seeming unwilling to let him go anytime soon. "Was it the heat or the shock?"

Sam noticed that Marcus had removed Sam's backpack and winter coat and laid them on the closest step. He did feel better without the heavy, hot garment tied around his waist and the weight of the backpack on his shoulders, so he nodded. "Both, I think. Or maybe too much oxygen…? I can't remember what it's called. Hyper… oxygenation…? No, that's not it. Regardless, disorientation is one of the symptoms of exposure to increased oxygen levels, which I think there are here. Not awfully high but… definitely there. Anyway… I'm sorry. I didn't mean to scare you."

Marcus nodded grimly. "It doesn't matter. Let's just get the hell out of here, okay?" He escorted Sam toward the stairs leading down to the underground chamber, pausing only long enough for Sam to grab his coat and put his backpack on.

They descended back into the dark, dirty, ruined chamber where the air was cooler but the smells of earth and vegetation grew in strength. Sam staggered on shaky legs, but thankfully Marcus never released his hold on him, which made Sam feel safe and excited at the same time.

With determination Marcus led them to the black recess of what they now knew to be a portal of some kind. Marcus stretched his hand forth to feel his way around as he stepped into the niche.

"Ouch!" he gasped, backing out fast and running into Sam in the process. They both stumbled backward, nearly falling and colliding with the floor.

"What the hell?" Sam muttered, rubbing his nose where it had made painful contact with Marcus's shoulder blade. "What's wrong?"

"I… I couldn't pass through. There's nothing in there but a stone wall."

"What?" Frustrated, Sam pushed Marcus aside, stepped into the opening—and slapped his palm against a cool, roughhewn stone wall.

Whatever doorway, portal, or passageway had been there for them to use was long gone. "Why isn't it...?"

His voice faded as he felt along the crude surface, moving up, down, and sideways. No opening appeared. He made quick work of the rest of the niches along the circular chamber's walls. A few had their back walls collapsed into rubble, but the rest were the same as the first— nothing but impenetrable stone walls.

"Fuck!" Marcus cursed behind Sam, and Sam heard him stomp or kick the stone floor or wall.

Sam retreated to the center of the chamber and studied the framework of the recess, which was made of the same metal as the other, cleaner chamber from before. Nothing seemed out of place. Except... no blue light glimmered in the oval lamp above the opening. A blue beam had appeared in the light fixture above the alcove back in the other chamber on Earth when Marcus had pressed his hand on the holographic screen. Now there was nothing.

"There's no light," he said, pointing at the unlit horizontal oval shape above the portal. "I... I think... we don't have power. Whatever makes this place, this chamber, these openings work—electricity, alien energy, or damn magic—this place doesn't have it."

Marcus drew in a sharp breath. "But... that means... we're stuck here."

Sam let out a sigh so deep and profoundly desperate that he actually slumped with the force of the emotion. "That about sums it up." Quickly he straightened up and recollected himself, saying with resolution, "Unless we find a way to fire this thing up."

Marcus inched closer, his voice filled with a trace of hope. "You really think we can?"

"It's either that or we buy ourselves beach property on this deserted coastline." He gave Marcus a scathing glance over his shoulder, lifting his chin resolutely. "I don't know about you but I'm not ready to admit defeat or the prospect that we'll never see home again."

Marcus offered him a shaky smile. "Neither am I. We'll whip this rust bucket back into shape and find a way back home. I promise."

Even though Sam was reluctant to believe Marcus's assurances, he nodded in response. "We should take stock of our new surroundings since we're going to be here awhile. At the very least we'll need to find shelter, water, and food. The five protein bars and one bottle of water in my backpack won't last indefinitely. And... we need to figure out our place in the food chain. Because I seriously doubt those ozzies are the only animals around here."

They slouched up the stairs to the landing where they had stopped before, temporarily resigned to their stranded fate. The odd and confounding view hadn't changed. A bright sun had risen over the horizon, casting its yellow glow over their new stomping grounds.

Marcus shook his head in bewilderment and said, "My God, we're on an alien planet, Sam. I still can't wrap my brain around it."

"Let's focus on the positive, shall we?" Sam looked around. "Alien planet—or moon, actually, since it seems to be orbiting another planet—there's air we can breathe. The atmosphere seems to be oxygen-nitrogen, like Earth, and there's a yellow star like our sun to light our way, and we're surrounded by an environment that should have abundant sources of nutrition. We can only hope there's an easily accessible source of drinkable water too."

Frowning, Marcus nodded toward the ocean. "Are all oceans salty?"

Sam had to admit he didn't know the answer. "The salt in Earth's oceans comes from land as slightly acidic rainwater breaks down the rocks, creating ions, which are—"

"Electrically charged atomic particles. Yes, I know." Marcus gave him an admonishing glare but his smile never wavered. "And in oceans, ion concentrations build up over time, forming chloride and sodium. I took advanced chemistry, Sam. I know how salt forms in *our* oceans. What about the oceans *here*?"

Sam blushed with embarrassment. He'd assumed jocks like Marcus didn't have either the time or the inclination to take advanced anything. But that was a gross generalization, not true of Marcus at all, which Sam well knew. Marcus had a talent for math and physics, which Sam knew from having overheard (or eavesdropped on) many a conversation between Marcus and Simon over the years. Then he realized he didn't even know what Marcus's college major was....

"I haven't a clue," Sam admitted finally. "Same process?"

Marcus regarded the ocean with a skeptic eye. "Don't know about you, but I'm less than enthusiastic about putting anything in my mouth while we're here. Drinking seawater, even to test a theory, falls into that category."

Sam chuckled at that, surprising even himself. "Let's cross that bridge if and when we get there. For now, we should try to see where we are, if there's anything we could use to power up the machine, and if… if there's anyone here."

Marcus swiveled around to face him, eyes wide. "You mean like… aliens?"

"I doubt H.R. Giger ever set one foot on this planet," Sam replied, making a jest of it. They were in dire straits, but humor could uplift their mood and overall morale. Though Sam often found Marcus's banter annoying, now a positive attitude was a valuable commodity.

Marcus actually chuckled at the joke. "That's a relief. Okay, seriously now. You really think some… thing or someone could actually be here?"

Sam hesitated before replying warily, "I think tropical climes are better for permanent settlements than frozen tundras. Beyond that… your guess is as good as mine." He whooshed out a breath. "Best to have a look around before jumping to conclusions. Though I doubt there are any sentient aliens living here, considering the wrecked state of that chamber."

Sam tucked his coat inside his already full backpack as best he could and then threw the bag over his shoulders. Marcus had abandoned his backpack in the woods by the tree stump where they'd fallen in. Too bad Marcus didn't have it with him, though it was unlikely he had anything more useful in it than what Sam had in his. After all, they'd planned for a day of classes, not a trek to an alien planet. As a result, they had scarce resources.

The stone deck where they stood, where the stairs from the underground chamber came out, seemed to be a halfway point, as the stairway continued up and down the mountainside. As before, Sam noted that the slabs were cracked, blades of grass and tree roots twisting their way to light. Chips and pebbles had broken off, and a few had moss growing on them.

Obviously no one had maintained the stairs or the underground chamber in ages.

Marcus pointed downhill and uphill. "These stairs go up and down. If we go up, we'll have a better vantage point to determine what kind of place this is. You agree?"

Sam nodded. The idea had merit. He'd always known Marcus was smarter than the stereotypical jock. Otherwise Sam wouldn't have been so into him, as he wasn't attracted to fools. Not that all jocks were idiots by definition. After all, in order to play sports they needed to maintain a decent grade point average. But Sam liked big brains more than big brawn—and Marcus had both. Though he was a bit reckless for his own good.

The upward-trending staircase rose in a straight line. Soil, moss, roots, grass, and gravel made travel precarious, and there were no railings to aid in the steep climb. Sam stumbled every couple of steps, but Marcus kept him steady with a hand on the small of his back. His companionship made the trip immensely better, and Sam felt relieved he didn't have to be trapped on this alien planet alone. Or rather, moon. Sam wasn't normally afraid of the dark or being by himself, but surely an alien environment fell into the exception category.

Though it was far from quiet, Sam needed some human sounds. "On heavenly bodies that are smaller than Earth, like planets, moons, and planetoids, the atmosphere will be dense, with heavy cloud cover and unpredictable weather patterns. However, the gravity's our main concern here because lower gravity means not only weakness in our muscles but bigger plants and animals. So we need to be careful."

"Check." Perhaps out of impatience or curiosity, Marcus sidestepped Sam to walk ahead of him. Sam was fine with that. It reassured him to have a well-built jock in front of him to block any threats that might arise.

"The height record for tropical trees on Earth is less than ninety meters. Here trees are way taller. The vegetation and atmosphere resemble the Mesozoic Era, with giant plants and humid heat and…. No, maybe not. That period also had high levels of carbon dioxide in the air, so it's not really comparable. Hmm…."

Marcus chuckled. "Check two."

"The air seems to be a bit more oxygen-rich than Earth, even though it smells like an oxygen-nitrogen atmosphere. There can be symptoms we need to look out for, like dizziness, vision problems, difficulty in breathing, that sort of thing. Too much oxygen is toxic in the long run."

"Check three." Marcus glanced at him over his shoulder. "How do you know all this?"

Sam's aspirations covered several areas of interest, and he hoped one day to become an archaeologist, an astrophysicist, or one of those scientists studying exoplanets. He was smart enough to have skipped a grade, graduated high school a year early, and gotten into college at the age of seventeen. He loved books, reading, learning, studying, and using big words with big ideas. But he didn't tell any of that to Marcus. He didn't think he could handle the ridicule, though it was unlikely Marcus would ever be so callous or cruel.

But Sam didn't know for sure, so he kept his answer short. "I like to read, is all."

Their perception of the flatness of the mountaintop proved to be correct as they reached the last few steps. The top of the mountain was flat and mostly bare, obviously deliberately cleared at some point, although the jungle was making inroads in the form of brushes, vines, and undergrowth. A faint cool breeze blew across the plateau. It picked up speed, causing their clothes to billow in the wind.

They encountered what appeared to be an old street made of square stone slabs. The road seemed to serve no purpose, and to their left it vanished into the jungle at the edge of the flat terrain. If there once had been something there, it was gone now.

At the right end of the narrow street, however, stood a formidable structure, though it was ancient and mostly in ruins. Constructed of amber-hued stone, the monument had four stylized towers, one in each of the four corners. Instead of a straight sugarcane shape, the towers appeared conical, like closed flower buds.

And from each of them a blue beam of light rose straight up toward the sky, the glow faint but detectable even in the increasing sunlight. The source of the beams wasn't apparent.

"Could that place be harnessing some kind of energy?" Marcus's optimism was endearing.

Sam smiled, and positivity bloomed inside him. "We can always hope."

They walked closer warily, keeping their eyes on both the remarkable building and the surrounding area. No animals stirred in the underbrush, but the foliage of the palm trees, giant ferns, flourishing tamaracks, and other leafy plants encircling and encroaching on the plateau rustled with a bevy of ozzies, their color-rich feathers vibrant amid the greenery. They seemed intrigued by the newcomers, rarely taking their eyes off Sam and Marcus.

Sam wasn't naïve enough to believe these small furry and feathery creatures would be the only fauna around. Where there were harmless animals, there would always be predators. Or more to the point, herbivores, carnivores, and scavengers. So he skimmed the jungle with his gaze constantly.

"Shit." Marcus stopped dead. "We're on a freaking island."

Sam had been so busy watching the stirring of every leaf and the approaching shadows of an otherworldly structure that he'd neglected to take note of their wider surroundings. Now he looked up and saw what Marcus had pointed out.

The balmy, cyan-hued ocean encircled the small island in all directions, and from the flattened summit unfolded a view to all compass points. The peak seemed to have been cleared as the only habitable area, and the rainforest-covered bluffs fell all the way to the beaches below. Now that the two of them had briefly ceased moving and talking, Sam could hear a rush of water that sounded promising. Then again, the constant drizzle all around proved without a shadow of a doubt that they were in a rainforest. Every warm drop sliding down his spine had the same effect, reminding him their new surroundings were far from the wintry mountains of home.

"Fuck." Marcus huffed angrily, whirling about with hands on his hips, kicking up dirt and pebbles. "No other islands in sight. And on this stupid rock, nothing but an abandoned ruin."

Sam could relate to his frustration. Not that he'd been eager to confront alien life-forms but the inhabitants of the island might have been able to help them turn on the traveling machine or restore power to it. He scanned the horizon, going full circle. The mountainous jungle island seemed to have risen out of the ocean alone, without any other land around. Scattered lone islands weren't uncommon on Earth, but Sam had prayed for an exception here.

"No such luck. This must be the Isle of Suryan mentioned on the holoscreen." Sam glanced over his shoulder. The sun had risen higher, the sky now more turquoise and aquamarine. "We have no idea how long days here last, so let's make good use of the present sunlight. That building is the sole structure here, so let's check it out. If even parts of the roof and walls are intact, it'll provide adequate shelter."

They resumed their trek toward the construction. As they got closer, Sam detected unusual symbols carved over the arched entrance. It didn't resemble the language they'd seen on the holoscreen. That suggested the builders of this site might not have been the same as those who had created the chamber with the portals. Or they might have had several languages on their world, same as humans on Earth. But at this point it was all pure conjecture.

"Marcus, can you read that?" Sam asked, pointing at the text full of elaborate curls and curves. Though he didn't know what it said, he recognized writing when he saw it.

Marcus cocked his head, but his expression was more puzzled than focused. "Yeah, I can. But... it's weird. The last word keeps... I don't know, changing." He shook his head then, perhaps to clear the cobwebs of confusion. "Anyway, it says Temple of Anissa." Then he harrumphed loudly. "But it also says... Temple of Love."

Sam frowned, switching his gaze between the writing and Marcus. "Well, maybe... what if the name belongs to a... a god or a goddess of love? Like Aphrodite or Venus or something."

Marcus's brow smoothed, and he nodded, shrugging. "Sure, okay. Works for me."

Sam looked back at the straight path they'd walked along, the other end disappearing into the lush green. "If this place is a temple, then the path we took could be a kind of ceremonial street. Many cultures have them."

Marcus chuckled, casting Sam an odd look somewhere between amused and bewildered. "How'd you come to know so much about stuff like this?"

Sam frowned, getting defensive. "I'm a scientist."

Marcus quirked an eyebrow. "You're a freshman in college."

Sam blushed fiercely. "I mean, I... I'm *going to be* a scientist."

Marcus wrinkled his brow while continuing to smile lopsidedly. "Really? I thought you wanted to be a—uh, never mind." He turned back to the imposing edifice, leaving Sam teeming with questions and curiosity. But the timing was wrong for a heart-to-heart. It was far more important to establish their bearings.

The Temple of Love burned golden now that the sun illuminated the otherwise dark amber stone. The structure dominated the landscape of the mountain island.

Sam guessed that the absence of other structures meant that beyond this ancient place of worship, the island served no other purpose. Perhaps the deities or spirits once venerated in the temple had been lost over time, the religion forgotten and the place too as a result. The other possibility was that the creators of this place had died off, maybe in some widespread cataclysm or an extinction level event.

For some reason Sam found both options kind of sad. Maybe the aliens had left the star system instead? That was a more positive notion.

The dense atmosphere, for example, could've provided the aliens a means of gathering hydrogen from water vapor to fuel the engines of spaceships and thus leave the confines of their world? Maybe....

Man, he read too much science fiction.

Sam also found it kind of curious that the temple's entrance didn't face the direction of the rising sun. Maybe in this world sun and love weren't paired in terms of worship the way fire and passion were on Earth. But since the original builders didn't seem to be around anymore, Sam's theories were all guesswork.

Even from the outside, Sam was able to tell that beyond the threshold was the main hall and that it appeared to have a square floor plan. Nonetheless, his attention quickly veered off to the external stone walls full of intricately carved reliefs.

And they were all erotic in nature.

"Holy shit," Marcus murmured at his side. Sam's cheeks flamed, thinking Marcus had observed Sam eyeing the artwork. But Marcus soon proved him wrong. "What are those things? Sam, did you see them? They're vaguely human but... not."

At first Sam had only noticed the figures entwined, but now he realized that the beings were not human. They had two arms and two legs—but they also had long, lizardlike tails, twisted horns on the sides and tops of their bald heads, and they emanated a luminescent glow. An aura seemed to surround their bodies, but the color remained indeterminate thanks to the stone's single hue.

"What the heck are they?" Marcus asked in awe. He chuckled loudly out of the blue. "Fuck, that's not even the main thing. I mean, Sam, you and I are now the only ones who know that aliens are real. They're freaking real!"

Sam couldn't breathe. His chest compressed, feeling two sizes too small. They were on an alien moon, yes, but learning about intelligent life-forms that could build structures surviving the ages? That was a whole other ball game.

"When we get back home, this discovery will change the world." Marcus continued to speak, unaware of Sam's state of imminent collapse. "You and me, Sam, we'll go down in history. The great explorers of unknown alien worlds."

That comment brought Sam back from the edge. He rolled his eyes. "Since you've got our whole future figured out, pray tell what means of returning home have you got in your back pocket?"

Marcus faced Sam, blinked hard in confusion, and then his cheeks turned red as he cleared his throat bashfully. "Oh. Right, yeah. Sorry." Hot dayum, but Marcus looked sexy when all sheepish and flushed. Sam couldn't take his eyes off the gorgeous guy. Then Marcus snapped out of his funk and apparently picked up on the sensuality of the images portrayed on the temple walls. "Jesus, are they…?"

"Well, according to your weird universal translator, this is supposed to be the Temple of Love after all." Sam coughed awkwardly. He didn't have a problem with sexual imagery. But he did consider seeing them in the company of his crush, as unrequited as the feeling was, awkward and unpleasant. "In our own human history, lots of societies combined shrines of love deities with brothels, and they shared the same kind of taste in explicit art."

Marcus snorted. "How convenient." Sam had to admit he was pleasantly surprised by Marcus's annoyed tone. His attitude toward prostitution, even of the hypothetical variety, made him more attractive in Sam's eyes. Sam realized he not only liked Marcus but admired and respected him.

Marcus whistled low. "Wow, those pictures are pretty shocking."

Sam stepped closer to one of the walls. He told himself the act was scientific curiosity. And surely it was just common sense to determine what kinds of life-forms might appear out of the blue. It wasn't arousal, no sirree.

Despite their tails, horns, spine spikes, and ethereal glow, the beings had features in common with humans; they were bipedal and had hands with opposable thumbs. And they also seemed to have at least two differing genders, one with external genitalia just like human males. Or maybe they weren't two genders, Sam mused, not knowing for certain. Perhaps there were more than two. Who knew? Nonetheless, he dubbed the lean beings with a pretty obvious penis as males and the curvaceous and graceful ones without a penis as females.

Marcus pointed at the reliefs. "Looks like these lizard-folk have men and women too, same as us."

Sam glared at him. "Lizard-folk? I'm surprised you aren't calling them… dino-people, or something equally ridiculous. Just because they have a tail, that doesn't make them reptilians. I mean, they don't have scales or armor or anything."

Marcus gave him a wicked grin and shameless wink. "I thought it sounded cool 'cause then they would match. You know, ozzies and lizzies."

Sam was stunned, and his mouth hung open before he snapped it closed. "Okay, that's it. You're not allowed to name anything else on this moon."

Marcus pouted playfully. "Aww, you booted me off the scientific naming board? I'm officially offended and hurt."

Sam blew out a breath and prayed for patience. Marcus was clearly baiting him, so he refused to be enticed into a childish game. But his trick did boost Sam's spirits, bringing a touch of normality to their unusual situation.

"You're such an ass," he grumbled quietly, not really meaning it.

For a while they both studied the sculpted and carved murals and reliefs on the walls. There wasn't an inch left unused. Numerous forms of lovemaking were depicted, ranging from oral to penetration and beyond.

In some, Sam observed the... fine, lizzies (*Damn you, Marcus!*) having sex with other creatures quite unlike them. Though they walked on two (apparently hoofed) legs they seemed to be dissimilar in other ways. They had tiny noses that reminded Sam of koala bears, big fluffy ears like bunnies, and striations on their furry legs. Sam surmised the lines might have differentiated colors in the fur, kind of like the dark and pale on the okapi or the zebra.

Judging from their expressions, the lizzies seemed conscious, aware, and intelligent, while the other beings... didn't.

"Are they having sex with... animals?" Marcus asked right then, startling Sam out of his own similar ponderings. It was eerie how similar their thought patterns and assimilation of news seemed to be. Perhaps they were viewing the same pictures at the exact same time.

"In ancient times, erotic imagery wasn't as censored as it became later and still is today," Sam replied slowly, not sure anymore what he was seeing. "The Catholic church, for example, destroyed and defaced a lot of irreplaceable erotic art in their time. There's this infamous sculpture—"

"This satyr-looking dude fucking a goat or a lamb, right?" Marcus snorted. "I kind of remember seeing a picture of it in a book or on the internet somewhere. Bestiality at its finest."

Sam stared at the temple walls hard to avoid looking directly at his companion. "Yeah. That one. Religious folk and conservatives purposely ignore the fact that those images don't mean anything like that happened in real life. I mean, satyrs don't exist, so obviously they never had sex with lambs or goats or whatever. And if individual men did fuck animals… well, that was their business. And maybe Greenpeace's or PETA's or some other animal protection agency's. It's art. Titillating, sure, but just art. And art should never be censored."

"The people who lived or worshiped here sure didn't practice censorship." Marcus's tone was level and composed.

Like Sam, he'd probably seen far more graphic things online. Unlike Sam, however, Marcus wasn't in the company of someone he had feelings for, so the sexual images probably didn't faze or trouble him as much as they bothered Sam. It was sort of tough not thinking about sex with Marcus while seeing these sensual illustrations.

"If this place is like the temples of love back home—on Earth, I mean—then the images were used both as stimulating sights and as a sort of formal sex education. Temples depicting sexual scenes in India, for example, were like sex manuals in 3D. The buildings complemented books such as the *Kama Sutra*."

Sam remembered reading the *Kama Sutra*. It illustrated proper sexual and social behavior in pictures. The book was also a guide to love, marriage, and family. Sam couldn't help but wish that their own schooling was far less repressed and judgmental, less concerned about religious views on sex and more focused on giving teenagers an accurate and factual sexual education.

Perhaps then Sam might have learned how to properly approach Marcus a long time ago, how two men were with each other, and how to give a man pleasure.

Of course, Marcus wasn't gay, so the matter was moot anyway.

"Yeah, I can kinda see it now." Marcus tilted his head and seemed to examine the reliefs with a more discerning eye. "It's amazing. All these sculptures are really well preserved. They must have been built to last. Too bad this place is abandoned. All these beautiful things forgotten, buried in time."

As the sun rose higher, the amber stone shone a burnished gold. The elaborate carvings and etchings formed lively plays of light and shadow, bringing the images to life in a magical way. The depictions were of strong, virile males and beautiful, voluptuous females, both young and old, individuals and couples, what appeared to be equivalent of gays and lesbians and straights, threesomes and foursomes and big orgies, and far too many sexual positions to count. And the aliens were remarkably limber too.

Not all the reliefs were fully intact, though. Some were chipped, flaked, or missing bits and pieces here and there. If they'd once been painted or decorated, nature and weather had ravaged them, leaving no trace of their full former glory.

"Let's check out the inside," Sam suggested, shuddering. He felt eyes on the back of his head, but upon glancing over his shoulder, he couldn't see anyone or anything.

Marcus nodded his wordless agreement. Together they entered the temple proper.

CHAPTER 4

BEYOND THE arched vestibule, a grand main hall opened before them. Judging from the size of the space, it had been the focal point of religious life. Although, Sam pondered, perhaps the aliens were more advanced and didn't view sex through the distorted lenses of religion and priesthood. That undoubtedly would simplify things immensely.

The square floor plan centered on a dais with a rectangular altar. Sam noted that the shrine resembled a bed. Since this was a temple of love, it wasn't outrageous to imagine that the altar had been used for sex rites. It wasn't a leap because the notion made sense.

"Huh. These aliens must have enjoyed the Great Rite."

Sam whipped his head around to see Marcus staring at the platform and the altar upon it, a lopsided smile dangling on his lips. Sam couldn't believe what his ears were telling him.

"What do you know about that?" Sam asked, frowning in bafflement.

Marcus merely chuckled enigmatically and shrugged. A hot tingling low in his body made Sam even more nervous, so he switched his attention back to his surroundings.

Apart from the central shrine, there wasn't much of anything in the hall. The walls and ceiling were adorned with ornate carvings similar to those on the outside walls. No furniture in sight, if any had ever been there. Seemed that the altar was all that remained, and it had survived because it was made of stone.

Regularly spaced square windows in the back and side walls brought light inside but had no glass or shutters, leaving the place open to the elements. Piles of fallen leaves, dry roots, and pollen had stacked in the corners, probably blown there by the wind. Vines grew on the walls, roots had spread across the stone floor, and the scent of various blossoms was sugary sweet, thick, and heavy in the hall.

Above them, the domed ceiling had a large, round opening, again without glass, wood, or anything to shield them from the sky and its whims. Sam pointed at the skylight.

"That's just like the one in the Pantheon in Rome. It's called an oculus."

Marcus harrumphed. "Like the Oculus Rift?"

Sam sighed impatiently. "Why do you act dumber than you are?"

Marcus gave him an odd impassive look. "Maybe I'm not as smart as you."

Sam hated that he got irritated, but he couldn't help himself. Words spilled out of their own volition. "That is not true. You're way smart. It's like being a jock is a role you play, and even now, when it's just us here, you can't take off the mask and just be yourself."

The emotional look on Marcus's face stopped Sam in the middle of his rant and broke his heart. Marcus's jaw quivered slightly, his lashes fluttered, and he looked away.

It wasn't like Sam could claim innocence either since he never showed his true self to Marcus or told him how he felt about him, what he dreamed of, what he was like when he wasn't running away. Blaming Marcus was cruel and hypocritical, and Sam had never felt more like a heel.

It was too bad for Marcus that Sam needed to vent his impotent rage at someone, with Marcus being the only other person in the room. As Marcus went stony and his typical smile faded, Sam knew he had crossed the line big time and hurt someone he really liked and admired.

"Marcus, I'm sorry. I didn't mean to—"

Sam's attempt at an apology was interrupted by a soft purr. Both men started and turned toward the sound.

A hunkering creature sneaked slowly toward them through the vestibule.

With black, gold, and green stripes on its fur, the feline-like beast resembled a tiger but was significantly bigger. Its height at the withers reached the guys' shoulders, a living testament to Sam's theory about low gravity and large animals. Its wide jaw held small, unassuming teeth, its round little ears resembled the delicate wings of a fluorescent green butterfly, and its long furry tail swished behind it carelessly. Its large, round eyes stared at Sam and Marcus with a dark glow, and right above them rose a single curved black horn.

"Oh shit. It's a… a big pussycat." Marcus's words were cocksure, but his tone wasn't. In fact, he sounded anxious, a feeling Sam more than shared.

The creature tilted its head as if focused on listening to their exchange. It didn't appear menacing, but Sam had chills up and down his spine.

Then the beast let out a low, menacing growl. Long curved fangs dropped down in its mouth, revealing the beast's true nature as a predator.

Marcus groaned. "Fuck. It's a vamp-puss."

Sam was on pins and needles. "You're not allowed to name things!"

But the brief banter calmed Sam minutely, for which he was grateful.

Then the creature's neck hairs ruffled and stood on end. Shimmers of electricity waved along its razor-sharp fur, as though individual hairs functioned as lightning rods or conductors. Sam had never seen anything like it, and he had no clue what could cause such an amazing thing in an animal. Bioelectricity?

"Oh my God, no. It's a flash-vamp-puss."

Though probably equally scared, Marcus kept his sense of humor firmly in place. Sam could have kissed the guy for laughing in the face of danger, and a short chuckle escaped his lips.

The alien feline hissed, its hackles rising, and tiny tendrils of electricity spiked in its fur, cascading over its length like rippling gold-and-green fluid. Its spiky tail rose high above it, like a lethal row of razors, whipping this way and that, ready to strike.

"Here's a thought. We should probably avoid touching that thing." Marcus's wise suggestion received 100 percent agreement from Sam, who nodded frantically. "Could we distract it somehow, or better yet, frighten it off? You got something in that backpack of yours that makes a loud noise or could work as a weapon?"

Sam spoke through gritted teeth. "Super sorry. I didn't know we'd be coming here, so I didn't get the chance to raid Cabela's today."

Marcus almost chortled, barely disguising the emergent sound with a cough. "Okay. Don't get your tighty-whities in a bunch."

As the beast approached, silent as a ghost, Sam feared this would be his last day alive. And he couldn't even manage to die on his home planet.

Moving out of the shadow of the vestibule, the creature stepped into the main hall. As soon as it was fully inside, a low hum filled the air. The hairs on Sam's body rose, and the odor of something burning floated around them. It smelled like… ozone.

The four corners of the hall sent a shower of sparks flying, blue and red streaks flashing bright around them. Then startlingly blue thunderbolts struck from all four directions and crashed together in the middle—and lightning cracked through the air and hit the floor directly in front of the creature.

Undoubtedly singed, the creature jumped back in reaction and growled. For a moment, it seemed to consider advancing again. Then a second prong of blue light struck the floor in front of it, startling the animal until it backed off and sprinted out of sight.

The hum faded as the electric jolts dissipated. Sam and Marcus breathed a sigh of mutual relief.

"Oh my God," Sam murmured, barely standing on shaky legs. "Looks like we just met the top of the food chain." Then he pointed a finger at Marcus. "And we're *so* not calling it a flash-vamp-puss."

Marcus chuckled. "Razor beast works for me. You know, razzies?"

He winked at Sam, who tried not to fume at the ridiculousness. Whether he liked it or not, he had to admit he was captivated by Marcus's resilient spirit.

Marcus stared at the four corners of the main hall from where the electrical current had seemed to emanate. "What the hell was that anyway? Some kind of alarm system on automatic? And more importantly, why aren't the two of us vaporized? Does it only work on those things?"

Sam let out a whoosh of breath. "I don't know. Maybe the automated system doesn't recognize humans. And maybe those bud-shaped towers act as some kind of energy collectors or something, discharging the power only in cases of animal attacks."

He winced. He hated conjecture; like all scientists (even future ones), he preferred to work with facts instead of fiction. Unfortunately that was all they had for now.

"You mean power like, say, static electricity?" Marcus rubbed his chin, apparently lost in thought, so the question must have been a rhetorical one. "Or maybe they retain a residual charge from some source of energy we don't yet know about?" He whooshed out a breath as if impressed. "Huh. Maybe the temple acts like some kind of, you know, a Faraday cage? That'd be... wow. Oh, yeah, that'd be something new."

Sam confessed he wasn't an expert on electricity, conduction, or power in general. He knew the basics, like everyone who'd finished high school, gone to college, and paid a modicum of attention in physics class. He was pleased that Marcus knew more because that might come in handy. Sam hoped his new best friend was equally skilled at engineering and the use of tools.

"Since we now know from personal experience that there are indeed predators on this island and that they can't enter here, we should probably search this place from top to bottom," Sam suggested.

Marcus nodded firmly. "Yeah, I totally agree. We need to learn more about whatever kinds of animals are here. We only know about the ozzies, razzies, and lizzies, and the latter aren't even real animals." He waved at the images on the walls. "I mean, heck, these lizzies have four fingers and four toes, but they have opposable thumbs too, which means they could construct tools, right? Obviously, since they built this place. Judging from those carvings, though, they're way bigger than humans. What are they... ten, twelve feet in height?" He shook his head, as if to clear it of haphazard thoughts. "So what else do we need? Food if possible, drinkable fresh water (fingers crossed), shelter for the night, and... and weapons, if there are any." He glanced at Sam from under his brow, his expression unreadable.

Sam frowned with discomfort. He was against weapons on principle. Maybe he'd just seen too many school shootings and too many needless deaths of students and teachers on the news. The victims were people with their whole lives ahead of them—gone with a bang. Literally.

Nonetheless, Sam understood the need for protection, especially now. That alien feline was dangerous at any distance, and it was clearly carnivorous. Harsh words alone wouldn't work as a deterrent, and they couldn't rely on the constant aid of the temple's towers. If they worked based on a residual charge, then they now had less power than before.

And sooner or later predators found a weakness in their prey. They always did.

"Let's look around first and worry about bearing arms later, okay?" Marcus's tone was that of a person trying to placate his companion.

Sam understood, so without saying a word, he merely nodded.

Marcus smiled shortly, obviously relieved at the response. Sam wasn't aware what, if anything, Marcus thought about guns. But he'd never seemed like a sociopath, or even a hunting enthusiast. That was positive, surely?

While Sam had been busy pondering, Marcus had begun to look around. He pointed up first. "There's another floor above us. See?"

A wraparound balcony circled the main hall at a significant height. Well, of course the distance between floors would be greater for builders who were taller. Huge chunks had chipped and broken off, having fallen to the ground floor long ago enough that moss and vines grew around the pieces. But parts of it seemed accessible, and behind the balcony, open, dark doorways appeared, suggesting the existence of other, smaller rooms.

"Think those are the brothel bedrooms you mentioned?" Marcus asked, the corners of his mouth twisted in an expression of distaste. Sam found that uplifting. Much of their continued survival depended on their characters, and Marcus's seemed to be grounded in good taste and high morals.

Then again, would those things be useful to them in a struggle for survival?

Marcus pointed left and right. "Looks like the building expands out to the sides, down the mountainside in both directions."

Sam's gaze followed Marcus's gesture. There were no hallways in sight, only an arch that seemed to drop lower at regular intervals. "They're stairs in a gallery."

Marcus stared at him in clear bafflement. "Huh?"

Sam suppressed a chuckle. "These two galleries are basically passageways, or in this case stairways. They run along the left-right axis of the temple on several elevations of the mountainside. Apparently they're open on both sides. Even from here I can see plants, vines, roots, and flowers growing on the stone surfaces."

Marcus stared at Sam with a dreamy look Sam couldn't decipher. No one had ever regarded him with that kind of... admiring gaze.

Seeing it made Sam swallow hard and blush like crazy. Why would Marcus look at him in such a way? It didn't make sense. Did Marcus have a secret architecture fetish? No, that was just ridiculous.

"Places like Angkor Wat have similar galleries and enclosures," Sam continued, unsure whether to stop. But he kept on babbling because he was too nervous to shut up.

Marcus smiled more widely. "You've got whole books memorized in that big brain of yours, don't you?"

Finally a response. Sam blushed and looked away, worrying his bottom lip. Why did this heartthrob of a man have to flatter him? Couldn't Marcus see how Sam reacted to his praise? He had a feeling sooner or later Marcus would discover his secret, especially now that they'd been put in close quarters by circumstance. The years of careful avoidance had apparently come to naught.

"No. Shut up." Cheeks aflame, Sam tried to look anywhere else but at Marcus, but that simply ensured his gaze landing on erotic carvings.

Marcus shoved him in the arm playfully, chuckling in that infuriatingly sexy manner of his. "Don't get upset. It was a compliment."

Clearing his throat, Sam avoided a further lecture. "We should do a complete search of the premises. Just because this main hall is sort of protected against that… razor beast, that doesn't mean every area is secure."

Marcus shrugged. "Agreed." He looked left and right. "Which way, Sammy?"

Sam bristled. "My name is *not* Sammy. I'm going to the left. You can go wherever the hell you please."

With hastened steps, Sam made his way toward the square archway. Marcus was soon on his heels, smirking irreverently. "Best not to split up. You might need me."

"Yes, of course. 'Cause I'm a helpless egghead who can't do anything manly alone."

Marcus merely laughed at Sam's sarcastic tone and punched Sam on the arm again, though not hard enough to hurt him. "You're hilarious. Lead on, oh brave and wise master."

Choosing to ignore the smartass comment, Sam reached the threshold of the doorway. His estimate had been correct. Beneath them, steep stairs descended in a straight line toward a gold-sand beach far below. Tree roots twined across the stairs, dry leaves piled in the corners, and vines crawled up the walls and along the window openings, with flowers hanging from the vines winding across the arched ceiling.

As they slowly made their way down the practically vertical stair, Sam noted that the complex was built on several elevations. Grassy stone terraces protruded outward, each level expanding a bit more, much like the stairs they were using.

The construction reminded Sam of the many pictures he'd seen in books about Incan architecture, and in places like Machu Picchu, Ollantaytambo, and Moray. Incan architecture was integrated almost seamlessly into its natural surroundings. The constructions here seemed to blend in with the jungle mountain as well, making it difficult to see exactly where one ended and the other began.

Sam considered it fortunate he was so well versed in ancient cultures. They fascinated him, and he often used his knowledge of them in his artwork. Now he'd found another practical application for that same information. Who would ever have guessed it? Unfortunately, he had little knowledge of survival strategies.

"Look at those doorways." Marcus pointed at the closest terrace and the black opening behind it. He squinted as he tried to pierce the veil of darkness. "Maybe this whole temple complex is mostly underground." He glanced at Sam. "Should we check it out?"

Sam nodded. Going down the stairs would lead them to the beach but not much farther, so exploring the temple seemed like a better idea. "Be careful. The temple above might be protected against those... razor beasts, but these underground sections might not be."

Marcus quirked an amused eyebrow. "So you finally came around to razor beasts, eh? Although my original suggestion rocked too."

"No, flash-vamp-puss sucked." The second Sam uttered the words he knew he'd been set up. Marcus's chortling confirmed that Sam was indeed the butt of a ridiculous vampire joke. He closed his eyes and prayed for patience. "Funny ha-ha. Get moving."

Laughing, Marcus stepped onto the terrace. Overgrown trees, bushes, and flowers hid most of the stones the terrace had been built on. Marcus crouched, grabbed a stick from the ground, and tested its strength against the stone wall. A crack sounded sharply in the air, but the piece of wood didn't break, so Sam figured it would work as a temporary weapon. Sam armed himself as well.

Beyond the doorway only blackness greeted them.

"I don't suppose you still have that flashlight in that backpack of yours?" Marcus asked, casting a curious glance toward Sam's bag.

Sam snorted. "Do you even have to ask?" He reached for a side pocket, picked up the small flashlight he'd stashed in there so it wouldn't fall out of his coat pocket, and handed it to Marcus. "It's all we've got, so don't waste it. I don't have any more batteries."

Marcus nodded, this time appearing serious and focused. "There's a light on my iPhone, but using the app will eat up the battery. Let's both try to conserve as much power as we can. I mean, who knows how long the days and nights last here."

Sam agreed with a curt nod. Though he'd never been a Boy Scout, he habitually had important things in his backpack and pockets. Who could have foreseen that packrat quality would come in handy on an alien planet? *Okay, an alien moon. Big difference.* Marcus flicked on the flashlight. The beam was compact but strong. Marcus walked past the threshold and entered the underground passage, Sam following behind him. The air started to smell stale, dust and grit covering the stone floors like a crunchy rug. But Sam saw no cobwebs in the corners, for which he was grateful. On Earth, jungle bugs could kill with a sting or a bite. Therefore it was a good thing this moon might be lacking spiders or other insects. Unless the temple kept them out too....

All too soon into their exploration, they learned that underneath the mountaintop lay a vast array of passageways, a virtual maze that made navigation difficult. There were no writings or signs to indicate where to go or even where they were in the labyrinthine structure.

"Fuck," Marcus cursed after turning yet another corner and seeing nothing but a new, endless tunnel. "Where's Ariadne with her ribbon when we fucking need her?"

Sam gawked at Marcus's back, stunned. Greek mythology. Yet another thing he hadn't anticipated the hunk of a jock might be interested in. Given that they were lost in a labyrinth, the ball of twine reference was spot on.

Marcus gave Sam a shit-eating grin over his shoulder. "Gotcha, didn't I?"

Sam blushed for the umpteenth time in Marcus's company, caught red-handed with his disbelieving thoughts. "Shut up."

Chuckling, Marcus trod forward, and for a while neither of them spoke. The beam of the flashlight revealed numerous statues and reliefs along the stone walls, all of the same erotic nature as the ones above ground.

But what they didn't come across were rooms.

"Is there nothing else here but these unending corridors?" Marcus's frustrated harrumph reflected Sam's own feelings. "This is ridiculous. Didn't the folks who used to live here have any kind of quarters or chambers, kitchens or bathrooms or bedrooms, anything? Or are we fucking going around in circles without realizing it?"

Sam had begun to worry about that too. Was there something different about the way the lizzies lived in the temple? Or were the two of them missing something obvious?

He stopped and looked around with a discerning eye. "Let me borrow that light for a sec, will you?" Once Marcus had returned the flashlight to him, Sam shot the sharp ray onto the wall, inspecting it more carefully than before.

"See something?" Marcus asked behind him, his warm breath fanning over Sam's nape and giving him goose bumps.

"It'd be weird for there to be no rooms." Sam explained his actions as he continued to aim the beam at every curve and shadow on the wall. "Maybe we're just not seeing them."

Sam crouched closer. A small, almost imperceptible crack revealed a stone door embedded into the wall so seamlessly no one would see if they weren't looking for it or didn't know it was there. The elaborate carvings and graceful reliefs made noticing the door even more arduous.

"There *are* doors, so there must be rooms." Sam straightened and pointed. "It's there. But I have no idea how to open it. The whole thing has to weigh a ton. Maybe the lizzies are, or were, physically stronger than humans."

"In the carvings the lizzies do appear bigger, so it'd be normal to assume—"

Sam frowned, remembering an article he had read a while back, so he interjected, "No, that's not right. The lower the gravity, the weaker the muscles, bones, cells, everything. If we stay here too long, our muscles will slowly begin to... shit, what's the word? Oh yeah, atrophy. And our bones will get thinner."

Marcus nodded in agreement. "Understood."

"This isn't our natural environment. We shouldn't be here long if we can avoid it." Of those facts Sam was certain. He was less certain about everything else. "Of course, for all we know, for the lizzies this could have been their natural habitat, so the low gravity might have been normal for them...."

"Gimme the light." Marcus illuminated the statues by the door, one on each side. Both depicted raucous and lascivious lizzies engaged in acts of debauchery. Sam wondered why Marcus wanted to view them up close. But then Marcus sneered with amusement. "Believe it or not, the statue is the key. Or the lock. Or, um.... Shit, you know what I mean."

Sam suppressed a chuckle and hid a smile behind his hand. It seemed that Marcus still needed some work on his metaphors. How adorable.

Marcus pulled on the male lizzie's cock.

A sound of stones grinding and chafing against each other echoed through the empty corridors and Sam's bones, causing him to grit his teeth with discomfort and sprout goose bumps. Marcus grimaced and shivered next to him as well.

The heavy stone door slowly began to open. Apparently the movable penis of the statue functioned like a lever, activating a hidden mechanism buried inside the wall. The grating noise was loud, and Sam winced, praying the underground area was as protected from predators as the aboveground areas.

The new opening revealed a large dusky chamber, illuminated faintly by light wells in the vaulted ceiling. Though Sam couldn't see them directly, he suspected that inside the shafts were either conveniently placed mirrors that reflected sunlight or crystals refracting sunlight. Breathable air must have been a byproduct.

Considering how many light wells there were, Sam figured the chamber had to contain something important or serve a valuable role. The second he saw the walls lined with bookshelves, all filled with scrolls, he knew he'd been right.

"It's a library." Marcus whistled low and gave Sam an admiring and approving glance. "You've got great instincts."

Sam smiled, ducking his head to hide his flaming cheeks. "You too. I wouldn't have guessed to check the statues and their, um… appendages."

Marcus chuckled. "Looks like we hit the jackpot."

Sam agreed enthusiastically. He rushed to the closest shelf, gently took out one scroll, and unrolled it, inspecting the contents with great care. "It's kind of like papyrus, a bit brittle to the touch, but legible, I think."

Marcus let out a relieved breath. "That's good for us. I hope there's something in there we can use to our advantage."

He took a gander at the premises, his gaze glossing over the table, and he rubbed his chin in thought. A scratching sound arose from his slight stubble, and Sam found it particularly hot. Marcus was already a man in every sense; Sam wanted him so much the urge unnerved him. He knew the feeling was both unrequited and hopeless, yet he couldn't shake his heart loose.

Then Marcus said, "You should stay here with the books. I'm gonna search for stuff we can use."

Sam frowned, baffled and disagreeing. "Why do I have to stay here when I don't even understand the language? How will I be able to tell what could work in reactivating the portal in the chamber?"

Marcus shrugged. "You're better able to recognize the kinds of books we need."

"What? Two pairs of eyes are better than one. And you read too."

"Yeah, but not as much as you. You'll be able to tell what's more significant. I don't know a drama classic from a computer manual."

Sam shook his head with disbelief and suspicion. "You're exaggerating—or lying."

Finally Marcus whined out loud and brought up his hands in a gesture of surrender, which seemed to be full of frustration. "Okay, fine. You got me. I'm not good at sitting on my hands doing nothing. I need to do something, anything, even if it's just walking aimlessly down hallways in search of… whatever." Then he licked his lips anxiously and looked away. "Or… maybe I'm just scared of failure."

As surprised as Sam was about Marcus's admission of restlessness, he refused to believe the latter could be true. "That's ridiculous. You could never fail at anything you put your mind to. And you, afraid? You're not afraid of anything."

Marcus smiled ruefully, hiding his eyes behind a thick veil of lashes. "I wish that were true…. But who knows, right? Maybe you'll get lucky and some of these scrolls will have pictures in them, you know, like comics, where the pictures sometimes tell you more than the text."

Sam frowned in bafflement. Marcus was into comics too? Did he somehow know about Sam's interest in them? If anyone had suggested it to Sam before they ended up on this alien moon, he would have denied the mere possibility of Marcus being a fan of comic books. Cool guys didn't do comics, or at least so the unwritten rule of popularity went in high school.

"Okay, fine," Sam acquiesced at last. "But be careful, for God's sake. And don't go setting off any Indiana Jones or Lara Croft type traps either. I swear, if I see a giant boulder rolling my way, don't think I won't leave you down here to rot under it."

"Rolling stones don't gather moss," Marcus quipped and chuckled. "Besides… booby traps? This seems more like a revered brothel than a military fortress. But I'll be careful traipsing on my tippy-toes, quiet as a church mouse."

Before Sam could get in a word in edgewise, Marcus had already nodded his goodbye and left the library with the flashlight.

Sam did holler after him, though. "Shut up!"

Vexed at Marcus's rash actions, Sam was nonetheless now alone, confined in a strange room, at least until his companion saw fit to return.

At the very least he wasn't completely in the dark, thanks to the light shafts above.

Since he had nothing better to do for the time being, Sam sighed in defeat and started rummaging through the countless scrolls in the library.

CHAPTER 5

"WHAT THE hell did I get us into?" Marcus murmured to himself as he trudged down the long, winding, utterly deserted hallways. A simple human voice echoing in the silence went a long way in comforting his troubled soul.

With only the faint glow of Sam's flashlight to guide him through the darkness, Marcus couldn't help worrying about how every horror movie and game he'd ever seen and played started out like this—a person alone, with only a flashlight to aid him. Shuddering, he stopped every couple of steps to listen. It was silly because surely no one still lived on the island, no one sentient anyway. Every trick of the light and shadow play caused him to stumble and swallow nervously.

Marcus began to feel it had been a mistake to leave Sam behind in the library.

He smiled at the thought of the morose geek boy who seemed so troubled by Marcus's presence and attention. Marcus had witnessed and relished each and every endearing blush, lip bite, and eyelash flutter. Sam was so cute, far more so than he even knew. Marcus wondered if the nerdy boy was still a virgin…. He was only seventeen, almost eighteen, so it was possible.

Marcus confessed to himself that he hoped Sam was untouched. He really wanted to be the first to do any touching with Sam.

But getting close to, or simply approaching, Sam had proved much harder than he had anticipated. Sam thwarted every effort on Marcus's part, appearing sullen, withdrawn, and hurt, as though Marcus had done something to offend him. Marcus couldn't fathom what he'd done.

Was the cause maybe that Marcus was best friends with Simon, Sam's older brother? Surely Sam couldn't hold that against Marcus. He and Simon had been best friends since fucking daycare. Marcus could do a lot, but turning back time was not in his bag of tricks.

His ponderings about Sam's reticence ceased when Marcus heard the gush of water. A beam of light on the floor grew as Marcus walked closer to another terraced balcony overlooking a wall of green vegetation and offering glimpses of a golden beach far below.

On the side of the mountain, a waterfall rushed down a steep vertical incline, vanishing in the jungle beneath a cluster of sharp rocks.

Marcus wasn't a religious guy, but he prayed the water was fresh, sweet, and clean. He stepped closer to where the stone-and-grass terrace turned into the natural cliff's edge, extended his hand into the stream, and waited. It wasn't acid, he concluded with a smirk, since his flesh didn't burn and peel off. He pulled back, smelled the moisture on his fingers, judged it fresh and harmless, and sipped a few droplets. The liquid tasted like fresh water, so he congratulated himself for such a beneficial find.

"I rock, uh-huh, oh yeah." He did a little victory dance in celebration.

Marcus wasn't ashamed to admit that when Sam had been down, Marcus had searched his backpack for supplies. He'd found a half-empty plastic bottle. Now he screwed open the cap and refilled the bottle with fresh water from the waterfall. Seemed like a sensible thing to do.

"And now to be brave and do a blind taste testing," he muttered aloud, for what it was worth since he was alone after all.

He lifted the bottle to his lips, took a sip, and gulped the liquid down nervously. Then he waited. His throat didn't burn off, his stomach seemed perfectly settled, and the aftertaste was the same as that of the tap water back home.

"Score." Marcus was glad he could at least check off one item on the list of things they needed to survive. "Next up: food."

Sam had been right. Protein bars wouldn't last them for more than a day or two, even if they did their best to conserve supplies and fight off hunger. How long could a human survive on water alone? A week, maybe? Surely not as long as a month, Marcus figured.

Around them spread a jungle. That was a pretty fertile environment, and Marcus decided to search for edible fruit. How would he know what wasn't poisonous? Well, if the animals on the island could eat them… then maybe they could too? Marcus decided to cross that bridge when he came to it.

First order of business: find out if there even *was* any fruit.

Farther in the jungle, the gigantic palm trees rustled in the winds that had apparently picked up speed, making Marcus's T-shirt flutter and wave about. He welcomed the cool breeze as the humid heat gave him bouts of nausea. In the thick foliage, the winged monkeys—ozzies—sang like birds, chirping and squawking. Marcus couldn't see them clearly, but every once in a while, he caught a flapping of wings or a flash of bright colors.

Marcus wondered what the creatures ate. He decided to follow them as best he could.

But he stayed mindful of Sam's warnings. Every ecosystem had a food chain, and they didn't need to end up a part of it as some alien animal's lunch.

There were no clear paths through the jungle; only steep inclines muddied by torrential rains and made impassable by crisscrossing webs of roots and underbrush. And all the ozzies were flying about high above or hopping agilely from tree to tree and beyond. Marcus had zero chance of tracking them down on foot. And Tarzan he wasn't.

"Shit." He leaned closer to the edge of the terrace and peered below in search of a safe passage down. There wasn't one.

A sharp, short coo startled him, the sound emanating from behind a bush.

Marcus gripped his stick tighter and readied for battle. Even if the creature was a small rodent, on this alien moon it could be massive. Marcus swallowed hard and prayed that whatever it was it wouldn't be an enormous bug or spider.

"We need fucking bug spray by the truckloads here," Marcus murmured to himself, hoping the sound of a human voice would either grant him courage or frighten off the source of the sound.

The fact that he hadn't noticed any bugs flying or creeping around didn't exactly help. For all Marcus knew, these creatures could possess camouflaging capabilities like chameleons and be invisible and stalk their prey unseen.

In his head he heard Sam's voice, clear as day, saying, "Surely there have to be insects. This is a jungle after all. Yeah, there should be bugs here the size of Buicks."

Marcus shuddered in disgust and instinctive nervousness. Of course Sam would never say anything like that. He'd probably never uttered the word Buick in his life. Then again, this was an imaginary Sam living inside Marcus's head, so real-life accuracy wasn't required.

The leaves of the bush rustled, and Marcus waited with bated breath, stick in hand.

A tiny furry face appeared between some leaves and grass. It sniffed the air cautiously before hopping out of the safety of the bush, revealing its small size.

Marcus let out a relieved breath. Unless this animal could magically turn into a bigger form, it wasn't much of a threat. In fact, it was kind of cute, resembling a squirrel with its bushy tail and whiskers, floppy rabbit-like ears and big round milky-white eyes.

But it was no ordinary squirrel. Its little legs resembled those of a kangaroo, so it must be a great jumper. Six tiny horn stumps stuck out on top of its head, and the collar area of its gray-and-white striped furry coat was composed of sharp quills like those of a porcupine. It had a flat pink button nose, and equally pink little paws, like a baby kitten.

In its sharp-nailed paws, it held a brown nut. Sniffing and gnawing at the nut, it finally smashed it against the rough rock by the waterfall. It kept at it until the hard shell cracked, exposing a soft, honey-hued center, which it ate, licking it with a green snakelike tongue.

"Nuts, huh? Guess I'll try those." Marcus saw the same nuts growing in the bushes and figured he could gather a few into his pockets.

The little critter raised its head suddenly, at last seeming to notice Marcus's presence over the gush of the waterfall. It cocked its head left and right but didn't look directly at Marcus. He surmised the creature's eyesight wasn't great. Maybe it was nocturnal.

Then its quill collar stood on end and vibrated, changing color to green. It had to be an effect of sunlight refracting within its hairs, Marcus guessed, since he knew only chlorophyll could create natural green, and that was a feature of plants, not animals.

The creature's bushy tail also sprang up, elongated, and spread into a wide furry fan, like a peacock's tail. Instead of round spots, though, the tail revealed a complex array of silvery hairs or fibers, like pappi on a flower. Along the fuzz ran a cobweb of blue electric current.

"You seem to be charged, little one," Marcus observed with a whisper.

The creature buzzed and cocked its head sideways, not fearful or hostile.

"Hmm, you're like a tiny squirrel and a peacock. Should I call you... squeecock? Nah, Sam would bust my balls. Squizzies? Cool. That works."

The critter's tail fluttered, as if catching Marcus's voice in its sensitive hairs. Perhaps the animal saw or heard with its tail, Marcus thought, vowing to mention this encounter to Sam.

Or he could do way better than that. Carefully, with slow movements, he fished out his iPhone and took a couple of pictures of the fan-tailed, fluffy little critter.

The squizzie's tail shivered, glimmering almost blindingly white. Then small lightning shocks traveled across its tail that looked like the seed form of a dandelion. Any minute now Marcus expected to get a bolt up his butt.

The quivering of the tail soon stilled, though, and it retracted back into its curved bushy shape. The creature snatched an orange-colored fruit from the bush behind it. Marcus figured it had a nest in there.

The oval shaped, amber-hued fruit, however, looked mighty promising. With its sharp, nail-like little claws, the squizzie ripped open the soft skin and sank its teeth into a ripe, glistening, purple-colored pulp. Marcus's mouth watered at the sight, and his rumbling stomach reminded him that he hadn't eaten since lunch at school.

Again the squizzie's head came up, and its tail fanned out. It was definitely listening or seeing with its sensitive tail. This time, however, the critter didn't return back to its serene form but hopped back into the shadows of the underbrush and vanished from sight.

"Okay, nice to meet you too," Marcus murmured, pleased with the encounter. Now he had information about another animal in the food chain, this one most likely fitting in the herbivore end of the spectrum. "And thanks for giving me hints about food."

If the squizzies were anything like rodents back home, Marcus had a feeling they had sharp nails and teeth. Therefore he made sure to ruffle the bushes with his stick before picking and pocketing a few orange-colored fruits and acorn-looking nuts. He decided to try and break them open later when he was with Sam again.

Sam. Marcus sighed when the image of his best friend's younger brother rose to his mind unbidden. And as usual, his arousal spiked. Sam had a tempting allure Marcus couldn't quite explain and Sam didn't even seem to be aware he had.

Sam was so cute. Marcus hummed to himself, unable to keep the smile off his face. It never ceased to amaze him how Sam could be two such different people. The enthusiastic one with a big smile, though never in Marcus's company, and the sullen, grumpy one who scowled at everything Marcus said or did while trying to run away from him.

Of course, it wasn't a total mystery to Marcus why Sam behaved the way he did. Sam clearly liked Marcus way more than he would admit even to himself. Sometimes he forgot, though, and acted nice and funny and smart. Then Sam remembered again and became either awkward or sullen with Marcus.

While Marcus was busy thinking about what to do with Sam, he scoured the bushes and trees for nuts and fruit. He wasn't that distracted by his musings about Sam, mostly because Sam wasn't with him. Marcus considered eating a nut or a piece of fruit but decided against it in the end. It'd be better to experiment when he wasn't alone. In case there was a need for CPR.

Naturally, that thought led Marcus straight to imagining Sam giving him mouth-to-mouth. And lo and behold, Marcus popped an untimely boner. Adjusting his dick in his jeans, he focused on harvesting and foraging for food instead.

Sam had been right about everything thus far. The low gravity made movement easy and allowed Marcus to jump higher than normal to reach for the branches and fruit of the tall trees. He could actually leap three times his own height. It was insane and cool and useful as fuck.

Soon he had his pockets full of nuts, berries, and fruit. The animal tracks on the jungle floor were fresh, and bits of these forest foods had been chewed and left to rot in the thin soil. Since they'd been consumed, Marcus felt confident he'd found edibles.

"Sam's gonna be pleased. At least we won't starve or die of dehydration."

Once he'd gathered enough provisions to last them a day or two, he wavered between returning back inside the underground temple or exploring the vast jungle growing on the steep sides of the mountain. He had nothing but a stick to defend himself, and those razzies were too big for him to deal with on his own. Who knew how many more of them lived on the island. Well, obviously two at least: a male and a female. How else would they reproduce?

Marcus sighed. It was better to leave questions like that to the resident egghead.

He walked along the edge of the long terrace and studied the jungle below. Overgrown thickets of underbrush. Liana, hanging moss, and colorful flowers peeked out here and there, adding different textures and hues to the otherwise verdant wall of vegetation. In some directions, the foliage was so thick he couldn't even catch a glimpse of the ocean beyond.

Going back underground didn't appeal to him. Marcus wasn't scared of cramped spaces, but the sensation of the mountain on top of him caused bouts of claustrophobia. So he stayed on the terrace, following the edge carefully.

As his eyes grew accustomed to the nature around him, he began to descry more than just the ozzies zipping from tree to tree, colorful feathers flapping.

Tiny, light green creatures that reminded Marcus of hummingbirds darted around beautiful orchid-type flowers. But whenever they stayed in place long enough to drink nectar with their long pink tongues, he could see they weren't birds. Not with those long curved tails.

Their four wings glimmered transparently in the sunlight, resembling dragonflies. But other than that, they looked like puffy versions of seahorses, only gem-studded. Their skin glittered as if they were covered by microscopic jewels. Whatever it was—Marcus pictured armor of some kind—it seemed to be rock-solid.

"Sea horse hummingbirds." Marcus snorted. "Gonna call you... humzies."

He snapped a couple of zoomed photos of the humzies for Sam's analysis. If they were aware of Marcus's presence, they didn't seem to mind. Then again, with their speed and agility they could undoubtedly outrun any threat they perceived. He didn't think even the razzies could move fast enough to catch one of these for lunch.

For a while he observed the humzie flock scatter about, scouring impressive flowers for their nectar. Soon, though, Marcus took note that the humzies avoided one of the plants.

This particular blossom was huge, like the tree it grew from, on average at least six times bigger than the other flowers. Heck, it had to be more than twice the size of a human.

Its large, elegant petals and blossoms appeared in various shades of red, ranging from light pink to dark burgundy. In fact, Marcus believed that it was one huge flower, with dozens, if not hundreds of buds and blooms around a hidden center. It was stunning, like a majestic collection of red roses in one gigantic bouquet.

Marcus took some pictures, not because he was specifically into flowers or plants in general, but because one never knew in advance what might be useful. Weren't orchids edible? Or was that just a random memory from some movie? He pondered hard and realized he was thinking of *Barbarella*. He harrumphed to himself and disregarded the idea of eating flowers.

The scent of the blossom grew heavier in the air the closer he got. Sickeningly sweet, the odor permeated the already humid atmosphere, making Marcus grimace and become nauseated. He started to back off, waving a hand in front of his nose to clear the syrupy perfume from his nostrils.

Something brushed by his foot.

Marcus stopped and looked down, praying it wasn't a bug or spider or whatever.

It wasn't an insect of any kind. It appeared to be a slithering liana. Marcus frowned, not having expected a vine to move on its own. He'd never heard of such a thing. He took a picture and decided to ask Sam.

The vine snaked forward in an instant and wrapped itself around Marcus's leg.

"What the fuck?"

He crouched to unfasten the creeping thing, and another one shot out of the bush and wound around his left arm.

"Jesus Christ," he called out in shock, trying to disentangle both his arm and leg.

Then he saw the jungle floor crawling with new liana, all headed his way.

"Oh shit."

That was when he noticed that the huge red flower the animals all avoided had turned his way. All the blossoms now faced him. In the center of the sea of blooms, a flap opened to show what looked like a cup. And inside something… bubbled and boiled?

"Fuck." Marcus knew he was in trouble. He'd never seen a pitcher plant in real life, but he'd seen pictures in biology books. Inside the trap of the apparently carnivorous plant was a vat of acid that would melt him into nutrients for the flower—very slowly.

If he didn't break free soon, he'd never escape. Sam would be trapped alone on this alien moon forever. Marcus couldn't let that happen.

He tried to avoid the vines twisting and coiling in his direction, the ground almost full of them now, like a heap of mating snakes. He still had his stick, so he hit the liana attached to him and those getting closer with all his strength. He was an athlete, so he had some power behind each strike.

"Let go of me, you stupid plant. I don't want to fucking date you."

The liana entwined around his leg burst apart when the stick's coarse surface ripped it open. Green fluid spread onto Marcus's leg and onto the ground in thick droplets.

Though it lasted no longer than a blink of an eye, Marcus saw blue electrical impulses wave across the rivulets until they faded away. Apparently the animals on this alien world weren't the only ones with curious bioelectric properties.

The other vines stilled for a moment. That brief instance granted Marcus enough time to yank off the liana wrapped around his arm. The vines felt slippery and resilient in Marcus's grip, like rubber. Malleable but tough.

Then he ran like a bat out of hell, dodging swinging liana and jumping over crawling ones. Once he got back in the shade of the underground temple, he heard a sharp electric rattle and hum.

Whisking around, Marcus saw the eyes of a standing lizzie statue on the temple wall shoot a lightning bolt at the ground. Several more followed in rapid succession.

Vines burned, erupted, and spilled green fluid on the thin soil. No sounds came from the flower, but the vines retreated, and the blossoms turned away to face the sun again.

Marcus breathed a sigh of relief, bending to lean on his knees and gasp for air.

"Shit. That was way too close."

He rubbed a hand over his sweaty forehead and took a deep breath to calm his frayed nerves. In the trees, ozzies flew about and humzies danced with the swiftness of magical sprites.

"Now I know why you avoid that flower. Thanks for the warning."

He inspected the damage the liana had inflicted. He'd worn only a T-shirt and jeans, as he'd left his winter coat with Sam at the library. His unshielded arm had bloody striations where the vine had gripped him. His trouser leg had a sliver of a tear too, his skin scraped and bruised.

Thankfully he'd escaped virtually unscathed.

Stepping out on the terrace and gazing down the hillside, he saw that the vines had all disappeared back into the jungle's dense undergrowth. Nothing in particular slithered over the terrain.

The bushes rustled, though, and Marcus crouched, readying himself.

Another squizzie came into view and hopped about, snatching nuts and berries from the ground and bushes and stopping every once in a while to listen, probably for predators.

Marcus might have been hungry, but he wouldn't even consider capturing the tiny thing and killing it for meat. Maybe if he and Sam ended up being stranded on the island longer, he might end up reconsidering. But not now, not yet.

A low growl emerged from a different direction a mere instant before an animal jumped through the air from the greenery and attacked the squizzie. The movement was so chaotic it was a blur, but Marcus could faintly make out a curved gray horn, black and green and gold stripes, and a set of fangs flashing in the light.

A razor beast. Only significantly smaller, perhaps the size of a household cat.

Marcus didn't think. He acted on instinct. He picked up a couple of pebbles and tossed them at the alien feline. He missed a few times but finally managed a blow to its side. The razzie let out a sharp yelp, released the squizzie, and ran into the jungle.

Marcus hurried toward the squizzie, his intention to lend aid. But the squizzie merely righted itself and spread its flashy tail, a bioelectric charge building till it sparkled blindingly white. Marcus shielded his eyes from the brightness and backed off.

When the shining faded from behind his eyelids, he opened his eyes and found the tiny critter gone. No more movement in his field of vision. Marcus could only hope the squizzie wasn't too wounded, or it would simply die elsewhere and likely get eaten.

Sighing, he returned to temple complex and started back toward the library.

Yes, Marcus had been successful in finding food and water.

But he'd also discovered that the feline razor beasts weren't the only predators on the island. That beautiful carnivorous plant was without a doubt dangerous and highly aggressive. From his short-lived encounter Marcus hadn't been able to determine what triggered the flower's hostile responses. Whatever it was, they couldn't afford to make that mistake again.

Marcus had managed to escape by the seat of his pants. Ripped pants. Next time they might not get so lucky. And at that exact moment, Marcus couldn't think of a worse way to die than being incrementally digested by a plant.

"Fine. I can take a hint. Enough exploring on my own."

Brushing off dried leaves, dirt, and flower pollen from his clothes, he headed back to Sam and the safety of the library.

CHAPTER 6

"OH, THIS is hopeless."

Sam tossed a scroll to the table and reached for another. In the past half an hour, he must have gone through a hundred scrolls or more.

Thus far, he'd only found two that seemed to be of any use. One of them described the temple complex they were in. That much Sam could tell because the scroll contained detailed floor plans. The other scroll had artistic renderings of the razor beast they'd encountered, as well as other creatures, so Sam kept that close. Learning about the food chain was their only chance of not ending up *in* said food chain.

The rest of the vast literary collection… well, Sam had no idea if he was reading a unique, brilliant classic or a recipe for homemade cookies. Without any pictures or recognizable symbols, Sam was at a loss.

For the umpteenth time, he growled at Marcus leaving him alone to this task.

And then there were the carvings, reliefs, and statues around him. Over and over, they kept drawing his gaze, distracting him from his mission.

For one thing, since the images were monochromatic—mostly anyway, as the outside of the building had no colors left, but in here scattered traces were occasionally visible—he had no idea what these lizzies were like in real life. Were they black or white or gray, red or green or blue? Did they have skin, scales, armor, or fur? The scientist in Sam was fascinated.

He hazarded a guess that the lizzies had green skin, like frogs, because if they were anything like the reptiles back on Earth, they would be exothermic. Tropical environments, therefore, would suit them. Continuous sunlight year-round and green skin to absorb the maximum amount of heat. Of course, frogs and other reptiles that appeared green actually weren't. Their cells filtered out other colors besides green. So… perhaps the lizzies weren't green either.

Sam pursed his lips in annoyance. His own deductive reasoning led him down a path that refuted his initial assumptions. But that was how science worked. First people had theories, and then they set out to find evidence that either proved or disproved said theory. Regardless of the findings, knowledge took a leap forward once the scientific community verified the facts.

With all these alien wonders around him, Sam felt compelled to document everything he saw. Who knew if anyone else would ever get to witness these stunning ruins again before the jungle claimed them forever.

So he fished out his iPhone from his jeans pocket and started taking pictures of all the amazing artwork. The wall reliefs and murals had to be hundreds or thousands of years old, but the sculptures, their shapes and few remaining hints of colors, jumped out at the onlooker, still vibrant. The carvings were astonishingly lifelike, practically three-dimensional.

But the statues sprawled throughout the complex were magnificent and imposing with their realistic depictions, each muscle and tendon in its proper place. Their jeweled eyes glimmered eerily as they stood on stone plinths and raised daises, carefully observing Sam wandering about.

Their positions appeared far from threatening, though. Each and every mural, fresco, relief, carving, and statue depicted sex in some form.

The images appeared shameless, lifelike, and graphic, nothing held back. At any minute Sam half expected the shapes to come to life and step out of the walls and stone bases as living, breathing beings. He wondered what they might have thought of humans, who were smaller, weaker, and weird-looking. Would they wish to engage in love or war with Sam and Marcus?

Love certainly seemed to be their predominant pastime on the island. He saw singles, couples, threesomes, foursomes, and more, all the way to wild orgies. He saw things he had zero experience with and no name for.

Male members were accentuated to the levels of hyperbole. Surely they couldn't have been that big in real life. Penises jutted outward, hard and proud and impossible to miss. Blushing, Sam couldn't look away from the most prominent features depicted as they stretched out, almost as if trying to reach the viewer. What Sam needed was a measuring tape so he could verify for himself that the penises he saw averaged about nineteen or twenty inches!

Holy hell. No wonder these lizzies were taller than humans if that was the size of their reproductive organs. How did the females handle that?

The creators of the artwork had been ingenious, able to capture fleeting moments of time and space, managing to show not only anticipation, temptation, lust, and love, but distinctive features as well so that every model was their own person. Sam guessed he might actually be able to recognize individuals if they walked up to him in real life. Alien lizards or not.

Sam bore witness to ancient, alien marvels and understood he was privileged to see them. He snapped shots on his iPhone. If they ever got back home, they'd have a pictorial journal of the wonders they'd seen.

Delicious details abounded, their bounty rich and rewarding. A hint of a quirky smile, a handsome or beautiful profile half in shadows, hands touching and fingers interlacing, lips parted in gasps, screams, and moans, luscious curves of breasts and cocks, backs arching, tails rising, heads thrown back, taut muscles, sweat droplets on flesh, hands gripping hard bodies, fingers digging into soft skin, kisses on intimate places.

From simple sensual and sexual acts to wild reckless debauchery with groups, animals, even what looked like fruit. Nothing was apparently forbidden or too unseemly to show. Despite Sam's squeamish, shy attitude toward most matters of the sensual variety, he was still pleased to learn that these aliens, these previous occupants on the island, hadn't viewed sex as sinful or a vice, something to be condemned or censured. Perhaps only humans disapproved or reproached their own kind for a completely natural act and equally natural behavior. The lizzies sure weren't shy.

Sam felt out of breath and hot in his skin. He longed to run his fingertips across the carvings and statues, to touch lips, to trace curves, to find a detail too small to see but one that could be felt, tangible and undeniable. And yes, perhaps even to feel the stony rigidity of a rock-hard cock against his palm, to follow the length of the shaft from root to tip, to examine the manhood of these alien beings. A tempting thought.

In the end, though, Sam didn't dare. So he settled for looking and taking photos.

A female with her mouth open accepted a cock while another female on all fours was being taken from behind by a male. Rough stuff, Sam thought, shuddering. She sucked on another cock while handling two others with her hands, while another female beneath her sucked on one of her nipples while twisting the other into a hardened peak.

The image was far more graphic than anything Sam had seen so far. He wasn't into porn, gay or otherwise. A flustered sweat made him uncomfortable, and he yearned to rip off all his clothes and simply be buck naked in the humid heat. He'd undoubtedly feel better and less close to having a heatstroke.

Sam wondered if the images were actual people caught in the middle of sex acts by the artists or if they were the products of a fertile, dirty mind.

If they had once been real people, then seeing these images was tantamount to peeping into intimate moments, sharing hours of private passion with them, and reliving their affectionate touches, sweet smiles, loving gazes. Perhaps the artists and sculptors had known these individuals personally rather than as mere subjects of the art. The artists had certainly been able to capture their models' personalities, emotional quirks, physical pleasure, and facial features with such detail and flourish.

Maybe they were... lovers.

After all, these depictions weren't crude renderings of violations. They seemed more like... lovemaking. Perhaps these artists loved all their models.

Surely no one person could have done all these reliefs? It would have taken centuries.

Sam realized suddenly that because this place had been abandoned, he'd likely never know the answer. It would forever remain an unsolved mystery.

Faint traces of minute mistakes and tiny flaws appeared here and there. Lips intended to smile that rose in a flirtatious sneer instead; hands that gripped with intensity but appeared unfinished and crude; cocks where the veins curved oddly, as if the sculptor's hands had slipped. Little details that showed that no one, not even an alien lizard artist, was perfect.

The presence of so much sexual imagery left Sam turned on to the point of horniness. He briefly contemplated rubbing a nut to get off quickly, no fuss, no muss. But.... Marcus could come back at any moment and witness Sam masturbating over sculptures, and he'd never be able to live down that embarrassment.

An instinct to get up close and personal grew inside Sam, however. His senses longed to learn all the secrets of these sculptures, wall reliefs, and murals, their hidden vows of love, their forbidden language of pleasure. Would hands and fingers be enough to satisfy his needs? Could he use... his body? Could he wrap himself around these images and those gigantic stone cocks, like an animal clinging to a vine? The impulse was crazy, more insane than any thought he'd ever had.

He closed his eyes and prayed for patience and endurance—and an ice-cold shower. But images of cavorting nudes flashed before Sam's closed eyelids anyway, like a salacious movie he couldn't stop playing over and over, exciting him without any hope of a climax. Worst of all, the male hotties started to look like Marcus. *Dammit.*

Shaking his head, angry at himself for getting distracted while they continued to be in dire straits, Sam stomped back to the table and the stacks of scrolls, pocketed his iPhone, and went back to work.

Time flew by without him being consciously aware of it.

When Marcus stumbled in through the door, clothes torn and skin scraped, Sam started and jumped about a meter in the air.

"Jesus fucking Christ, you scared the shit out of—oh my God, what the hell happened to you?"

Sam rushed over to Marcus, wrapped an arm around his waist, and helped him down onto a stone chair by the table, a chair so big Marcus looked like a Lilliputian sitting on it.

Marcus groaned, grimaced, and then gave Sam a full account of what had happened to him, the animals and plants he'd encountered, and why he was so roughed up. Sam made soothing circles over his upper back as a means of consolation while mulling over the details of a tale fraught with danger.

"I guess we know now there are more of those razzies on the island, even if that one was so small," Marcus said, cringing no doubt at the aches and pains of his ordeal.

Sam half shrugged, half nodded. "Must have been a cub. Maybe the gray color of the horn turns black when it's fully grown into maturity."

Marcus harrumphed, squaring his shoulders. Then he handed his partner his phone and showed Sam the pictures he'd taken of the animals and the flower.

Sam let out a yelp. "Wow. That's one bigass plant."

"Yeah." Marcus sighed, apparently unwinding at last. "That razzie isn't our only threat on the island. And this flower thing, it's insidious. I didn't even see how bad the situation was until I was almost consumed. Oh, and by the way? That's now officially the worst possible way to go."

"I believe you." Sam frowned, shivering as he stared at the image of beauty and death in one shot. "And you said the vines on the ground were a part of the flower?"

Marcus nodded, closing his eyes and leaning back. "Sure seemed like it. I mean, they did try to drag me toward the flower, and all the blossoms turned toward me." He shook his head, as if pissed off. "I just wish I knew what the fuck I did to attract the thing's attention. I mean, on Earth the carnivorous plants, they eat insects and small animals, right? They don't attack big animals or large prey, right?"

"Yes. But everything's bigger here, so...."

Marcus grunted, sounding displeased and rubbing his wounded arm. "Well, that damn thing's as big as a house. We better not get in its way again." Suddenly his eyes flew open and, wide-eyed, he gazed at Sam in alarm. "Could there be more of those plants on the island?"

Sam had no clue. But he said, "Probably not. Too many of them about, and there'd not be enough food. I mean, this isn't that big of an island. Competition is bad for predator species like the flower and that razzie. In fact, I doubt there are many of those beasts here either."

Marcus let out a relieved breath and visibly relaxed again. "Good. 'Cause I doubt we would be able to combat more than one of either."

Sam studied the images on the phone. "That squizzie's fascinating."

"Yeah, its tail... wow." Marcus rubbed his sore arms and thighs. "Maybe every one of these animals has some sort of bioelectrical—"

"That's weird." Sam frowned, perplexed. "I mean, photons *are* the quantum particles of light and other electromagnetic energies but... they have no electrical charge themselves. Hmm, maybe the light emitted by this animal's tail is a... a byproduct of whatever bioelectric or chemical process creates the charge?"

"Uh-huh." Marcus regarded Sam with curiosity. "Did you find anything useful?"

"Oh. Yes." Sam cleared his throat and rushed over to the table, picked up one of the scrolls, and gave it to Marcus for inspection. "That one's about the animals on the island, I think. It has some sketches."

Marcus's eyebrows rose up to his hairline. He nodded with enthusiasm and started to go over the scroll. "You're right, Sammy. This is a catalog of indigenous flora and fauna." Then he cocked his head and frowned in bafflement. "Yeah, I can't pronounce that. Too many *M*s and *R*s for my tongue."

Sam stared, confused, unable to see anything but weird squiggles. "What's too hard to pronounce?"

"The humzies. The real name for them in here? Impossible."

Sam glanced at Marcus, amused. "How come you didn't call them hummers?"

Marcus harrumphed in obvious distaste. "'Cause hummers are big dumbass cars that are too fucking noisy, take up too much space whether parked or mobile, and pollute. And those little critters were way too cute for that association."

Sam snickered. "You take this naming business too seriously."

Marcus snorted. "Untrue. I don't take it seriously at all. It's all fun and games—till I get eaten by a giant plant I named wrong and it took offense."

"Okay, smartass." Sam gestured at the scroll. "Is there anything useful in there? Forget the pronunciation."

Marcus exhaled heavily as he went through the written and drawn catalog. "Actually, yeah. I think this describes the animals in relation to each other." He gave Sam a knowing look. "In the food chain, that is." Sam waved his hand in a rush to get him to hurry up. Marcus chuckled, seemingly undeterred by Sam's haste. "Okay. Anyway, on the bottom rung are the humzies and… another little thing I didn't see while I was out there."

Sam leaned over Marcus's shoulder to see a sketch depicting a small, round creature. Its skin resembled wood bark, tiny mushrooms grew on its head, and big round eyes and a darling smile gave it a cute childlike look. Its petite paws and furry tail intensified the doll-like impression. Its size was in the mouse department, so it could hardly pose much of a threat.

"Aww. It's so adorable. It's like a Beanie Baby." Sam sighed, loving the sight of the little animal. "What's it called?"

Marcus hesitated. "Lots of *B*s and… letters I can't identify. I guess the translation bug inside me isn't foolproof. I'm gonna call it… a barkzie."

Sam rolled his eyes. "I swear, Marcus, you're trying to drive me mad." Then he sighed in resignation. "Fine. Barkzie it is."

Marcus chuckled in obvious victory. "It kinda looks like a… a human, doesn't it? Tiny hands and feet, pink and fuzzy and cute as a button."

"Anthropomorphic," Sam added automatically. When Marcus laughed, Sam huffed in exasperation. "Shut up. I'm so tired of using single syllable words or dumbing myself down so that jocks won't kick my ass or the cheerleaders won't laugh at me or—"

"I'd never do that," Marcus cut in, his eyes narrowing. "Besides, most of the time no one gives a flying fuck what anyone else does.

Maybe they did in high school, where everyone was put on the spot. But not in college. Everyone's got their own shit to deal with." Then his eyes softened. "But if anyone gives you a hard time when we get back home, I'll kick their ass."

Sam rolled his eyes. "Thanks, but I can take care of myself." That was a bold-faced lie. But Marcus's protective instinct made Sam feel like a weakling. He decided to steer the discussion away from himself. "So that's the bottom rung of animals. The humzies drink nectar from flowers and these barkzies... well, who knows what they consume at the end of the day. But they all seem to be at the docile herbivore end of the spectrum."

Marcus frowned. "That means they're... food for predators."

"That's usually how it works." Sam kept his tone light, but he could tell Marcus didn't like the idea of these animals getting devoured. He quickly raced ahead. "What's on the next rung?"

Marcus flipped forward. "The ozzies and the squizzies."

Sam rubbed his forehead, pensive. "On Earth, animals like chimpanzees and squirrels are omnivores. They can eat anything, same as humans. These ozzies and squizzies could very well be similar. That could be what the next level is about."

"You mean, like, scavengers?"

"No, that's not the same thing." Marcus shrugged, so Sam went on. "What's next?"

Marcus grimaced. "The razzies and... and something I really hope we never meet."

Curious and nervous at the same time, Sam leaned closer to see the image next to the description text. His eyes widened in shock, and his heart skipped a beat in pure terror.

The creature was nothing short of colossal. Next to it, perhaps to provide scale, stood a lizzie. And it was like comparing an ant to a bear. They weren't even in the same category.

At first glance, the beast resembled a whale. But on closer inspection, echoes of times past when dinosaurs walked the earth came to mind. Long and wide, with fins and flippers, it might have appeared cute if its stature were less gargantuan and it didn't have rows of sharp spikes on its back. Its jaw was filled with huge teeth, and judging from the overall width of that mouth, it could have swallowed hundreds, maybe thousands of razzies in one single bite.

"T-that, uh… it looks like it's a… a sea creature," Sam said, swallowing hard. "I don't think it could come on land. So if we avoid any moonlight skinny-dips in the ocean, I'd say we're safe and sound."

Marcus huffed out an incredulous breath. "Look at that skin, man. That's not scales like with a fish. It's some kind of armor, like a crocodile. And look at the size of that thing. It must be as big as a skyscraper, for fuck's sake. If we ever encounter it… we're boned."

Sam agreed wholeheartedly. "Uh-huh. Guess we're not going fishing anytime soon."

"I'm gonna dub it… mazzie. As in massive." Marcus shuddered, then frowned as he flipped the scroll back and forth. "Why aren't there more animals? Aren't jungles supposed to be thriving ecosystems?"

Sam shrugged. "Maybe these few are the only ones the lizzies were interested in since they obviously didn't establish a presence on this island to conduct biological surveys or observe the fauna in their natural habitat. Or perhaps most of the animals are so good at hiding, the lizzies weren't aware of their existence."

Marcus harrumphed, handing the scroll back to Sam. "Anyway, that's the gist of it."

"What? No mention of the flower?" Sam asked.

"Oh shit. Yeah, you're right." Marcus yanked the scroll from Sam's grip and returned to it with a vengeance. After a moment, he said, "A-ha. Got it. Here it is." He blew out a frustrated breath. "Jeez. Lots of hissing sounds in that one."

"Never mind that. What does it say about the plant? What triggers it?"

Marcus scanned the text, scowling, as though the scroll was the plant and he'd sworn an oath of vengeance. "There are a few, apparently. Vibrations of the ground—"

"That means not much activates it. The biggest creature we've seen was the razzie, and felines can move real quietly." Sam worried all over again.

"—high-pitched sounds," Marcus carried on as if there'd been no interruption, "touch, and sunlight." Sam groaned inwardly. That didn't leave a lot of room for weaknesses. Then Marcus chuckled in pleasant surprise. "Wait. It seems sunlight is really important to that thing. According to this text here, the flower sleeps at night."

"Huh." Sam had never heard of such nocturnal behavior with plants. Sure, some plants turned toward the sun, and a few even closed their buds when the sun went down. But a meat-eating flower that actually slept at night? That was unique to be sure. "That's good news at least. So if we tiptoe, keep our voices down, and avoid the area where it grows during the day, I think we might be okay."

Marcus smiled up at him, his eyes bright. "Awesome." His gaze went hazy as though he were lost down memory lane. "It was so weird. When those vines grabbed me, it felt like… like when you're standing in wooly socks on a rug and get a spark."

Sam frowned. "You mean, like, static electricity?"

"Yeah. Only… milder. It tickled more than it hurt." He regarded Sam with a frown of bafflement. "Is it normal for plants to be, like, electric?"

Sam shrugged slowly, mentally searching his biology classes and websites he'd perused that involved biology. "If exposed to an electrical current of say, twenty thousand volts, many plants reveal having electrical properties. Firs, cress, and common yarrow to mention a few. You see, some plants are susceptible to electrical conductivity, which can even be used to help growth and—"

"Amazing." With one sarcastic word, Marcus conveyed to Sam he was less than interested in a lecture on botany, or possibly he already knew all that. He cocked his head, again as if remembering something important. "Those vines were damn thick, though. Like fucking rubber. When I broke one trying to get free, that green ooze sloshing out of it had sparks too. They dissipated pretty quick, though."

Sam started at the news. He'd assumed that the animals and the lizzies were the only ones to possess bioelectric qualities. Now it seemed that all the living beings on the island, perhaps the whole moon, had those same features.

He pondered the implications carefully. "Some nutrients that the flower digests or the very soil beneath us must contain solutions with ionic properties."

Marcus quirked an eyebrow. "Salt?"

"Yeah. Salts conduct electricity when dissolved into water or when in a liquid state."

"Like the green stuff inside those vines?" When Sam nodded in reply, Marcus pursed his lips in thought. "Is that important? As long as that green goo is inside those vines, it's not going to help us in any meaningful way. Unless you're thinking of fetching vine necklaces."

"Au contraire, mon ami." Marcus rolled his eyes, and Sam hurried on. "You said the outside of the vines felt like rubber, right?"

Marcus frowned at first in confusion, but then his brow cleared and he started to smile. "And rubber is an insulator." But soon his brows scrunched together again. "But just because those vines *felt* like rubber, it doesn't mean they *act* like rubber."

Sam nodded. "True. That's why we need to conduct field tests to determine—"

"Wait a sec. Hold up." Marcus raised a hand to stop Sam, only then asking, "Are you suggesting we somehow use that incredibly dangerous plant's vines to power up the portal in the chamber? Like using jumper cables?" When Sam nodded firmly, Marcus hesitated. He obviously had doubts about the success of the mission.

Sam jumped back into the conversation. "I have no idea if it'll work. But I don't see a lot of other options for us." He looked up, picturing the temple main hall before his eyes. "Those temple towers act like lightning rods. And if everything else on this moon has a strong connection to electricity—"

"Then maybe the weather has one too," Marcus finished Sam's sentence for him, a slow smile spreading across his lips. "Okay, yes, that makes sense. I guess we have a possible escape plan."

CHAPTER 7

"OKAY. WE'LL work out the details later. What other info did you find?" Marcus asked Sam, curious to see how he had fared in his time alone. Marcus did feel slightly guilty for leaving the seventeen-year-old by himself. He vowed to make amends in the future.

"Here." Sam handed Marcus another scroll. "I think it's about this temple. But since I don't speak the language...."

Marcus could take a hint, so he avoided an argument by studying the scroll carefully. Like the first, it wasn't long. Apparently these lizzies could be quite succinct when the mood hit them. He'd hoped Sam would find more information about the lizzies so they could at least answer the question whether they'd died of extinction or if they had simply left for who knows where.

"Hey, Sam. This *is* useful," Marcus commented after he'd perused the scroll from top to bottom. "Here's a complete floor plan of the temple, plus short descriptions about each area, hall, and room. Looks like we're in luck."

Sam let out a relieved breath and chuckled shortly. "Glad that wasn't a total waste of time. What does it say?"

"Blah-blah, yada yada. Aha! Here we are." Marcus pointed at a specific section of the scroll. "We can check out the rest later, but this part talks about, and I quote, a peculiar chamber found underneath the temple mountain, end quote." Marcus frowned in confusion. "I don't get it. Why describe the place in such a fashion?"

Sam let out a long sad sigh. "Unfortunately that's obvious. They didn't build the portal chamber. The lizzies didn't create the portals, the chamber, or the technology. 'Cause if they had, they wouldn't have abandoned such a strategic spot, a beachhead."

Marcus had to admit Sam's deductions were likely correct. No one who built a piece of technology capable of traveling the universe would leave such a place to be reclaimed by nature. "You think they also destroyed the chamber and the chair and then left it to the elements?"

Sam nodded slowly. "Sounds logical. If the lizzies were afraid of what that chair and room might do, then yes, they probably did ransack the place on purpose." He sat down on one of the hard stone seats and looked defeated. "We needed to know and understand how the damn thing works in order to power it up with our makeshift jumper cables. Instead, now we've learned that the previous occupants of this planet had no idea what that machine did or what the room was there for. We're screwed."

Marcus shoved him in the arm hard enough to almost knock him off of the chair. "Oh boohoo. Stop being such a negative Nellie. We're gonna figure this shit out on our own. God, show some backbone, will you?"

Sam's face darkened like a storm cloud; he was clearly pissed off at the name-calling. But then he deflated, nodded, and sighed. "You're right. I'm sorry."

Marcus flung an arm around Sam's shoulders and squeezed. "Hey, c'mon. We're in this together. We're going to be fine. Just keep up your spirits, okay? I need you on this." As an athlete, Marcus had both given and experienced countless motivational speeches and pep talks, so he had this part down.

Sam nodded a few times, leaning slightly away from Marcus. "I'll try." His voice was small and meek, and Marcus felt bad for the things he'd said. But he didn't get the chance to voice his regrets because Sam straightened up and said, "So thanks to the scroll, we now have the lay of the land. Is there anyplace we should check out right away?"

Marcus removed his arm and returned to the text. Sam had been right in his estimation that most of the temple complex had been devoted to love and sex. There appeared to be numerous private quarters—like bedrooms—but few other spaces. The library was one of the few exceptions.

"There's a bathing area on this same level," Marcus said. "It's not far."

Sam looked skeptical. "You think it could still be… functional or clean or…?"

Marcus shrugged. "No idea. Stagnant water…. We could take a look if we have time. I found a waterfall outside anyway, so we can get fresh water there and wash up if we need to."

"Good." Surreptitiously Sam sniffed his armpits while Marcus did his best to stifle his laugh. No need to embarrass Sam, who was such a cutie.

"Oh shit." Marcus almost bolted out of his chair in a rush of excitement after reading a passage of valuable information. "There's something here about the lizzies too."

"I'm sure they have another name for them," Sam commented dryly.

Marcus waved a hand about impatiently. "Yeah, yeah. Anyway according to this text, the lizzies could handle electric shocks and lightning bolts without getting killed."

Sam frowned. "So? We already know the indigenous life on this moon has a curious symbiotic relationship with bioelectricity."

"Yes, but remember the main hall?" Sam nodded, so Marcus went on. "That altar that resembled a bed? Well, it was used as such." Judging by Sam's rosy cheeks and carefully bland expression, Marcus figured he had already made that connection. "As the, uh… lovers did their thing on the altar, they were doused with salt water and that goo from the mazzie flower. When the storm hit, the lightning struck them as they were… you know."

"Wow." Sam's eyebrows rose in surprise and fascination.

"Amazing." Marcus shook his head, his gaze riveted on the scroll. "The lightning bolts didn't kill or hurt them. According to this, it heightened their sexual pleasure. Rain coupled with lightning acted like an aphrodisiac. They engaged in that kind of mating a lot. It was apparently one of their most revered customs, at least on this island. Oh, and get this? When they had an orgasm from lightning, they actually turned translucent. Wow. It must've created one hell of a light show if all these lizzies having sex lit up with full-body halos."

"Do you know what kundalini is?" Sam asked out of the blue.

Marcus grinned. "Does anybody but you?" Sam blushed at the words but said nothing, so Marcus added, "Wait. Let me guess. Gunga Din's baby sister?" Sam blinked and stared. Marcus laughed seeing the stunned expression. "What? I've read my Kipling, same as you."

Sam's blush darkened, and he shrugged. "Anyway… kundalini is the flow of primal energy inside a person."

"And? What's the significance of that little tidbit of random fact?"

"Well, I think these lizzies have a similar concept. Had. From the imagery around the temple, from what you've read, and from what we've observed, energy and electricity means a lot to their culture. And it ties in with their, um… sexual practices, as you just read."

Marcus grinned at Sam's bashfulness. "I love how you start talking all fancy-like when you get to awkward topics, like sex. Even something as peculiar as alien sex on an alien planet. Oh, excuse me. Exoplanet."

"Considering we're orbiting a gas giant, we're technically on an exomoon," Sam said prudishly.

Marcus rolled his eyes. "Excuse *me*." He regarded the light shafts above them. "With that sun blazing up there, looking so much like ours, it's easy to forget we aren't actually on some tropical paradise back home, heading down to the beach in our bathing suits, carrying drinks with little umbrellas and pieces of fruit in them."

Sam smiled, longing in the rueful expression that Marcus could relate to. "We should be glad that the star above us appears to be yellow. After all, the most common star in the universe is a red dwarf, and that would emit infrared radiation. We'd be screwed, then. The star above this moon, though, appears to be like ours, midrange and midlife, so I think we're good."

Marcus shook his head in amazement. "How do you even know that?"

Sam blushed again but ducked his head and said nothing in explanation. Marcus was curious and desperately wanted to ask more. But he felt the timing was off.

"I guess that's something we humans and lizzies share," Sam said all of a sudden, his gaze rising to the light shafts as well. "Most human cultures share the myth of a paradise. The deep-seated yearning for peace, tranquility, eternal life, and abundance. Perhaps that quality is inherent in our genes, common ground to all sentient life. Like a universal myth, a drive toward perfection and advancement of our lives. The hopeful dream of a better place and a higher state of being. A shared experience in our hearts and souls."

As Sam stopped talking, Marcus stared at the pensive seventeen-year-old using the words and phrases of an ancient sage, an old soul. Marcus had known from the start that some elusive quality lured him to Sam. Was it this, the wisdom in his outlook? Sam could be withdrawn, pessimistic, and downright cynical, that much Marcus knew well, but maybe that was a defense mechanism for a fragile dreaming spirit.

Was it Marcus's imagination that Sam appeared incandescent, a pure light in the darkness of their unfamiliar surroundings?

Then Sam said, "It's getting darker," and Marcus realized perhaps his impression was just his imagination.

He glanced up and saw the light shaft was indeed getting dimmer. "We better head back up while we can still see two feet in front of us."

They gathered their belongings and the two useful scrolls and made their way swiftly back to the main hall. Once they reached the large room, it became clear from the oculus on the roof and the windows on the walls that the sun was setting.

"Already?" Sam asked, staring out through the windows in the direction of the horizon, which blazed red, orange, and gold. "We've only been here for, what, a couple of hours?"

"The day's shorter than ours, even our short winter days," Marcus said. "Six hours and a couple of minutes."

Sam stared at him in bafflement. "How do you know that so exactly?"

Marcus bared his arm, showcasing his wristwatch. "Thanks to this. I'm an athlete, so I use a stopwatch a lot. After practice or a workout, I often forget I have it on. I started the countdown clock when we arrived here and the sun rose. If I didn't have my watch, I still have a stopwatch app on my iPhone, and I could've used that."

Sam smiled at him with admiring eyes. "That was smart thinking. Forethought."

Marcus beamed. It wasn't often he got such high praise from his secret crush.

Outside, the tree canopy rustled and crackled in the increasing winds. Huge trees, old long before either of them had been born, sprawled around them to form the dense jungle, complete with vines and moss dripping lazily from the branches, now all swinging and shaking in the rough breeze. Clearly night wasn't a good time to be outside.

"Looks like we might be getting a storm tonight," Marcus said, not liking the rapidly darkening sky and growing gusts. The temple interiors became increasingly shadowy as the light waned. "We need to find shelter for the night. It's gonna get real dark real soon."

"What about those rooms up there?" Sam pointed at the balcony wrapped around the main hall.

"If any of them are still intact, they should do." Marcus scanned the room. "Where are the stairs, or did they just jump up there?" At the exact same moment, Marcus and Sam glanced at one another. "Okay. Let's try that, then." Marcus backed up toward the farthest wall, searching for the sturdiest rubble to act as a bouncing board. "If I fall down to my death—"

"If you leave me to handle this on my own, I'll follow you to hell just to berate you to a second death."

Marcus laughed. Sam did lift Marcus's mood, if not his feet. "Cool. Stand out of the way, chipmunk."

As he started to run, he heard Sam muttering about that not being his name. Sprinting and vaulting from a toppled pillar turned out to be effortless, and Marcus landed on his feet on a broken section of the indoor balcony. A few small chunks chipped off, but nothing more.

"I'm good," Marcus hollered back down to Sam. An audible sigh echoed in the room. "I'm gonna check some of the rooms. If none are usable, no need for you to come up. We'll retrace our steps underground and find shelter there, okay?"

"Fine. But hurry up. Soon I won't be able to see my feet, let alone jump up there."

Chuckling, Marcus did his best to work fast. Again Sam had been right. Each of the rooms had a stone bed and sex reliefs on the walls and ceiling. Nothing organic, like mattresses or pillows, had survived, proving the temple had been abandoned centuries ago. The spaces Marcus surveyed had crumbled chunks of wall or ceiling, piles of dried-up leaves, tree roots or branches growing in, and what looked suspiciously like animal droppings.

Marcus cringed. Unless they found a room without crap in it, they wouldn't dare sleep in any of them.

Finally, after checking out over a dozen rooms, he caught a break. This one had a slab of stone in front of it, acting as a makeshift door. Was that what the lizzies had used back then? Or had they been satisfied with curtains? Could they have been exhibitionists too?

Thankfully the stone slab wasn't too thick or heavy. Or Marcus's newfound agility had a connection to physical strength as well. Considering how Sam had warned him, that seemed most unlikely. The other option was that the slab wasn't actually made of stone but some unknown light metal.

He decided it wasn't worth thinking about right then and grabbed the sides of the slab and lifted. With some maneuvering he was able to slide it through the gap and into the room behind. The chamber wasn't exactly homey, but it was kind of cozy, a small square space with a stone bed and a window. But the window was blocked by a tree trunk, so only tiny slivers of detritus had gotten in. Dried plant matter had gathered in the corners but no animal droppings, no dead animals, and no alien skeletons. Plus the ceiling was intact.

"Thank goodness for small miracles," Marcus muttered. He returned to the edge of the platform and hollered for Sam to throw his backpack up. Sam complied, then backed up to get a running start for his jump. "Be careful," Marcus called out to his sole companion.

"Y-yeah." Sam sounded anxious, his voice cracking.

He sprinted through the hall, used a piece of broken pillar as a stepping-stone, and took a high leap—only to fall short. His hands scraped the balcony, but that was all.

Marcus reached for Sam's arms and grabbed on, preventing him from dropping back down. "Hold on, bae. I've got you."

"Marcus." Sam's voice was fraught with fear, but his grip remained strong.

"Not gonna let you fall," Marcus promised, pulling Sam up by his arms.

Pebbles rained down, clattering onto the stone floor, as Sam kicked them loose from the rough edge of the balcony. Finally he seemed to get a firm foothold, and Marcus could yank him to safety. They tumbled backward onto the balcony, Marcus on his back and Sam on top of him.

Damn, but it felt heavenly to hold Sam flush against him. Marcus practically purred in delight. He really needed to find a way to declare his feelings to Sam, despite their awful circumstances. Holding out as long as he had—liking the guy for years, even when they'd both been too young to contemplate sex—had been torture. Of course, Marcus's childhood feelings for Sam had been far more innocent. He had treasured the sight and sound of his best friend's younger brother, admiring his smarts and quirkiness and enjoying his company even if he had to share those moments with Simon.

Marcus hadn't become friends with Simon because of Sam. They'd met first. His passion for Sam had come later and grown over time. But Sam persisted in acting either skittish or peeved in Marcus's presence, hindering what could become an epic romance.

"You okay?" Marcus asked, holding on to Sam's waist.

Sam reddened, glanced away bashfully, and gulped hard. Marcus could feel Sam's body respond to his, and that raised his spirits—and other body parts. But Sam moved off quickly, as though he were on fire. He looked around, rubbing the back of his neck self-consciously.

"Wh-where's the room?"

Marcus stood too, disappointed but not surprised by Sam's swift denial of what they could mean to each other, but he kept those thoughts to himself. Wrong place, wrong time. But perhaps not all was lost. Marcus hid a grin. Their new temporary accommodations had a single bed. *Promising.* He gestured toward the room and then followed Sam in.

"Wish we had a broom," Sam commented as he placed his backpack on the stone bed.

Marcus snorted. "That's only one thing in a long list of things we don't have and could use."

Sam smiled shortly. "True." Then he regarded their surroundings, biting his bottom lip. "Should we start a fire?"

"There's plenty of broken branches and dry twigs around for that." Marcus studied his companion. "Please tell me you've got matches or a lighter in your trusty backpack."

"Duh." Sam dug into the front pocket of his pack and produced a matchbox. "It's not full, so take care not to use too many."

"Get it right the first time. Got it."

"Wait." Sam grabbed Marcus's arm to stop him, then withdrew in a flash. "Uh, what if the smoke or flames attract the animals?"

Outside, the waxing night produced a cacophony of animal noises, ranging from the songs of ozzies to the chirping of other creatures they'd yet to encounter. Crickets or their alien equivalent? Marcus had no clue. In the distance there was even a chorus of croaks resembling that of frogs. Clearly the jungle did indeed teem with unseen life. Awfully loud life.

Marcus frowned as he listened and reconsidered the plan. "Shit. Hadn't thought of that." He rubbed his jaw thoughtfully. "If the night's as short as the day, perhaps it won't get too cold. Maybe we shouldn't risk a fire after all."

Sam nodded firmly, appearing relieved. He looked down at Marcus's bulging pockets but immediately looked away, his cheeks turning pink. "Did you find anything to eat?"

Marcus snapped his fingers. With everything else going on, he'd forgotten what he'd collected. Sam's near fall had given him an adrenaline rush, so he didn't even feel hunger. First he dragged the stone slab back in front of the doorway, ensuring that nothing as big as giant flowers or predatory felines could get in through the remaining slivers and cracks.

Then he fished the nuts, fruits, and a couple of blue berries he'd gathered from his pockets. "The squizzie I saw cracked the hard shell of the nut and only ate the soft part within. The fruit and the berries? No idea. But from the leftovers on the ground, I think they're edible."

"It's a myth that if an animal eats something in the wild it's not poisonous," Sam said wisely. "Birds can eat pokeweed berries, and deer can eat poison ivy."

Marcus raised a surprised eyebrow. "Really? I didn't know that." He stared at the nuts, berries, and fruit on his palm. "Should we try these anyway?"

"There's no one-size-fits-all rule for nuts. Unless they smell like almonds. That's bad because they might contain, you know, cyanide."

Marcus huffed out an admiring chuckle. "You're like a walking Wikipedia."

Sam blushed. "With fruit and berries, testing is easier, though there are no hard and fast rules. You could place a few drops of their juice on your skin, corner of your mouth, and finally on your tongue. If there's no burning, stinging, swelling, redness, nausea, vomiting, etcetera, then… then it should be okay… ish."

Marcus placed the nut in his palm, made a fist, and cracked open the shell. A cream-colored soft core became visible, and a delicious fresh fragrance rose in the air. He glanced at Sam, who sported a worried frown.

"Here goes nothing." Marcus popped the nut in his mouth, chewed carefully, and then swallowed. From the taste, he wouldn't have been able to tell what grew on an alien moon from what grew on Earth. "Tastes okay. Same as any nut, really."

"Do you feel, I don't know, queasy or nauseous? Wanna throw up? Burning, tingling, anything weird? Cramps, diarrhea? Breathing problems, weakness in senses or limbs, blackouts, seizures?" Sam bombarded Marcus with questions, his expression so anxious it was a small miracle he didn't spontaneously combust.

"Easy there, chipmunk." Marcus calmed Sam down with his tone and a hand over his shoulder. "I'm fine." A moment after he'd swallowed, though, a weird tingling sensation coated his tongue and a cooling airy feeling crept down his throat. "Um…."

Sam seemed immediately alarmed. "Um what?"

Marcus tried to put the sensations into words. "I'm salivating like a dog, and my mouth's sort of… buzzing and tingling, sizzling and boiling, like I ate Pop Rocks. It doesn't hurt, though. It just feels odd. My tongue's vibrating, and going a bit numb. And it feels like I'm breathing in frozen air. But… it still doesn't hurt, and I don't feel sick."

Sam frowned, studying him carefully. "That sort of sounds like… buzz buttons."

"Uh… like what now?"

"Buzz buttons or electric daisies. It's a flowering herb, used as a medicinal plant. It has a grassy taste and a musty odor, but it's used in salads because of that mild stinging sensation. It's a culinary specialty. You just described the sensations to a tee. Never had them myself, but they're not bad for you. Guess this place has its equivalent of buzz buttons, and you found them. Hardly surprising that even edible plants here have bioelectric properties."

Marcus chuckled. "It feels like a live wire in my mouth, like electricity. Super weird." He shrugged. "But not bad. Still not nauseous. That's good, right?" When Sam nodded, Marcus took the rest of his collection in hand. "Let's try the fruit next."

The skin of the oval fruit was smooth and broke apart with ease as Marcus dug in with his thumbs. Inside, purple pulp dripped a little, a sweet scent reaching his nose. With a few reservations, Marcus nonetheless let some drops fall on his forearm. It didn't sting or burn, and the skin didn't turn red. He tried some on his lips and then over his tongue, but nothing bad seemed to happen. So he snatched a bit of pulp with his fingers and ate the tiny piece. After a moment of chewing, he gulped down his bite. A few seconds later, the same buzzing sensation as with the nuts emerged past the aftertaste.

"Refreshing. Tastes a bit like papaya, only sweeter. Tingles again. Here. Have a taste."

He offered Sam a share, and they sat down on the stone bed and munched on their tiny but apparently safe meal. A citrusy flavor preceded the by-then familiar vibe of tingling and sizzling. The effect didn't last long, though.

"Too bad your measly five protein bars are all we have for, like, a substitute for meat," Marcus said absentmindedly, frowning. He already missed meat more than he ever meant to admit out loud.

Sam chuckled. "We could always try insects, if there are any."

Marcus grimaced. "Eww. Pass."

Sam flicked a tongue at him in between bites. "Haven't you ever tried Chapul bars?"

"What the hell is that?"

"Crickets. They're a good source for protein. And from Chapul cricket flour you could make, like, cookies or—"

"Are you fucking serious?"

Sam rolled his eyes. "You don't think there's, like, cricket legs in there, do you? They're ground into a flour. You won't nibble on any pieces of cricket corpses."

Marcus shuddered, chills running up and down his spine. "Please, stop talking before I hurl what little food I managed to find today." Sam giggled but left the topic alone after that.

When Marcus made a move for the berries, though, Sam slapped his hand away. The few berries dropped to the floor and rolled into the corner.

"Hey. What gives?"

"Did you pick these from trees or bushes?"

Marcus frowned in bafflement. "Bushes. Why?"

"Because berries from trees tend to be poisonous. Also, if they're white or yellow—"

"These aren't," Marcus cut in, vexed that the rewards of his arduous search had been so callously swept aside. But he also knew they were in an alien environment and couldn't take too many precautions. "I'll do the same test as with the fruit."

Sam nodded. "On Earth, less than ten percent of white and yellow berries are safe to eat. With red berries, the percentage is about fifty, and with blue, purple, and black ones, around ninety percent. But this isn't our world."

Marcus accepted Sam's warning. On his arm, the purple droplets glided down without producing any weird sensations. After he smeared a few drops on the corner of his mouth, though, a mild stinging occurred immediately, and he wiped the daubs away and spat to be on the safe side.

"Stung a little," he explained to an alarmed-looking Sam. "Best to avoid." He shoved what few berries were left out through the cracks in the doorway. "You were right. We do need to be careful."

Sam's soft smile made Marcus hungry for a different savory dish. Sam could have come off as arrogant considering he was batting a thousand with each theory, guess, and estimate that came out of his mouth. But no, Sam remained shy and grateful whenever Marcus praised him in any way.

Marcus sighed with longing. Being in such close quarters with the object of his desire for the duration of their off-world adventure might just be the death of him.

CHAPTER 8

"I KNOW these are hardly conventional circumstances but… you wanna talk?" Marcus suggested in a low, empathetic voice that seemed to hone straight in on Sam's insecurities. They were still in the middle of their repast, so it wasn't like either of them were trying to sleep yet.

"Not really. I… I don't need friends to talk to," Sam replied defensively.

Marcus smiled with a shrug. "That's fine. I read in some science journal a while back that people without a lot of social relationships, such as friends or boyfriends, actually have above average intelligence. You're not antisocial; you're just really smart."

The compliment only served to confuse Sam more, and the boyfriend reference made him jump inwardly. "I… I never mastered the art of chitchat," Sam confessed, humiliated by the reluctant admission. He craved normalcy in the maelstrom of their current situation, but he didn't know how to start a conversation that was purely random and pure fluff. He was a bookworm, and he didn't have any friends—too shy to approach people and apparently too morose to attract any to him.

Marcus smiled kindly at him. "I don't believe that for a second. What you need is a little practice. How about… music?"

Sam hated talking about his preferences. No one else ever seemed to have heard of the bands or the genre he liked. Sure, it had become popular in the past ten years or so, but it was an acquired tasted. Still he ventured to ask, "Do you listen to pop music from other countries?"

"Yes. I used to listen to and watch a lot of visual kei, but not that much anymore. I still like it for the varying genres and flashy androgynous styles, but some of their videos have become way too freaky for me. If I wanted to see people eating humans, I'd watch *The Walking Dead*, which I don't. I'm so done with zombies." Marcus's grin was as usual irreverent and self-confident. Sam stared back in shock. "Why do you look so surprised? Both K-pop and J-pop have been an ongoing trend since the early 2000s. Or are you just stunned it's *me* who likes them?"

Sam recalled Marcus mentioning something about comics. Anime comics? K-pop and J-pop hailed from the same region originally after all. He was flummoxed, not having even dared to dream his crush might be into the same things he was. The thought boggled the mind. "I... I don't know. Which do you prefer?"

Marcus shrugged. "They kind of sound a bit similar. I like girl groups, like AKB48 in Japan, and 2NE1 and 4Minute in South Korea. AKB48 is such bubblegum pop, even if the girls are overly sexualized and all look awkwardly young. 'I Want You' is their best stuff. 4Minute was disbanded but I loved their attitude as kickass women. 'Hate' is one of their best songs, but—"

"But you can hear Skrillex's influence in there," Sam cut in, practically on autopilot as he was well acquainted with the same genre of music.

"Yeah, pretty much. CL of 2NE1 is my favorite. She's got moves and awesome vocals, and she's got spunk. Their song 'I Am the Best,' proves she's freaking amazing. She alone can rap a song like 'The Baddest Female' and be totally believable."

Sam stared wide-eyed and mouth agape. "You like their videos?"

Marcus chuckled. "Duh. K-pop and J-pop videos are sick. Their quality, production value, and storytelling, it's all dope. It's kind of funny, really, to look at them. There's like a gazillion members in each group, whether male or female—"

Sam got into the topic fast, smiling eagerly. "Yeah, and all the guys have really high-pitched voices—"

"—But they're awesome dancers, you know. They all pretty much dance something fierce, even with the compulsory rapping of late and the extensive use of ridiculous hip thrusts."

"—And they've got magical superpowers, melodramatic gestures, luxury cars, trendy fashion clothes in every video."

"Don't forget all the makeup every guy uses: fabulous eyeliner, glossy lip gloss. And please don't even get me started on all the ludicrous hairstyles that they change every two minutes."

Sam worried his bottom lip, ashamed for his secret desire. "I like their hair."

Marcus grinned, giving Sam a leisurely once-over. "You'd look fantastic with those hairstyles. Hmm, maybe green or blue. Like T.O.P. from Big Bang in 'Fantastic Baby.' Yeah, I'd like to see that."

Sam blushed again, which seemed to be his typical response to everything Marcus said. He couldn't say out loud to Marcus that he'd wished for years to be brave enough to do exactly that. But he also knew that would, in effect, out him. Not that straight guys didn't listen to K-pop or that they didn't dye their hair, which a lot of guys did these days. But since Sam had never been seen with a girlfriend, a public act would effectively shove him right out of the closet into the limelight.

"Which is your favorite boy band?" Marcus asked, snapping Sam out of his musings. "Hate calling them that, but sometimes their dance videos can be so ridiculously retro, even if technically skilled and stylish."

Sam wasn't sure if he should admit who he found totally hot. "Well, I like Big Bang, BTS, B.A.P., EXO-K, TVXQ—"

"Okay, who's your fave guy in a boy band?"

Sam ducked his head, rubbing his neck, so edgy and nervous he felt like he was sitting on an anthill. What was Marcus suggesting? That Sam was… gay? Marcus couldn't possibly know that—unless he had eyes and half a brain and had seen every embarrassing reaction Sam had ever had to him.

He decided to answer. Perhaps Marcus wouldn't even recognize the names.

"I like Jungkook and Taeyang…." He racked his brain for more names, but his memories evaded capture. He'd chosen the names on instinct because they reminded him of Marcus, bad boys with swagger, strength, flirtatiousness, and sex appeal in equal measure (even if sometimes they were so androgynous in appearance they could be mistaken for girls).

Marcus whistled low. "Jungkook, eh? Let me guess. 'Boy In Luv' from the *Skool Luv Affair* album? Still… only bad boys? I didn't expect that. I assumed you'd go for the more… pretty guys."

Weren't all K-pop and J-pop boy band members pretty and dreamy and smoking hot? Sam frowned, bristling defensively. "What's that supposed to mean?" Before Marcus could answer and make the situation even worse, Sam snapped back, "Who do *you* like, then?"

Marcus tapped a finger on his chin, obviously feigning serious pondering. "V's cute in his schoolboy shorts. So's T.O.P. with his blue hair and posh attitude, not to mention Zelo's awesome dancing skills in 'One Shot.'"

Sam licked his lips nervously. Was it a coincidence Marcus had picked the names of all the cuties from exactly the same bands Sam had named as his favorites, and in exactly the same order? Obviously

Marcus knew the subject well enough not to be fooled by Sam's attempts at deflection.

"I.... This is too surreal." Sam couldn't believe he was having this conversation with his secret crush. None of it made any sense. Marcus referred to these guys as cute—but as far as Sam knew, Marcus wasn't gay.

Could K-pop and J-pop make Marcus gay? No, that was preposterous. Unless... he'd been gay all this time. No. Impossible. Sam shook his head at the mere notion.

Marcus stretched his back and arms to pop his joints. "It's well after sundown. We should get some shut-eye. The sun's probably going to be up in a few hours anyway."

It seemed Marcus had decided to move on from the subject. Perhaps he'd figured out Sam was so boring he couldn't even make an interesting topic exciting and worthwhile. Naturally Sam felt rotten, his mental image of himself as sucking at small talk confirmed.

Then Marcus said, "We should probably sleep next to each other on this stone bed for warmth and safety."

Sam gulped. Sleeping next to his dream guy all night? He'd lose his mind—or bust a nut. Either way, it was trouble with a capital T. Nonetheless, it wasn't like they had a lot of choices when it came to their sleeping arrangements. Sam didn't want to sleep alone on an alien world in the dark.

Marcus laid their winter coats on the stone bed, folded the clean towel Sam had in his backpack from his cancelled gym class into a pillow for them both, and sat down to take his boots off. Sam followed suit. Once they'd stripped down to their socks, jeans, and T-shirts, Sam lay back on the wide, long stone bed, using his coat as a sheet and partial blanket. Then Marcus lay down next to him. Sam swallowed and turned away from Marcus, hoping the position would hide inopportune boners. But then Marcus spooned him from behind, and Sam knew his plan had royally backfired.

"Sammy? It's okay to miss home." Marcus's words were at once soothing and... not.

"Yeah." He had nothing else to give at that moment or he'd break apart.

"Good night, Sammy," Marcus whispered behind him, snapping off the flashlight he had used in the growing darkness to guide their way around the small space.

"G-good night, Marcus." Sam hoped he hadn't sounded too squeaky. As Marcus's arms tightened around him, keeping him warm and safe, Sam decided he was in a special hell reserved for losers like him. Shaking the thoughts aside proved difficult, but in the end he managed.

Sam had initially foreseen trouble falling asleep on an alien moon. But Marcus's warmth behind him, the soothing sound of singing ozzies, and the darkness blanketing them soon sent him on his way to dreamland.

SAM STARTED awake, a booming sound above scaring the shit out of him.

"Oh my God, what the fuck?"

"Calm down. It's okay. It's just a storm, that's all." Marcus's soothing tone placated Sam's frayed nerves, even though he could barely make Marcus out in the dimness.

"The sun came up hours ago, but only for a moment," Marcus continued. "Then clouds rolled in out of nowhere. You were right about everything. The weather's unpredictable. And the cloud cover is pretty damn dense. Can't see the stars at all."

Sam wiped the sleep out of his eyes and sat up. "You've been outside already?"

"Uh-huh. When the sun rose. Now it's pitch-black. Decided to let you sleep since we can't see two feet in front of us." Marcus handed Sam the filled water bottle. "Went to get some more food and water. You should drink some. You didn't drink enough last night."

Sam didn't feel like arguing. Truth was, he was thirsty. Greedily he downed half the bottle in one long gulp. "Thanks." He stood, pressing his palms on his back to straighten his spine. "It didn't get as cold last night as I expected."

Marcus smiled shortly. "No. It was warm and comfy. Maybe the weather's to blame. I mean, heat gathers, and then we get a storm, right? That's usually how it works, isn't it?"

Sam shrugged and stretched his legs. He needed to do his yoga but didn't want to exercise in front of Marcus. "On Earth, yeah. Here? Who knows."

Marcus nodded absentmindedly and sauntered out the door. Nothing blocked it; he'd moved the slab aside. Sam followed him, needing to relieve himself. But he couldn't very well take a piss in a holy place, could he?

Once he got to the edge of the balcony and got a good look at the sky through the roof oculus and the windows, Sam figured they could be stranded indoors for days.

A bright blue light flashed on the dark horizon without warning. Surprisingly low lightning painted a silhouette of gigantic trees in the black-and-blue sky. Then the pace of the strikes quickened, and soon the midnight-dark sky blazed every few minutes. The electric pulsing of the clouds was like a bubbling witch's cauldron.

Yet it was eerily quiet at first, with no thunder, as though the stormy show was muted. Then the lightning dwindled and a dark blanket of clouds returned, covering the island with gloom.

But the spectacle was far from over. A low rumble heralded the full awakening of the storm. Sam's and Marcus's eyes could no longer track how many lightning flashes burst forth above their heads. Looked like hundreds in the span of a single minute, both horizontal sparks between clouds and vertical streaks from the clouds to the ground and back up again.

The wind picked up speed, and then came hot waves of rain, beating down the jungle with ferocity. Rustling from the brutally assaulted foliage grew louder. The hammering of the rain on the building almost drowned out the thunder's roar, and Sam shuddered, thinking about how the deluge would have pelted them had they been outside.

A black cloud cover churned and swirled menacingly above them and shot lightning bolts every few seconds. The stormy skies appeared like rivers of fire or bright lanterns, twinkling and sparking.

Lightning formed inside thunderclouds when static charges accumulated, and Sam surmised that the charge difference between the ground and the storm clouds had to rise into the hundreds of millions of volts. He was both a tad scared and a lot inspired by nature's raw power performing before his very eyes.

He wasn't sure what could cause such an awesome display of nature and its elements, but he ventured a guess (thanks to Marcus) that the wind, the sun, the ocean, the rain, and the island mountain together created the effect. It was a logical deduction since the tropics on Earth often suffered from hard monsoon rains, violent thunder and lightning storms, and rough winds.

The storm's ferocity reminded Sam of what he'd read about the Roaring Forties, a phenomenon of stormy air currents in the southern hemisphere, where there was little to no land to work as a windbreak.

"Insane." Marcus sounded awed, clearly amazed by nature's violent spectacle.

Sam was more afraid than fascinated. He wished he were as brave as Marcus, but he wasn't. "I need to… you know."

Marcus glared at him. "You're not going out there. What if that rain is, like… acid or something? We don't know."

Sam growled. "I'm not peeing inside, or just wherever like an animal. But fine. I'll find a safe spot, close to the outside but not quite there. Okay?"

Marcus narrowed his eyes in suspicion. "If you're not back in two minutes—"

"Got it." Sam made a mad dash toward the other end of the balcony in search of a convenient spot to take a leak. Why the heck were there no stairs to or from this level? Didn't the lizzies like them?

"There's a small window with a ledge near you," Marcus yelled after him. "I used it. So can you."

Darn know-it-all. Sam found the window and the tiny protruding ledge. He stepped on it and found it solid but kept a firm hand on the wall the entire time. He unzipped and did his business. As he emptied his bladder, he stared out into the jungle that was being shaken and stirred by the raging storm. Sam felt exposed and vulnerable in the face of so much hostility from the environment. He finished quickly, zipped up, and rushed back to Marcus, who at the moment equaled safety.

"In here, Sam," Marcus called out softly from the relative privacy of their quarters.

Sam dashed in and sat on the bed, watching as Marcus studied the scrolls they'd taken with them with Sam's flashlight, set on low to save the batteries. "Found anything good?"

Marcus harrumphed and chucked the scroll onto the bed. Sam huffed indignantly. The scroll had survived the downfall of the temple but might not survive one pissed-off jock.

"Nope," Marcus said. "This is fucking useless. There are no panic rooms, no armories, no power or generator rooms, not even a damn pantry in this temple. Just loads of bedrooms, a couple of bathrooms, and ceremonial areas where the lizzies could play stuff the sausage and get hit by lightning."

Sam blushed and cringed at Marcus's words. But since Marcus sounded sullen and defeated, he decided to steer their conversation elsewhere for general morale. "Earlier… you mentioned… comics."

"Did I?" Marcus slumped against the wall, eyes closed.

"Uh-huh." Sam puzzled how best to coax some answers from Marcus. "So… you like comics? Like, um, anime or manga…?"

Marcus shrugged. "They're okay. I mean, sometimes I think mixing sweet innocence and little girls in school uniforms with sexually explicit, ultra-violent, bloody and gory imagery is too much. It gets a little… been-there-done-that after a while." Then he smirked at Sam. "But that's not what you really wanted to ask me, is it?" Sam gulped, and Marcus chuckled. "What you really want to know is if I like a specific subgenre of anime: yaoi and BL."

Sam gasped and went beet-red.

"It's okay. Simon told me what you're into."

Sam squeezed his mouth into a disapproving line. "Oh, did he now?"

"Only 'cause I asked him. I was curious about what you kept reading so intently on your laptop. So Simon did a bit of cybersleuthing for me."

"You mean snooping into someone else's private business."

"That too. But he only did it because of me, so if you want to be angry, be angry with me."

"Oh, I am." Sam chewed on the inside of his cheek. "So… *do* you like yaoi?"

Marcus shrugged. "It's okay. Some are good, some aren't. I admit, though, that I like boys' love comics more than strict yaoi, where things get a bit predictable after a while."

Sam disagreed. He thought the plotlines were different and unique each time.

"I follow a few BL webcomics religiously. Such as *Avialae*—Gannet's too cute for words even if he can be obnoxious. *Transfusions*—Joa's hot for a vampire. *Demon of the Underground*—Pogo kinda reminds me of you. *Buying Time*—so adorable and sad that I cried for like an hour. *The Less Than Epic Adventures of TJ and Amal*—these two are so realistic and just a hoot. *Light Romantic*—that kissy-face janitor is too funny, and that witty banter rocks! *Teahouse*—too bad it was discontinued 'cause it was awesome—"

"Oh. My. God." Sam was blown away. He wasn't sure if he was furious, exalted, or a mixture of both. "How the hell do you even know about those?"

Marcus laughed. "You of course. Who else? But, like I said, I found a few on my own. As you can see, though, I prefer BL to yaoi, like *A Foreign Love Affair*. I just feel like they've become too violent and gory. All those guys having sex but never admitting they're gay. Maybe I've outgrown yaoi. I mean, I still follow a few, like *Maiden Rose,* but I liked the original video animation better than the actual comic. That said, it's not that I mind yaoi, if and when I'm in the mood, but—"

"Name even one yaoi comic right the F now," Sam insisted, even though Marcus had already mentioned two. Sam couldn't wrap his brain around the likelihood that Marcus was into the same things he was. That'd mean the world had gone surreal while Sam had been busy blinking and running away.

"*I do not want to play around because I like it*—the whole collection of stories was so hawt and cute and dirty in a titillating way. *Yatamomo*—Momo's such a slutty goofball. *Electric Delusion* and *Peach Boys*—hot best friends getting it on. These spring to mind," Marcus retorted.

He was clearly undeterred, as cool as a cucumber, while Sam felt like he was sitting on a hill of fire ants. Marcus cringed for a blink of an eye when he mentioned the names of the ones he liked. Sam understood. He'd reacted the same way to the yaoi manga that were all filled with lots of explicit sex scenes. And both *Electric Delusion* and *Peach Boys* were stories of friends who had sex and loved each other.

"What about you? What's your favorite boys' love?" Marcus asked.

Sam went through his mental Rolodex. "*Ten Count* is good. It's got depth, intriguing characters, and some spicy... uh, sex scenes." He ducked his head and tried to get a handle on his feelings. He licked his lips and went on. "The psychology behind the plot is fascinating, and it's one of my favorites. But... like you, I'm into *Yatamomo* by Harada. It's lighthearted and fun."

Marcus nodded. "Yeah. Then there's *Under Grand*—"

"—*Hotel*," Sam finished for him, breathing out the word in shock.

Marcus nodded, not appearing to have noticed Sam's shaken state of mind. "That was kind of brutal in many ways, the setting being a prison and all. But of all the stuff I've read over the years, that one had the greatest impact on me, making it memorable. I suppose the reason is Swordfish and Sen as seme and uke, the traditional roles firmly in place."

"Yeah." Sam frowned, more in puzzlement than anything else, saying anything to say *something*.

Marcus shrugged. "I didn't think Swordfish would ever give a blow job to anyone. But love changed him. However, like in pretty much all the yaoi and manga I know, the role switch for him was a rape scene. Disappointing, though instrumental to the plot. Nonetheless, I thought it was interesting how the comparison was made between how Swordfish fucked Sen and how the Warden raped Sen. That showed well that anal sex doesn't have to be brutal and that it isn't rape if both men are willing—and use plenty of lube."

Sam heard Marcus's voice and words faintly, echoing inside his head like a dream or a distant memory. The whole conversation felt unreal; Sam couldn't grab ahold of his sanity. Both of them had reacted with the same cringe to yaoi involving friends and/or neighbors falling in love.... Sam didn't think that was a coincidence. They were on the same wavelength. The same topics spoke to them both.

"You draw comics too, don't you?" Marcus asked, startling Sam.

"Huh? H-how'd you know about that?"

"Same way I know everything about you. Made it my business to find out since you're always busy running away from me."

Sam blushed with embarrassment and looked away. Then he remembered something. "Is that what you meant when you doubted me wanting to be a scientist?"

"Yeah. I assumed art was what you were into the most."

"No. That's just a hobby. I mean, I've thought about maybe writing and drawing my own boys' love comic but in the end I want to be a scientist. When I was twelve, at summer camp we got to participate in a dig within an ancient Native American burial ground. It was amazing. For the longest time I wanted to become an archaeologist."

"Huh. I had that phase when I watched the Indiana Jones movies."

Sam smiled. "That too. If my math and physics scores were higher, I'd want to be an astrophysicist. I'd love to study exoplanets."

Marcus snorted. His laugh wasn't mean or derisive. Sam thought it must have been his way of encouraging Sam. "We're on one, in case you missed it. Well, on an exomoon."

"True." His curiosity piqued and he just had to know. "Marcus, this might sound kind of stupid but... I don't know what your major is."

Marcus chuckled. "What? You haven't been keeping tabs on me?"

"Shut up."

"I can hardly do that and answer you," Marcus teased softly. "But if you must know, I'm majoring in classical studies and history. I was happy Whitefish Lake College offered courses on both. In any case, I would have thought talking about *hieros gamos* and Greek myths would have made my scholarly interests obvious."

Sam stared, eyes wide, mouth agape. No, he hadn't known that. And just what the heck was—oh, *hieros gamos* had to be the Great Rite Marcus had mentioned earlier. He flushed with heat and was unable to offer an intelligent comment.

Marcus went on as if unaware of Sam's weird thoughts. "I always wanted to study ancient civilizations. They're fascinating. The history, the religions, the society.... Cool stuff. And we Americans owe so much of our cultural heritage to them." Then he chuckled wickedly and winked at Sam. "Although, if and when we get home, I'm going to take some new minors, like... electrical engineering or forestry or... or fucking survival skills."

Sam laughed at that. Marcus was great, no doubt about that.

"What's your major?" Marcus asked then, shaking Sam out of his reverie.

"Oh, uh, natural sciences, with a minor in art." Two things he loved combined. How could Sam resist?

As the moment of silence stretched between them, Sam replayed the talk they'd just had—and he realized he'd mentioned boys' love a number of times. Basically he'd left the door wide open for Marcus to deduce that Sam was gayer than a unicorn riding a rainbow.

A rumbling thunder rolled above them, shaking the ground and the temple. Lightning flashed, turning the room briefly bright as sunlight. Sam jumped at the sudden sound, trembling and rattled.

"Everything's going to be okay, chipmunk."

Sam shook his head in frustration. "First of all, you don't know that. I'm a realist, and the kind of ridiculous and unfounded optimism you display is what landed us in this mess and will likely get us both horribly killed. So how can you possibly believe everything's magically going to turn out sunshine and roses?"

Marcus ducked his head. "Well, I don't believe the universe is out to kill us, for one. I don't expect the worst-case scenario to befall me every second of every day. I think the universe, gods, spirits, magical mojo, whatever, is giving us every chance to come out on top."

Sam hesitated. "I don't think I could be so...."

"Sanguine?"

"How do you even know that word?"

Marcus looked away. "You mean why aren't I a brain-damaged jock with a learning disability and the mental faculties of a fetus?"

Sam hadn't meant that. He wasn't surprised that Marcus knew the meaning of the fancy word, but rather that someone as active as Marcus had such a philosophical turn to his thinking. Come to think of it, though, maybe that was just as poor an assumption. Sam guessed he had failed to deliver his message. Again.

Confused, Sam backpedaled as fast as he could. "I didn't say that!"

"Maybe not. But you were thinking it."

Sam bristled at the accusation. "Oh, you're a mind reader now?" Marcus gave Sam an admonishing look. To hide his own delicate emotional state, Sam continued, "Firstly, I don't think you're stupid. Even if you are a jock—which doesn't mean anything. I know I might not always act like it, but... I respect you and your intelligence even when you try to hide it." When Marcus opened his mouth to intervene, Sam hurried to get ahead and add, "Second, I really, *really* hate it when you call me chipmunk."

"Why? It's an affectionate nickname."

Sam stared at Marcus in gobsmacked disbelief. "What?"

Marcus smiled softly, casting weird goo-goo eyes at Sam. "The nickname reminds me of when you smile. Your cheeks get bigger. It's cute. I've seen it a few times over the years, though you rarely do it in my company. Nonetheless, I've stored the images in the old memory banks." He tapped at his temple and winked.

Sam might have squeaked. He kept opening and closing his mouth, his brain fried, the words on the tip of his tongue practically glued on. "But... why?"

This time when Marcus smiled, wide and seductively, there was zero chance anyone, even an inexperienced dum-dum like Sam, could misinterpret his intent and meaning.

Sam swallowed hard. "Are you saying you're... gay?"

Marcus nodded. "Yes. Yes, I am. Well, I suppose I'm bi since I've been with chicks *and* dudes. But I'm leaning more toward dudes. Funny but I'd have thought us talking about yaoi and boys' love would have been a dead giveaway...."

Sam balked, full of disbelief, and stammered, "But... what about all those girls you've dated over the years?" Marcus frowned and cocked his head, looking confused, so Sam added, "Like, uh... Zoe?"

Marcus's brow smoothed as he chuckled. "Oh, her. When I went out with her, she was in her rebellious phase 'cause her parents wanted her to date an egghead or a rich dude. I wasn't considered either, so...."

"Okay. What about, um, Kayla?"

"She preferred older guys, like in their twenties or thirties, and still does."

"Mindy?"

"She's a lesbian and dating Una in secret. I was her beard."

Sam shook his head in bafflement at all this news. "*Glee* has lesbian cheerleaders, so Mindy being attracted to girls shouldn't really be a shock anymore."

Marcus laughed. "How do you know all their names? Even I don't recall the names of every girl I've dated over the years. But you... you have them memorized?"

Sam coughed to hide his embarrassment. The truth was, he'd been keeping a close eye on the girls surrounding Marcus. It wasn't like he wanted to be a girl and seduce Marcus (though he had once or twice had a sex fantasy like that), but he had wondered what Marcus saw in them. What aspects in a person was he drawn to?

And could Sam somehow maybe reproduce those aspects in himself?

"So, um, are you sleep—uh, seeing anyone from school?"

Marcus shook his head. "Nah. I don't shit where I eat."

Sam admitted he was both relieved and disappointed. Marcus wasn't currently having sex with any girls or guys at school. But... he also wasn't dating anyone from their school, and apparently wouldn't as a general rule. That school chum category included Sam—and disqualified him from the prospective boyfriend pool. *Dammit.*

Then Marcus grinned seductively. "Of course, I've had to revise that rule since...."

Sam frowned with expectation, sitting on pins and needles. "Since… when?"

"Since you grew up so cute and fine." Marcus's flattering smile widened into a naughty grin. "Just. My. Type."

Sam seriously considered having a stroke.

CHAPTER 9

MARCUS WATCHED Sam reel from the news. He started to think he'd phrased his desires improperly and scared the guy off. "You okay there, Sammy?"

Sam swallowed and blinked, repeating the moves several times. His mouth opened and closed, but nothing came out—not so much as a peep. Marcus got anxious. Had he unwittingly caused Sam to lose his shit completely?

Marcus decided to soften the blow. "I'm sorry if I freaked you out just now. It's just that I… I like you. I've liked you for a few years now." His hope faded. "I… I thought you might feel the same. I'm sorry, Sam. I didn't mean to upset you this much. Just forget it, okay? Forget I said anything."

Sam's brow scrunched in a desperate frown, and his eyes watered. "Y-you didn't mean it then…?"

"I did." Marcus was out of his depth. Every girl and guy he'd ever dated had been way less trouble than this. They'd all been pretty willing to fall flat on their backs for him at the drop of a hat. But Sam wasn't like that, and Marcus knew it. "Look, bae, I really am sorry. I did mean it 'cause I do like you, a lot, but… it's not like you're obligated to…. You shouldn't feel pressured to…."

"I think that's about the third time you've called me bae."

Marcus stuttered to a halt, which was probably good since he was rambling without a clue as to where he was headed. He'd never been this much at a loss for words before. "Huh?"

Sam hesitated briefly, as if unsure. "You did call me bae before, didn't you? The first few times… I thought maybe I'd, like, misheard or something. It barely registered 'cause we were in pretty serious situations at the time. But this time I'm sure." Sam had never looked so utterly confused and sad, and Marcus didn't know what to do or say to make him feel better. "H-have you called lots of guys… bae?"

"No. Never. Only you." That reply gave Marcus back some of his self-confidence. The truth had a calming effect on him. "You're my one and only bae, Sam." Briefly he wavered over the foolishness of saying that when they weren't dating and Sam might not even want to be with him.

Sam frowned, disbelief and suspicion evident in his haunted gaze. "How many g-guys have you... been with?"

"Three. You don't know them. They don't go to our college. And it wasn't... I mean, it was just getting off and basically me figuring out what my body wanted. None of us were, you know... in love. We just...."

"Fucked." Sam spat out the word like something vile from his mouth.

Marcus had to accept he'd totally misread the situation, Sam's feelings, and maybe his orientation too. Guess the guy wasn't gay, or if he was, he wasn't into Marcus. "Yeah."

Sam said nothing. He simply stared, his expression closed off, his lips thinned and his eyes ablaze.

Blinding flashes of the storm periodically illuminated the confined space, which started to feel claustrophobic to Marcus. He couldn't explain the accusation he saw in Sam's eyes. Regardless of the motivation behind that look, perhaps it was time to admit defeat.

Marcus stood awkwardly, feeling like his limbs weren't his own. "I'm, uh, gonna take a look outside to see if the storm's clearing anytime soon." He stepped to the doorway, not daring to look at the sole other person on the island. "I won't go far so... if you need me or anything, just holler." Their relationship had just become a hell of a lot more awkward, and it was all Marcus's fault. He'd gambled and lost.

Before Marcus could walk out and be alone with his depressing thoughts, Sam stood in a rush, gripped his arm, and prevented him from leaving. "Wait."

Marcus stopped but didn't look at Sam. "What?"

Sam released him slowly. "I... I'm your... bae?"

Finally Marcus faced Sam, resolve in his heart. "Yeah."

Sam worried his lower lip, hesitating before asking, "So you... like me?" he asked, his tone tentative and small.

Marcus smiled shortly. "Yes. More than like, actually." When Sam remained silent too long for his comfort, Marcus added, "Look, I'm sorry if I made you feel uncomfortable. It's okay if you don't feel—"

"I've wanted you since I figured out I like guys, which was when I was nine."

Sam's sudden outburst warmed Marcus's heart so much it skipped a beat. "Really?"

Sam looked terrified, his eyes wide, his skin pale, his stance rigid. But he nodded despite the deer-in-the-headlights expression.

Marcus smiled joyfully, a great weight lifted from his shoulders, relief washing over his senses. Leisurely he rested his hands on Sam's hips and drew him closer, till their bodies touched. It was amazing and powerful and intoxicating and world-changing.

"Really?" he repeated, wanting to hear Sam say the words out loud, to confess he liked Marcus as much as Marcus liked him. But his smile never faltered because he doubted that any amount of nervousness would force Sam to take back his admission.

Sam swallowed and nodded, a tiny frown between his eyes, as though he still wasn't sure of the reception. "Y-yes. I... I like you a lot too."

Marcus could have sworn that wasn't what Sam had intended to say. The second that thought hit his brain, his heart supplied the answer. *Sam's in love with me.*

And that idea sparking to life in his head made Marcus dizzy with want.

Voicing his desire, however, proved arduous. "Look, Sammy—uh, Sam. I don't want to rush.... I mean, I know this is hardly the time or place for... you know. But I—"

"Sex?" Sam blurted out of the blue.

At that straight-to-the-point utterance Marcus could only laugh and nod. "Yeah. That's what I was going for. Unless you don't want—"

"I do. Right now." Despite his red cheeks, sweaty paleness, and withheld breath, Sam looked steadfast, determined, and... totally freaked out.

Marcus swallowed hard, desire buzzing in his brain and body. "There's some stuff we won't be doing." Sam frowned, tilting his head in obvious puzzlement. "You're only seventeen—"

"Yeah, seventeen, not seven," Sam cut in, pouting.

"—and I'm twenty, so—"

"You've been twenty for, what, two weeks?"

"Three. And a half." This time it was Marcus who pouted.

Sam rolled his eyes and snorted. "Well, I'm sure those three-and-a-half weeks make *all* the difference in the world now that you're not a *teen*ager anymore."

"Legally—" Marcus argued.

"Are you kidding? Look, I'm already legal at home in Montana. And even if that weren't the case, we're stuck on an alien moon for who knows how long. No cops here to arrest us, no lawyers to sentence us, no parents to scold or ground us."

"Regardless," Marcus said emphatically, "we're not doing anal. For one, no lube, and two, no condoms."

Sam blushed, his irate state vanishing. "Well, even if we had those things, I… I'm not ready for that. It's not that I don't want to, you know, someday, but at the moment…."

Marcus smiled in relief. "Well, good. 'Cause neither am I, having never done it. Before we do… that, I need to do, like, research and stuff."

Sam chuckled, a twinkle in his eyes. "Like what? Gay porn?"

This time Marcus blushed. "Did I say that?" Yeah, he'd totally meant that, but no way in hell was he going to admit it to Sam, the annoying know-it-all.

Marcus wound his arms fully around Sam's waist and back, pressing them together in full-body contact. He rested his forehead against Sam's and for a moment just let himself revel in how good Sam felt, their skin touching, their breaths mingling, their bodies growing hotter and harder by the second.

Then, without warning, Marcus's mouth was full of Sam's insistent tongue. In fact, Sam pretty much jumped him, climbing Marcus's body like an ozzie up a tree. Marcus was forced to cup Sam's butt in order to prevent him from falling.

Hot damn, but Sam was a great kisser. Marcus could never have imagined such talent and power behind Sam's kissing skills. Sam sucked on Marcus's tongue and lips, upper lip one moment, the lower a heartbeat later. He licked over Marcus's teeth and across his palate; he fused their mouths together so tight not even an air molecule could have snuck in uninvited.

Marcus was instantly suspicious.

Tearing his mouth away, he breathed out, "Where'd you learn how to kiss? And with whom?" He couldn't keep the burning jealousy from his tone.

Sam blinked as he pulled back to look Marcus in the eye. "A-are you… jealous?"

"No. …Maybe. …Yes!"

Sam's eyes shone with amusement, and his smile could have lit up the night. "Oh, Marcus, you're mad. There's no one else. There's never been anyone else."

"Kissing's not the kind of skill one learns on their own, if you know what I mean."

Sam blushed fiercely and coughed to clear his throat. His gaze darted around the room without settling anywhere. "Well, that's not exactly true...."

Marcus frowned, puzzled by the response. Then it hit him. "Hand or fruit?"

Sam ducked his head farther, hiding his face. "F-fruit. P-plum and... m-mango."

Marcus smiled softly, though Sam couldn't have seen the gesture with his downcast eyes. "I bet they didn't taste as sweet as I know you taste. Oh, and by the way? Nothing to be embarrassed about. Or do you think I came up with those choices out of thin air? For me, it was the hand. In fact, I learned to do most sex things with my hand before doing anything with a real person."

Finally Sam looked up, hesitantly, as if trying to be as small and inconspicuous as any guy possibly could. "R-really?"

"Yeah." Marcus kissed Sam because he had to or his heart would stop beating. "And bae? You've learned some mad skills. Kiss me again. Kiss me like you mean it."

Sam apparently didn't need to be told twice. He smashed his lips against Marcus's and sealed them together. His tongue delved, his teeth nibbled, his lips savored. Marcus was fast losing control. He wanted Sam naked, the way he'd imagined for so fucking long.

Marcus slipped his hands underneath Sam's T-shirt and felt an expanse of smooth skin he couldn't wait to put his lips to. Sam moaned into the kiss, and Marcus felt weak in the knees. He craved everything with Sam, but the last remnants of his sensibility stopped him. The recent memory of their frank discussion about anal, among other things, was fresh on his mind.

"Um, anything you don't wanna do? What's off-limits, Sam? 'Cause I want you so bad it feels like my blood's boiling. But fuck if I want you to regret anything we—"

Sam whimpered and went lax in Marcus's arms. "Naked. Now. Please."

It wasn't much of an answer, but it was a start. Marcus chuckled as he yanked Sam's T-shirt off and dived straight for the button on his jeans next. They hadn't been in the jungle long enough for their clothes or bodies to stink yet, so Marcus scraped his teeth against Sam's neck, needing to taste his skin and flesh.

"Oh God," Sam murmured, throwing his head back to give Marcus better access. His hands roamed wildly over Marcus's back, gripping at times, flailing at others. "Need...." He didn't even finish his sentence before he fisted Marcus's T-shirt and began pulling it off.

Marcus finally relented, released Sam, and raised his arms to aid in the undressing. As soon as his torso was bare, Marcus cupped Sam's cheeks and kissed him again, his hunger growing with each second. Sam's shaky hands reached for Marcus's belt, unbuckled it, and then unbuttoned and unzipped his jeans. Marcus followed suit, shoved Sam's jeans halfway down his thighs, and gripped his erection through his underwear, stroking the hardening length.

"Oh, sweet Jesus, *yesss*...." Sam's voice cracked into a high-pitched noise that rang in Marcus's ears as proof of a perfect act.

He pushed Sam toward the bed. It wasn't soft or springy, but it was convenient. Their winter coats and a single towel had to be enough. Marcus laid Sam down on the bed and then finished removing his jeans, socks, and underwear. Sam's hard, red dick rested heavy in the groove of his thigh and abdomen, throbbing visibly, a translucent bead of precome dangling from the slit.

As he stared, momentarily mesmerized, Marcus knew without a shadow of a doubt he was in love and in lust with Sam.

"D-did you change your mind?" Sam asked nervously, rising onto his elbows. "What's wrong?"

Marcus smiled. "Nothing. You're perfect."

Sam blushed and smiled shyly. "You... you make me feel beautiful."

His sweet statement sent Marcus's heart into a fluttering frenzy. "I love you, Sam."

Only when Sam's eyes widened and his jaw dropped in shock did Marcus realize he'd spoken out loud. He'd not intended to blurt it out like that. But the cat was out of the bag now. The truth wouldn't change over time, he knew, for want was such a weak word to describe the depth of his feelings for Sam.

"I feel like I've been saying weird shit a lot lately but... it's true. I love you." Marcus was proud of himself for getting the confession out without stammering or his voice cracking. He meant it with all his heart after all.

Sam lay on the bed so still it was as if he'd magically transformed into a resting statue. Finally he murmured, "R-really...?" Marcus could only nod, his mouth dry as a desert from waiting with bated breath. When Sam smiled, his cheeks turning rosy, Marcus let out a long breath of relief. "I… I love you too, Marcus."

As though in a hypnotic daze, Marcus finished undressing, climbed naked onto the bed between Sam's spread legs, and knelt there. He placed a hand over Sam's bent knee, unable to tell which one of them trembled more.

"I've wanted to touch you like this for so long," Marcus confessed, an unusual shyness causing his whispering tone and clunky actions. "Dreamed of touching you, being with you, holding you in my arms, kissing you."

Sam gulped, his skin glowing from fresh sweat and coloring crimson with arousal. Or at least that was what Marcus hoped for. With one outstretched arm, Sam beckoned Marcus closer. Nervousness bunching under his rib cage, Marcus lowered himself down over his lover-to-be. He'd never felt this anxious about the prospect of sex. Then again, he'd slept with girls and guys for no other reasons than being hard and horny, and them being ready, willing, and available.

Not the stuff of burgeoning love affairs or epic romances. Not like this right now.

Holding his weight up, Marcus leaned down onto his elbows, his hands hooked under Sam's shoulders. When their nude bodies came together, they both let out a long sigh of satisfaction.

Marcus smiled softly. "Been chasing you a long time, Sam."

Sam smiled back. "I won't run away from you again. I promise."

Marcus chuckled. "That's good to know. Although… it's been kind of fun. Besides, I'll just remember to wear my running shoes next time I come after you."

Sam giggled at that. "I'll promise to be easy prey."

The heat from Sam's body created a primal reaction in Marcus, one of possession and greed. The impulse scared him a bit, but he'd longed for Sam so long that he couldn't tamp down the effect. Even though Sam was beneath him, Marcus felt Sam somehow engulf and envelop him, like a magnetic current pulling them together, cocooning them inside a safe haven of love and drowning out the alien world around them. Sam equaled passion and beauty and love, and Marcus couldn't get enough.

Marcus shifted his hips, and their hard cocks nuzzled, pressed together shaft to shaft. Sam gasped, his eyes hooded with lust. Marcus petted Sam's hair while he touched Sam's body with his own, their skin kissing. Despite Sam's nerd persona, Marcus felt Sam's muscles, the strength hidden there, belying his geekiness.

"Are you...?" Marcus breathed out, starting to lose it. "Are you mine?"

Sam kissed him and wound his arms around Marcus's neck. "Who else would I ever belong to but you?"

Marcus threaded his fingers through Sam's silky hair. With surprised delight, he felt Sam slide his arms down to squeeze Marcus's asscheeks. Marcus dipped to suck up a hickey on Sam's neck, loving the catch in Sam's voice.

His own was thick with emotion when he said, "I can't believe how much I want you. It's like a drug running through my veins. Every damn day I need my intoxicating Sam fix, or I'll act like a fucking grouch or a bear shot in the ass."

Sam laughed, undoubtedly at the mental image, and hugged him tighter. "You know, I can actually picture you in an adorable teddy bear costume on Halloween, sitting on your porch like a grumpy—mm-hmm."

Marcus stole Sam's breath away and effectively silenced him with a tongue down his throat. Every touch of Sam's slick tongue was like liquid silk, hot and delicious. Marcus was so ferocious he feared he might hurt Sam, and he would never forgive himself.

"T-tell me if I'm too rough, baby."

"Mmm, you're perfect," Sam whispered in his ear, then sucked on Marcus's earlobe. Chills ran down Marcus's spine, and his hips bucked. Sam grunted, and an answering upward thrust of his hips followed.

Marcus wanted to be perfect for Sam—the hero who saved the day and the rescuer who brought them both back home safe and sound. He prayed to be able to deliver on his secret vow.

"God, you feel so good, so good," Marcus mumbled over and over.

"Marcus, I'm so close. Please...." Sam's voice cracked, and Marcus's heart skipped a beat. No way would he cause Sam agony.

He snapped his hips hard, meeting Sam's with a perfectly matched rhythm as they ground against each other, clinging together tightly. Sam's limbs wrapped around Marcus, who'd never felt such all-encompassing love and desire. They burned his senses and shook him to the core.

Sam pulled Marcus harder over him, and Marcus responded by surging against Sam. They were both panting roughly, words forgotten, reason obliterated. Only their lovemaking existed in this small room in a ruined temple on an alien world.

Their cocks lined up and rubbed along each other's lengths. The touch—not enough, but it had to be enough—was sweet torment. Marcus pictured his cock plunging in and out of Sam's ass, that beautiful soft nubile body bent, that channel stroking his dick, that quivering voice begging to come....

Marcus's climax took him by surprise. His hips jerked violently, and his cock erupted. He crashed over the edge, hurtling headlong into the blinding void where no thought existed. He slammed against Sam, who suddenly cried out sharply, grasped Marcus's back and buttocks so hard his nails dug in.

Hot juices from both of them rained down between their writhing bodies. Their mouths fused into a passionate, breathless kiss, and they clutched each other tight, neither willing to let the other go. Their hips kept thrusting lazily as they came down from orgasmic heights.

"Oh. Oh. Oh." Sam's sighs slowed eventually as his breathing calmed. "Th-that was... the best... ever."

"Right on." Yes, Marcus could indeed be eloquent when the occasion called for it.

For a while they just held each other. Marcus slid off Sam, and they cuddled side by side, their legs entwined, sluggishly caressing one another, tracing indistinct patterns on each other's skin, sharing smooches, smiling goofily, and staring into each other's eyes.

Then Sam grimaced, his nose scrunched. "I feel sticky, and we're starting to reek. You said there was a waterfall? We should probably wash up."

Marcus harrumphed. "Heck, we could just step outside for a minute and be pelted like animals."

Sam quirked an eyebrow. "Wanna take the risk that the giant plant's still chasing you, or the razzies prefer to hunt during stormy weather, or the rain is acid?"

"Ah. Good point. That's why you're the brains to my brawn."

Sam pursed his lips, clearly vexed. "Stop calling yourself dumb. Even in jest. I don't like it. After all, it's *my* guy you're badmouthing there."

The words made Marcus ridiculously happy. "Okay. Sorry."

Sam narrowed his eyes, appearing suspicious, probably due to Marcus's wide grin and soft voice. "Okay. Cool."

They decided to leave their clothes behind since the island was uninhabited and none of the animals probably cared if they walked around in the buff. Marcus did take his iPhone in case they'd need a loud noise to frighten away frisky or fearsome beasts. They made sure the stone slab was in place in front of the doorway so their stuff would be secure.

Treading carefully, they made their way down to the mountainside terrace onto which the waterfall partially flowed. Marcus soaked himself first. The tepid water was cool on his heated skin, but not for long. The moderate temperature of the water soon gave him a decent washing experience. Once he was done, he indicated with a chin lift that Sam should go next.

With a shy smile and pink cheeks, Sam did as he was silently instructed. He stepped under the cascade, his hair instantly glued to his skin, his body glowing with each lightning strike in the sky high above, the tantalizing curves and luscious plumpness of his buttocks in plain sight, the mesmerizing lines of his back, legs, and arms beckoning Marcus to get more familiar with them all in intimate detail.

In short, Sam looked divine.

Marcus cocked his head, thinking about his feelings for Sam. He knew he was in love. But what was love? Was it butterflies in his belly, weakness in the knees, surges in his groin, parties in his head, or the flying feeling in his heart? Or perhaps love was plainer and more mundane, like laundry or dishes: never-ending.

Marcus smiled when he figured out at least part of the mystifying equation. Love was Sam's bare feet next to his under the blanket, his head resting over Marcus's heart, their fingers interlaced. Love was memories of the past and dreams of tomorrow, and his beloved was a part of both.

Love was all that, and more. He wondered if even a lifetime was long enough to solve that mystery of the ages.

Marcus bit his lower lip to stop the moan threatening to burst out of him. Then an idea occurred to him. With a naughty grin, he set out to fulfill another unspoken fantasy with his iPhone, a testament to his desire for Sam.

Despite the gush of the waterfall, Marcus heard the rain cease abruptly. The looming dark clouds parted to reveal the rich, colorful stars of the night sky, a strange galaxy spreading out across the heavenly arc.

Then he understood. "We're in the eye of the storm."

The sudden serenity, silent and stunning, stilled Marcus in awe. Though he hoped they would get home sooner rather than later, that night sky was definitely worth capturing. Apparently the storm had already taken longer than they'd thought, swallowing up the whole day.

Or perhaps they'd simply lost track of time due to the awesome sex. Marcus's cheeks flamed just thinking about it.

A monstrous splash startled them both.

The noise was so tremendous, it was as if the seas had parted by magic.

Then Marcus saw… it. The pictures hadn't done the massive sea creature justice.

Gargantuan in size, the aquatic animal resembled a whale, a crocodile, and an extinct ocean dinosaur. Its skin had a blue-green tint, and it was heavily armored with rows of dorsal spikes and an elongated snout tapering toward the tip. It had numerous fins on the side and along its spine between the spikes and four large flippers low on its sides, like a plesiosaur. Obviously, despite its gigantic size, it could move swiftly underwater. The animal glowed as if tiny lights flickered all over its length, so it was obviously bioluminescent.

But… the incredible creature's existence alone wasn't the weirdest part.

Because the mazzie was no longer underwater. It was… flying.

CHAPTER 10

"IMPOSSIBLE...," MARCUS whispered, frozen in astonishment and primal dread, watching the sea creature glide along the sky as if swimming through the air. Its belly radiated a purple glow, and its flippers sparked an electric blue shower with each flap.

Then they heard it.

Magical tunes floated through the air. Bursts of high-frequency clicks, long waves of whistles, and tonal musical moans and groans created ethereal vocalizations clearly emanating from the mazzie, like the songs of humpback whales but far more complex. The modulations and amplitude shifted, exactly like in a song. The sweetest sounds rained on them. Marcus had never heard anything like it.

"Marcus?"

"Sam?"

"Are you seeing this, or have I just gone spectacularly insane?"

"Not unless I'm right there with you in the asylum." Marcus couldn't stop staring at the unbelievable sight, though he gathered himself enough to make use of his iPhone again. "How's it doing that? Staying up there like that? Gliding... and flying... and air-swimming... and singing."

"Electro... magnetic... levitation?" Sam suggested.

"Like a maglev?" Marcus figured the exomoon's lower gravity might have something to do with it as well. Plus despite its size, the creature could have hollow bones or some such.

Sam blew out a breath. "Please tell me you got a picture of that."

"Better. Got video footage."

"Wow. That was quick. Points for speed."

"I've got my finger on the button all the time, same as any tech-savvy guy." He waved his iPhone in the air, grinning. "Although to be fair, I already had my phone out to record your sweet ass under the waterfall."

Now Marcus had Sam's full, horrified attention. "You *what*?"

Marcus tried and failed to keep a straight face. "Well, I thought about just snapping a shot of your butt to use as my desktop wallpaper, but then you looked so hot, all wet and glistening, I just had to immortalize it on film."

Sam hurried closer, his hand outstretched. "You delete that this instant."

Marcus backed off, taunting. "If I do that, we lose the flying mazzie video forever."

That made Sam stop, but he still looked furious. "When we get home, you'll edit that video and delete all footage of my naked butt. Or I'll strangle you in your sleep. Got it?"

The threat didn't have the effect Sam must have wanted because the comment merely made Marcus giddy with joy. "So when we get home you plan on sleeping in my bed, then, eh? I've got no objections to that." He waggled his eyebrows suggestively.

The pissed-off look faded and was replaced by a sweet blush Marcus adored. "Fine. I'll let that one slide. This once." Sam wagged a finger at Marcus in warning. "'Cause, yeah, I do intend to stay in your bed a lot, with you in it."

"Already looking forward to it, bae."

Sam smiled, pushing strands of wet hair behind his ear. Then he straightened, inhaled sharply, and his eyes widened. Afraid all over again, Marcus followed his gaze.

By then, the mazzie had glided over the island, oblivious to the two humans observing its course through the skies—skies that were darkening once more. Dark clouds gathered, surrounding the gigantic sea creature on all sides, as though it somehow *was* the eye of the storm. The thought seemed insane. But everything about their current situation was beyond normal.

A rhythmic sequence of sounds, like an alien aria, flowed out of the mazzie.

Then it seemed to drop from the heights as if whatever forces had allowed it to levitate in the first place suddenly evaporated. Like a mountainous boulder or a stupendous asteroid, it fell back down to the ocean, the following splash an almost deafening boom, and the waves rose so high Marcus feared the whole island would be swept away by the tidal forces.

"Back inside!" Marcus shouted. He grabbed Sam's arm and ran toward the shadowy interior once more, his privates bouncing between his legs. Sam didn't argue, and they sprinted as fast as they could around the closest corner and waited to find out if they'd drown in the buff on an alien moon.

Sam shuddered, having gone pale. Marcus pulled him into his arms, and they hugged each other for comfort, neither speaking, both panting and yet trying to hold their breaths. Sam's heart drummed a rapid staccato beat against Marcus's chest, and he had an uncanny feeling that his own rhythm matched. The embrace tightened as the roar grew louder.

Sloshes of water streamed over their feet, reaching as high as their knees. But the gush of the current was already slowing down, and they remained safe. Slowly the water drained away. The stone floor was wet but no worse for wear, and neither were they.

"Jesus Christ," Marcus murmured, refusing to let Sam out of his arms.

Sam didn't appear in a hurry to leave them either. They waited until the trickle of water and their breathing quieted before they separated and took in their surroundings.

"We survived," Sam huffed out, his voice surprised. "I... I really didn't expect that."

Marcus barked out a laugh. "I hear that."

"Still got your phone?" Sam asked, and Marcus nodded, waving the thing at him. Was it an instinct of modernity not to let go of one's camera even during a crisis? Seemed so futile. But they had evidence of alien life-forms on it, so perhaps that was why Marcus had hung on to it.

As they slowly separated and returned to the terrace, rain and tempestuous winds had started again. Stormy clouds raged in the sky once more, puffy and somber. But the rain was less intense, and it was already clear the furor had begun to wane and would soon come to an end.

The sea creature had disappeared under the waves, not so much as a fin or a flipper in sight.

"Well... that was interesting." Marcus huffed out a breath, standing astride, hands on his hips, staring out to sea. His mind was blown away by all the wondrous things he'd seen over the past two days. Things he never would have believed could be possible or real.

"That's one word for it." Sam seemed to be short on eloquence too.

"We should get back to our room, for the time being anyway. Until the storm passes at least."

Sam nodded his agreement, and they swiftly made their way back to their small room above the main hall, even Sam managing the jump effortlessly this time. They dried themselves off as best they could and put their jeans back on. But neither did more than that, as they sat on the stone bed, side by side, their shoulders and arms touching.

Every time thunder boomed loud or lightning struck, illuminating the night sky, Sam flinched, shuddered, and inched closer to Marcus. Surely he couldn't be scared of some nasty weather?

"You know, you can't go through life like that. Being afraid of everything," Marcus said gently, hoping to convey strength to his friend. Sam's reaction, however, surprised him.

"That's easy for you to say," Sam murmured, leaning away. He behaved as if Marcus was butting in where he had no business. Marcus had thought their trust issues were in the past. Then again, when had sex ever replaced a much-needed conversation? And wounded pride repeated.

"What's that supposed to mean?"

Sam sighed. "You're rash and thoughtless. You leap before you think. You jump in the deep end before you even know how to paddle. You always seem to act before you consider the consequences." Clearly Sam wanted to go on. Instead he snapped his mouth shut, his lips forming a thin white line—but his jaw quivered, as though he were sad, not angry.

Marcus felt rotten, partly out of guilt, partly at the sudden reproach, so he tried his best to explain. "My dad and granddad…. Did you know my granddad wanted to be a pilot in the Air Force or an astronaut for NASA? But instead he worked over forty years in a tiny gray cubicle in an office selling insurance. And my dad, he wanted to be an architect, like that famous guy who designed the pyramid in front of the Louvre, or the guy who built Fallingwater, that cool house over the river and the waterfalls."

"I.M. Pei and Frank Lloyd Wright," Sam cut in to supply the missing information, a small frown of confusion on his face.

Marcus chuckled shortly. "Figured you'd know them. Anyway, my dad works as a mechanic in an auto repair shop." Marcus's family history weighed heavily on his shoulders, and he slumped. "They're my main influences in life, you know, my… male role models. But… neither of them pursued their desires. It wasn't like they had no opportunities to do so, because they did. But they always decided against them, turning their backs on their dreams. They were both born in the same town, they've never been anywhere else, and they'll more than likely die right there, in that same stinking town. It's like… they never lived a day in their lives.

When they die, nothing remains of them. No legacies of adventures. It's like they never were."

"Oh Marcus…," Sam whispered. Marcus was surprised by the watery catch in Sam's voice. He'd expected pity, not empathy. Sometimes the distinction was easy to miss.

"They've influenced me, but probably not the way they intended," Marcus carried on, sighing. "I don't want be like them. I don't want to end up an old man full of nothing but regrets and unrealized dreams. I suppose that's why I do what I do, the way I do. You say I'm thoughtless. That's not true. Every time I do anything, I think about them. I want to try everything to figure out what I'm good at and what I want to do with my life, to follow my dreams. I try to see everything as an opportunity, something that challenges me. That's why I leap before I think, as you say. I look around me, see all these wonderful, exciting windows of opportunity and chance, and I try to catch them before they fly away. Rash? Yeah, sure. But… I have to be. The alternative… sucks."

Next to him, Marcus heard a sniffle. Stunned, he turned to see Sam wiping his eyes with the back of his hand. Before Marcus could offer consolation or apologies, Sam shook his head.

"You carry around all that baggage, and you still let me give you such a hard time? Dammit." Sam's expression twisted with remorse and anguish, and Marcus felt bad. Then Sam added, "Fuck, Marcus. I'm so sorry for being such an asshole to you. You didn't do anything to deserve it."

Marcus scoffed softly. "You mean like getting us stranded on an alien planet without a means of escape? Sorry, I meant moon."

Sam snarled in anger, most likely aimed inward. "I did blame you for that, but the truth is, I'm as much to blame as you, perhaps more so. I'm the one who just had to get that damn beanie back. I'm so stupid. I'm sorry."

Marcus smiled. "It's okay. I forgive you. No harm done."

Sam started crying in earnest, visibly falling apart. Marcus raised his arm over Sam's shoulders and pulled him near, hugging him. Sam clung to him hard, his hands fisting in Marcus's jeans around his waist. He trembled as he wept almost silently.

Marcus offered him as much support and comfort as he could. Because that was what a man did. That was what a friend did. That was what a lover and a boyfriend did.

"It's okay, bae. I promise we're going to get home. One day all this will be nothing more than a distant memory." Marcus kissed the top of

Sam's head, ruffling his damp hair, the scent of fresh water strong but not overpowering Sam's natural body odor. Marcus liked it.

"These are man tears, by the way. Why didn't you ever tell me that's why you do things the way you do?" Sam asked, still wetting Marcus's neck with hot moisture.

Marcus smiled though Sam couldn't see it. "I had to catch you first."

Sam half chuckled, half sobbed and hugged Marcus tighter. "I've been such a fool."

"No, you haven't."

"I used to worry you were following me around to… to kick my ass."

"What?" Marcus was aghast at hearing that. He'd joked about that being Sam's reason, but he'd never believed it was true. "I'd never do anything like—"

"I know." Sam sighed, his crying diminishing. "I know that. I knew it earlier too, but I was afraid, mostly of shadows, things a violent, abusive, cruel world has taught me to dread—even though I think I believed all along I had absolutely nothing to fear from you. But before… I thought you could somehow see that I was… gay."

"And what? I'd give you a gay bashing you'd never forget? That I'd be upset you had feelings for me?" Marcus stifled the anger boiling inside him because he understood Sam's motives. Fear was a powerful emotion that could silence all the positive voices within.

"It was just senseless fear, irrational. I'm so, so sorry, Marcus." Sam breathed against Marcus's neck, the sensation ticklish. A moist warmth fanned over Marcus's skin.

"No, you have nothing to be sorry for. Sam, I get it. Being afraid of the unknown and being scared of what seems to be an everyday thing these days. Jocks and bullies beating up nerds and geeks *and* gays." He held Sam tighter, his arms wound around the scared boy. "I just want you to know that I'd never throw shade at you or hurt you. I'm in love with you. And even if I wasn't… I don't beat up on people, gay or otherwise."

Sam's labored breathing slowly returned to normal and his eyes no longer welled. "I used to have the biggest crush on you," he admitted quietly. "I was so nervous, all the time, that you could see it just looking at me."

"Used to?" Marcus teased softly.

Sam barked out a hoarse laugh. "It has evolved to love. Not just a crush anymore."

"Good. I'm happy to hear that." Marcus rocked Sam gently and rubbed his back up and down, soothing him, grounding them both.

Sam took a deep breath and seemed to straighten up even though he was still firmly in Marcus's embrace. "I'm tired of being afraid. Sure, we're on an alien world, and that thunder and lightning could be really different and more dangerous than the storms back home. But... I was thinking...."

"About?" Marcus coaxed, intrigued.

"It's night now. It's raining and thundering and flashing. Best distractions nature can buy. Best we can hope for, anyway, in order to... to gather the liana from the carnivorous plant. We should do it tonight."

Marcus pulled back to see Sam's expression and judge if he was actually serious. "But.... Are you crazy? We're half-naked, we have no blades, weapons, or cutting tools of any kind, and we haven't even measured the distance between the towers and the chamber to know how much liana we will ultimately need."

Sam nodded, his jaw set, his now dry eyes steadfast. "I know. But we should at least try and see how easy or hard it will be. The storm's the perfect opportunity. Either the flower will be asleep or it'll be practically blind and deaf from the noise and flashes."

Marcus had to admit Sam had a point. They had no idea when another storm might roll in to aid them in disorienting the flower. Could be hours, days, or longer. It was time they didn't have to waste.

They did, however, require tools. "What are we supposed to cut the liana with? Your pocketknife will hardly do the trick. And if we start yanking the liana in the hopes some will break loose, that thing will wake up and eat us. Slowly. Digest us really fucking slowly."

Sam smiled. "While I was down in the library, I noticed some of the imagery on the walls depicted warrior types, perhaps for some sort of... heroic sexual fantasy, or whatever. Now if we found a statue like that—"

"It might come with a weapon," Marcus finished for him, excitement starting to buzz inside him.

"Yes, that was my thinking. Plus if they are shown with rudimentary weapons, they'll likely be... um, you know... phallic in shape. Like, uh... spears or knives." Sam blushed cutely and blinked, and Marcus tried hard not to laugh, biting into his bottom lip.

"Check." Marcus stood and gave his partner a chin lift. "Let's go and see if we can get something useful from statues."

For the next ten minutes or so, Marcus and Sam scoured the two levels of the temple's underground, at least the sections that weren't crumbled or collapsed into ruins. The majority of the art, both reliefs and statues, showed only sexual positions and acts.

It wasn't until they combed the area adjacent to the library that they discovered a few warrior types who stood astride, holding long lances in their hands—while being orally pleasured. So not exactly warriors per se.

"You think we can remove those without destroying the statues?" Sam asked, his brow furrowed with worry.

Marcus thought Sam's concern was endearing, if impractical. The circumstances were less than optimal, and they might have to do some serious property damage to get the ball rolling. At least it looked like the owners wouldn't be around to lodge a complaint. "C'mon, Sam. They're stone. We're not. And we really need those spears. They don't."

Sam bowed his head. "I know that. I just… don't want to vandalize a place that's so close to vanishing off the face of the… the moon already." Then he shrugged, as if he didn't care, but he also looked away, perhaps to hide his telltale expression. "Do what you have to do."

Marcus rested a hand over his companion's shoulder. "I'll be as gentle as I can."

A flicker of a smile graced Sam's lips, as much as Marcus could tell from his profile alone. "Thanks."

Marcus inspected the artwork. If the javelins, made of reddish metal, were part of the statues themselves, then there would be no way to avoid hacking the statues to pieces to retrieve them—if that even worked. But the sculptures appeared to be carved from stone, not metal, so Marcus dared to hope the weapons had simply been slotted into the figure's hands.

The tip of the lance looked ragged but sharp, so Marcus figured it would require a little work with a whetstone to get it shiny and new. He gripped the rod with both hands, braced one foot on the pedestal, and pulled. His muscles grew taut and bulged as he strained with the effort. Beads of sweat popped out on his forehead, and his arms and fingers, not to mention his thighs, soon felt the stress of exertion.

"Is it working? Can I help?" Sam asked in a small, hesitant voice. Clearly the comic-book geek didn't feel confident about his physical abilities.

"Sure. Grab my waist and help me." Sam followed Marcus's instructions, wound his arms tightly around Marcus's waist, and began to tug. "Easy does it. Don't yank. Just one long pull, okay?"

Sam murmured something along the lines of understanding, so Marcus grinned. Then he resumed dragging, using all his strength and body mass to pry the spear loose.

A grinding sound echoed in the empty hallway as the metal started to chafe free from the stone's grip. Flakes of dust danced in the air, falling like gray rain on the floor, as the statue's hand began to crack.

The stony fingers broke with one loud boom, shattering into rubble. Marcus and Sam fell backward hard, with Marcus landing on top of his smaller friend.

"Sorry, Sam." Marcus quickly rolled aside, stood in a hurry, and helped Sam onto his feet. "You okay?" He scanned Sam's backside purely out of concern. Mostly.

Sam kept nodding, brushing his hands over the rumpled seat of his jeans. "Yeah. No worse for wear. Did you get it?" He did sound a bit breathless, as if the wind had been knocked out of him.

Marcus lifted the metallic lance between them triumphantly. "Uh-huh. Did you ever doubt me?" Sam chuckled, and Marcus scrutinized the tip of the spear. "Needs a bit of polishing, but then it'll be good as new. So… let's get another one for you."

Fifteen minutes later as the storm continued to rage outside, darkness still enveloping the temple, Marcus and Sam both sported smooth spears, the tips once again virtually razor-sharp, and without further discussion, they proceeded to put on their boots and sneak into the jungle and close to the flower that had almost made a meal out of Marcus.

As they skulked their way toward the carnivorous plant, Marcus asked, "When we cut the vines, won't the bioelectrical charge inside dissipate?"

Sam shrugged. "Yes, probably. Some of it more than likely. But I'm hoping the saline solution's properties remain and that the liquid retains its conductivity."

Marcus chuckled, more than a little impressed. "Geez, Sam, baby. You sound like a bona fide scientist already."

Sam blushed and ducked his head. "My math scores—"

Marcus waved his hand about dismissively. "Pfft. There's more to physics than math. You'll make an excellent physicist. No, scratch that. An amazing astrophysicist. Or astrobiologist, or whatever the title is for someone researching alien worlds. I know it."

Sam didn't reply, but his shy smile glowed. Marcus really liked the look on his new boyfriend. *No. My first, last, and only boyfriend.*

A few minutes later they could see their target. Like before, the flower appeared huge and bloodred in the near dark, all the blossoms and buds glimmering wet with rain. The sounds of drops landing on the leaf-covered jungle floor created soft little thumps Sam and Marcus could only hear thanks to their proximity. Nonetheless, nauseatingly sweet odors floated everywhere, emanating from the depths of the flower.

The terrain was covered in vines. None of them were moving. Even the flower itself looked like it was drooping. It seemed to be asleep. Marcus had seen flowers that had a sort of night mode, closing their petals at night. But an actually sleeping plant? That was new.

Could it… dream?

"I'll make the first cut," Marcus whispered into Sam's ear. "You get ready to yank the vine and run if that thing starts moving."

Sam nodded several times, his eyes wide, his breathing shallow, and his skin pale. He was clearly having second thoughts about their plan and its chances of success. Fear was a common response to an unknown threat, but they couldn't afford to get distracted or intimidated.

Marcus decided to get Sam's brain back on track and his nerves under control as fast as he could. "How many volts do you think is running inside the liana? Won't the liana burst apart, or burn up, or at least tear into a million pieces? I mean, so much raw power running through it. It's a violent current of electricity, after all."

"Amps," Sam corrected Marcus seemingly on autopilot, his gaze a million miles away. "Amperes describe electric current, volts measure electric tension, and joules are units of energy. They're not the same thing. But… all can be used to describe the energy in lightning."

"Right." Marcus smiled. His tactic had succeeded. He'd taken physics too, so it wasn't like he didn't know the difference between the three terms, even if physics wasn't his first choice of subjects.

"A single lightning bolt can develop an electric current of about ten to thirty kiloamperes, carry five hundred megajoules of energy, and have a buildup of anywhere between ten and one hundred twenty million volts, thus exceeding fifty thousand degrees Kelvin," Sam muttered absentmindedly, as if he didn't need to put that much focus on what he was saying. "If the voltage differential between the lightning rods and the portal's frame is too great, however… then you're right: The vines might explode before the current even makes it there." Sam sounded worried again. "The ionic radii ratio—"

Marcus harrumphed as quietly as he could. "Let's worry about that later. For all we know, we might get eaten in a few minutes anyway."

Sam snorted. "That's reassuring." But his stiff shoulders relaxed, and a small shy smile graced his lips.

"C'mon, bae. Let's do this."

Marcus stepped on the balls of his feet, trying to find a safe place to set his feet where he wouldn't be stepping on extensions of a plant that liked to eat meat. Once he'd found a good spot, he nodded back to Sam, who gently gripped one of the liana. The second Marcus cut it, they'd both take off running.

Spear in hand, Marcus crouched, glancing between the vine, the plant, and Sam. Then he raised his weapon and struck as hard as he could, not knowing in advance how much power he needed for the blow.

The tip of the spear hit the ground with a heavy thud and a metallic clink.

The liana broke, the edges frayed and jagged. Then thick green goo started oozing out.

The flower shook silently. The buds and vines stirred, flailing about blindly, searching for the intruders it clearly couldn't see or hear.

Without warning, something sharp shot out of the buds and blossoms, swift and vicious. Sam cried out in pain. Something burned his arm, leaving a singed red welt behind, as if he'd been kissed by acid.

Though equally wounded, Marcus didn't stop for answers. He snatched the cut end of the vine and dashed toward Sam, who was also sprinting, both on tiptoe.

Purple clouds of puffy vapor arose from the twitching buds and the biggest blossom. It spread all around, camouflaging the whole flower from sight behind an impenetrable wall of mist.

As the fumes rose high up into the trees and the foliage, a single ozzie groaned and fell to the ground with a soft thump, clearly out of it. The vines closed in on the tiny creature and pulled it toward the flower, swallowed up by the veil of fog.

Sam and Marcus didn't stop until they reached the safety of the stone terrace. Only there did they slow down to breathe and inspect their spoils and injuries.

"Bae, you badly hurt?" Marcus asked breathlessly, pressing a hand over his shoulder where he felt a burning sting and already swollen skin. Whatever had struck him, it must have come from the flower. Or perhaps the damn thing was defended by flora or fauna they were unable to see or hear.

Sam showed his arm where, just under the elbow, a slightly turgid wound appeared, fire-engine red in a whip-thin but deep mark. "Fuck, it hurts. But... I don't think anything's under the skin, and I don't feel weird or anything. Just in pain. You?"

Marcus waited for dizziness, nausea, or any other symptoms of poisoning. Other than the painful burning and stinging sensation, there was nothing. He shook his head. "No, nothing odd. I think we're okay. But we have to assume that whatever that was, it came from the flower."

Sam nodded. "It could have been a snake or something, but I didn't see one, so I think you're right. Guess we'll have to add that to the list of things to watch out for."

"What the heck was that steam coming out of it?" Marcus asked, waving generally in the direction where they'd run from.

Sam shook his head in bewilderment. "I don't know. Some kind of noxious fume that makes its quarry pass out? God, I hope it didn't eat that ozzie."

"Let's hope we're not next on the menu." Marcus straightened and blew out a breath. "How much did we get of the vine? Did we lose the liquid inside?"

"Bind the other end tight so no more is lost," Sam instructed, using a long thin strand of cloth he'd torn from the hem of Marcus's T-shirt earlier (with his permission) to tie his end of the vine. Marcus did as asked. Soon both ends were tightly knotted, not a single drop escaping anymore. Sam used his arm to measure how much of the vine they had gathered and finally sighed. "We got about... six or seven meters worth."

"Fuck." Marcus stomped the ground in anger. "That's not even a fraction of what we need to make this plan work."

"I know. We'll need to harvest more. Much more. And then we need to figure out a way to attach all the broken ends to each other without the electric current in the liquid dissipating."

Rolling his eyes, Marcus huffed out a sarcastic breath. "Sounds like a breeze. Okay. Back to collecting, then."

Sam left the coiled liana on the closest statue's outstretched arm. Then they returned to the flower. Thankfully, it appeared to have gone dormant again. None of the blossoms waved about, and none of the vines creeped, nor did any purple mist shoot out of the buds.

"It might be more touchy this time, so be careful," Marcus advised with a whisper.

This time when they cut one of the vines, Marcus caught a glimpse of what had struck them before a cloud of dizzying vapors hid the flower again.

"I saw it," he said, blowing out a breath once they were back to safety.

Sam's eyebrows rose to his hairline. "What was it?"

"They came out of the blossoms, poking out in a flash, like the tongue of a snake."

"Really? Flowers with tongues that burn and sting? Man, this place just gets weirder and weirder."

"Now we know what to avoid. They strike out perpendicular to the blossoms."

"Gotcha."

Bravely they returned to the flower, this time more than ready to confront their faceless foe of the plant kingdom.

For the next hour, while the storm continued to rage in the dark of the night, Sam and Marcus gathered more liana. The flower didn't seem to know what to do or how to react. Flashes of lightning and booms of thunder had to make it blind and deaf. It did awaken each time Marcus cut off a piece, striking out with its stinging tongues and letting out puffs of purple gas, but they escaped unscathed.

Finally Sam dropped to the floor of the terrace, breathing hard, his skin sweaty. "I think… we've got about… three or four hundred meters' worth…. That'll have to be enough for now." He lay on the ground on his back, closing his eyes and just breathing. "I don't think we should take any more. The plant might not survive losing any more vines. I sure hope for its sake it can grow new ones…."

Marcus knelt next to his supine friend and smiled. That was such a Sam thing to say. Even though the flower would have happily consumed them if it had the chance, the young scientist didn't want to kill or hurt the plant more than was strictly necessary. It was not simply being idealistic or ethically minded, but being a good, eco-friendly, nature-preserving person.

"I'm so fucking hot for you right now," Marcus said with a wide grin of pride.

Sam's cute blush was icing on the cake.

CHAPTER 11

"WHAT ARE you grumbling about over there?" Sam asked once they'd returned to their room above the main hall with their impromptu luggage.

Marcus harrumphed. "Nothing. Just thinking. Like I was wondering why we didn't do a Ben Franklin and build a kite with a piece of metal attached to attract lightning to harness it. But then I remembered that's what the lightning rods are there for. And since the lizzies didn't build the portal chamber, powering the temple somehow would do exactly diddly squat for the portal. Then I started thinking about which we need to attach the vine-turned-power-cable to: the doorway or the chair, which is broken."

Sam chuckled. "Geez, Marcus. Give your brain a rest. That's a lot to worry about." It was amusing, though, he thought, since he'd literally worried about the exact same thing less than an hour ago.

Marcus shrugged. "Not so easy to turn things off, you know. I keep thinking about all kinds of contingency plans. Like what I said earlier— what if the vines burst apart from the electric current? We don't exactly have replacement parts or a Home Depot next door."

"I know. But let's just stay positive, okay?"

"Wow. That's a change. What's happened to the pessimist I know and love?"

Sam blushed, smiling. "I'm trying to follow your example and not picture the worst-case scenario at every turn. This is a good plan, worth a shot."

"Agreed." Marcus sighed as he straightened up, grimacing. Sam could relate. His own muscles protested as well. "So how much vine have we collected?" Marcus asked.

"This is a rough estimate, you understand," Sam said hesitantly, frowning with displeasure. "But I figure we have about… three hundred meters for sure, plus maybe… a dozen or so more."

"That should be enough," Marcus commented with a nod. "I mean, this whole island couldn't be more than a mile long anyway. And the chamber is situated on the mountainside, about half the island's total length from the temple."

"We'll see." Sam wanted to believe, to stay positive and have faith that things would work out for the best. That fundamental change in perspective wasn't easy for him. But having Marcus around helped a lot. "I just wish I knew how we're going to measure the distance between the temple's lightning rods and the chamber," Sam groused, annoyed at the situation and his own sad point of view. "Steps, maybe?"

Marcus chuckled and fished out his iPhone. "Nah. I got a distance measuring app on my iPhone. Back home I use it when I go out running and stuff. Should be helpful here too."

Sam smiled, relief flooding him. "I love you."

Marcus smiled back, his eyes shining with happiness. Then his eyes grew dark, and he licked his lips, leaning closer. Sam giggled and did the same. Their lips met in a chaste kiss.

A deafening rumble of thunder sounded above their heads, shocking them both.

They hadn't pulled the stone slab in front of the doorway, so they had a clear view of the upper area of the main hall. At least one side and one corner of it.

Inside a stone recess the shape of a tube, the front of it translucent, the lightning rod glimmered in a cocoon of blue sparks and wild streams of energy. Sam guessed that the metal bar reached all the way to the top of the bud-like tower.

The semicircular base glowed azure, gathering electricity from the storm clouds above, which was what lightning rods did. Instead of grounding the power of the dark skies, though, the base seemed to collect the energy into a pool, possibly recharging power reserves they couldn't see, perhaps inside the walls or under the temple complex itself.

"The base," Sam murmured. "That's where we need to attach the vines."

"I see it too." Marcus sounded cool and composed, and Sam took that as a good sign. He relied heavily on his companion's strength. Not that Sam felt he was awfully weak, but strange space adventures weren't his forte.

Silently the two young men stared at the web of blue current that slowly dwindled and died. The thunder and lightning also faded, and the night grew still. Wind still rustled in the jungle's trees and underbrush, but the storm had clearly passed. Smells of wet earth and damp flowers rose fresh to their noses even inside the temple.

"I think we've seen the worst of it," Marcus said, rising to his feet and walking out to the balcony overlooking the great hall. Sam followed him. Together they watched through the roof oculus as darkness waned, and a deep rosy hue began to conquer the skies.

"It's already dawn." Sam was surprised so much time had passed. The days and nights moved so quickly on this alien moon. He knew that, but the weirdness of it still rattled him.

"Yeah." Marcus frowned. "It's getting light, but we've been up on our feet for a while. We should get some rest now, so we can measure the distance to the portal chamber and attempt a power hookup later, bright-eyed and bushy-tailed."

At first Sam considered arguing that they didn't have time to waste, since a new storm could brew in an hour or weeks from now. But right then a yawn he couldn't hold at bay damn near broke his jaw, so he conceded with a curt nod.

They returned to the room, reset the slab in the doorway, and settled side by side on the stone bed over their winter wardrobe. Sam rested his head on Marcus's chest, listening to his soothing heartbeat. The heat of Marcus's skin told Sam they were alive and well, and that counted for something.

Then Marcus murmured, "You asleep yet?"

Sam snorted. "Not with you yapping."

Marcus chuckled. Then he whispered in Sam's ear, "Wanna make out?"

Like flipping a switch, Sam was instantly on alert, his heart racing, his dick hardening, and his desire kindling. "Want more," he muttered back, arose over Marcus, and claimed his lips in a possessive kiss.

They both allowed their hands to roam, fondle, and grip. Sam straddled Marcus's hips, cupped his cheeks, and kissed him harder, his need growing by leaps and bounds. Marcus shoved his tongue in Sam's mouth and entangled them in a hot swirl of need. Soon they were both too out of breath to maintain a sealed kiss.

Marcus unbuttoned and yanked open Sam's fly, digging underneath to pluck out his cock. Sam blindly fumbled with his boyfriend's pants to do the same. They stroked each other, and none too gently either. Marcus pulled back just long enough to lick his own palm, and then his hand returned to Sam's cock, tugging roughly but more fluidly too.

"God, your hand on me…." Sam's voice failed him. He couldn't even finish his sentence, his brain muddled, his blood deafening in his ears.

"If you love that, my bae, you're gonna love it when my dick's inside you." Marcus's lewd words sent hot thrills and frissons of pure pleasure coursing through Sam's veins. Anticipation of what their relationship would eventually evolve into made his toes curl and the hairs on his body stand up on end.

"What if it's my dick inside you?" Sam teased, breathing hotly over Marcus's lips. He'd never imagined he would say such dirty words to his secret crush. Now Marcus was his boyfriend, and Sam could say what was in his heart *and* below his belt.

Marcus grinned wide, looking like a hungry wolf. "Yeah, that too."

There was stuff Sam knew he wasn't ready for yet. Sexual stuff. But he also knew full well that Marcus would do nothing to hurt or pressure him. He'd said as much earlier. No, this was sex talk, fantasies spilling into words, hot thoughts they'd both had about each other. And that was just fine.

Marcus pushed Sam's hand away and wrapped his fist around both their cocks, a fiery stroke mashing them together. Sam moaned, and Marcus half chuckled, half groaned.

After that, neither of them seemed capable of stopping. Their hips rocked in unison as they inched closer to climax, their limbs wound around each other, their bodies pressed together hotly.

Sam couldn't breathe properly. It was as if his lungs had shrunk. His heart hammered in his chest, the beat echoing throughout his body. His belly fluttered, his groin was on fire, and desire all he could think of.

"Marcus." Sam repeated the name, over and over, his eyes closing.

Then Marcus sought Sam's lips in a passionate kiss, and Sam was lost. His whole body jerked violently as his cock erupted, and he spilled his seed over Marcus's hand and between their writhing bodies. Marcus followed a blink of an eye later, a deep rumbling groan prelude to his cock discharging ropes of hot, sticky come everywhere. Sam reveled in the thick, earthy odors of male musk and spunk while hot flashes continued to cascade over his body and senses, unraveling him to the core.

Exhausted, they collapsed back on the stone bed, both panting hoarsely as they clung to each other, continuing to pet and caress, softly kiss, and quietly murmur sweet endearments. Sam was so sleepy he felt like he could dream for a month. Marcus didn't seem to be in a hurry to make Sam move off him.

So Sam lay there on top of his lover, ignoring the cooling gooey substance between them. His skin remembered, though, each kiss from Marcus, that tongue around his nipples, those lips traveling down his body, that moist breath fanning hotly over him, those strong hands holding his back and buttocks. With a goofy smile, Sam dozed off to sweet dreams.

"Love you...."

"Mmm, don't wanna wake up yet," Sam murmured drowsily, yawning and rubbing his eyes. "What time is it?"

"Best guess? Afternoon. Ish." Marcus stood, straightened, and pressed his palms over his back, grimacing. "Damn. Every muscle in me is fucking jammed. I need a weeklong trip to a hot tub."

"With me, I hope." Sam flashed an irreverent grin as he got up too. His body protested as well, yesterday's exertions taking their toll. Both the vine gathering and the later lovemaking. His welts had stopped stinging but still felt swollen.

"Naturally." Marcus turned on his iPhone, scratching his jaw where stubble had begun to form, a dark shadow on his skin. Sam didn't have to shave often since his bristle was still soft and dirt-blond like the rest of his hair, virtually unnoticeable.

"Okay," Marcus said. "The app's working. We can now start measuring the shortest distance between the closest lightning rod and the portal chamber. I'm relatively sure we can get a pretty accurate reading, with a couple of meters margin for error."

"Okay, then." Sam stifled another yawn and put his boots back on. He wore his jeans but decided to forgo his T-shirt. The humid heat wasn't going anywhere, so the garment seemed unnecessary. "Let's do this."

As they approached the see-through stone pillar housing the lightning rod where it rose through a corner of the balcony, Sam noted a crack in the surface. The transparent casing wasn't impenetrable. Sam took a piece of rubble off the floor and hit the crack. A few shards of the glass-like outer cover broke off, leaving a jagged-edged hole.

"That's not, like... radioactive, is it?" Marcus asked with mild concern in his voice.

Sam shook his head. "No. Electricity is movements of electrons, which can't become radioactive. We're fine. Plus, I think this hole is big enough to stick the vine in there."

"Awesome. Time to get started, then." Marcus pressed the app to activate it and moved toward the edge of broken balustrade, peering below and to the side. "I think we should try to get the vine through the open windows here instead of going around, over the balcony, and under the entrance arch."

"Agreed." Sam hopped down, the lower gravity giving his jump a touch of lightness and speed. "Man, I could get used to this. Feel like an athlete."

Marcus laughed as he jumped down next to him. "I already know for a fact that you'd qualify for the sexual Olympics for sure, bae."

Sam blushed. "Shut up." Marcus merely chuckled in response and winked at him.

They walked under the high vaulted entrance into bright sunlight. The air rippled with heat since even tropical winds seemed to be absent today, not a single leaf rustling around them. The warm moisture hung heavy in the air, and Sam was grateful he'd decided against putting on his T-shirt, same as Marcus.

Marcus blew out a breath, wiped a hand over his forehead, and blinked up at the sky. "Gonna be a hot day. You think this oppressive heat might bode another storm?"

Sam shrugged. "Back home it often does. Here? Who knows. We can only hope."

"Even though we didn't receive a jolt, there could be some residual charge left in the energy collectors from the storm last night," Marcus stated, frowning as if he'd just thought of it.

"Yes, it's possible," Sam concluded. "That's one of the reasons we should get on with this."

Marcus snorted and rolled his eyes. "Yes, master." Sam shoved him in the arm, but the guy was an unmovable object, clearly amused by the geek boy's effort. He swiped a hand across his forehead again. "Jesus, it's fucking hot out here."

"No wind yet." Sam studied the cloudless skies and the tops of the gigantic trees, and not a thing stirred. "As irritating as this heat is, the weather's promising for us. No wind means that the pressure's gathering."

The soles of their boots clopped against the stone slabs of the ceremonial pathway across the mountaintop. To Sam, the sound was awfully loud, and his gaze kept returning to the thick underbrush by the sides of the road. He wasn't sure if he was expecting rampaging animals or hungry vines, but he refused to relax even for a second.

"There. The stairs are close." Marcus pointed in the direction where they had climbed up the stairs from the underground chamber. "We're almost there, and according to this app, we've traveled about two and a half hundred meters."

Sam let out a tiny whoopee. "That means the vines we've gathered might be enough."

Marcus glanced at him over his shoulder, grinning lopsidedly. "Yeah, looks like. Now all we need to do is to figure out how to combine the cut vines to each other, and then we're home free. Man, I'm super glad we don't have to go back to that fucking plant with its tentacles and—"

A low growl stopped both of them dead in their tracks.

Out from the underbrush on the other side of the path, a razor beast sneaked, hunched and cautious, its long curved fangs bared. It inched toward them, menace in its slow, steady approach. Its gold-black-green striped fur stood on end, blue cascades of electricity covering it like a fluttering veil, and its butterfly-winged ears flapped rapidly. On its forehead, the single black horn curved backward instead of straight up, like that of a rhinoceros, and behind and above its body swished its long tail with its row of razor-sharp spikes.

"Oh. My. God." Sam couldn't breathe, and his vision blurred in pure panic, his whole body buzzing with adrenaline, his instincts crying for him to run or die.

"Slowly back away toward the temple," Marcus whispered, stepping in front of Sam, his movements appearing almost leisurely.

"We're over two hundred meters from the entrance. We'll never make it."

"Shit. Fuck." Marcus sounded breathless and more angry than frightened. "Why the hell didn't we remember to bring the spears with us?"

"Maybe that thing won't enter the chamber beneath us, same as at the temple," Sam said, racking his brain to find them a safe haven close by. "Could we make it?"

Sam backed off, his gaze glued to the beast creeping toward them, its growl growing louder, its hackles sending off sparks.

Because he was retreating with his back turned, Sam didn't realize how close he was to the edge of the path—until his foot slipped and he fell backward, flailing helplessly and quite comically. Not that he was in a laughing mood.

He caught Marcus's arm with one flailing hand, grabbing desperately for purchase. Shouting, they both tumbled and hurtled down the mountainside.

They rolled over bushes and rocks in a heap of limbs, unable to stop their rapid descent down the steep hillside. Not plants, mudslides, or even tree trunks slowed them, as they merely bounced off them like a couple of Ping-Pong balls thanks in part to the lower gravity.

Sam couldn't see anything but the jungle spinning madly around him. It was as though he were watching a rinse cycle through the round window of a washing machine. Everything was a jumble of green and blue, gray and brown, and Sam couldn't focus on anything.

He didn't know what he kept hitting, but he was getting tiny shocks, as though he were the target of constant static bolts of electricity. But he couldn't see what caused them.

A large paw smacked him in the chest and sent him cartwheeling through the air until he hit a huge tree trunk, fell painfully over the roots of a tree, and then resumed rolling, barreling down by the force of gravity, as light as it was.

Sam had no idea where Marcus was. It was clear the razor beast had jumped over the edge and dashed downhill after them, catching up with Sam along the way and swatting him away like an annoying bug. *Please God, don't let that thing eat Marcus.*

A loud hissing noise sounded close by, but he couldn't pinpoint the direction. Out of the corner of his eye, though, Sam detected puffs of purple vapors spreading high and wide.

Another meat-eating plant.

Sam shielded his face with his arms and tried to roll into a ball. That was what he'd been trying to do all along, and even succeeding, at least until the alien feline had hit him square in the chest. But he was aware he'd have scrapes, bruises, and perhaps even cracked or broken bones and internal bleeding before he hit rock bottom, wherever that was.

His final landing surprised him.

Golden-white sand welcomed him like a soft mattress as he spun helplessly onto the beach at the foot of the mountain. He lay there on his back, his vision dancing, his mind reeling, his body aching all over. His breathing was labored, but at least he could draw breath. His sides hurt, but he figured he'd be screaming in agony if he had broken ribs or limbs or internal bleeding.

Once his vision cleared and his head stopped humming, Sam pushed himself up until he sat upright. His jeans had tears and holes in them, and he could see bloody scratches through them. He still had his boots on, for whatever that was worth.

Sam peered around, but the beach was empty of animals and people. Slow waves sloshed against the shore, the turquoise waters glittering in the bright sunlight. If Sam had been at a tropical beach at home, he would have lain back down and relaxed. But here he couldn't.

Marcus was nowhere in sight.

"Marcus?" Sam hollered in panic as he staggered onto his feet, shaded his eyes with a hand, and scanned his surroundings.

A steep incline covered in green-blue trees spread out above him like an impenetrable wall of vegetation. Only everything was supersized. He couldn't even make out the cleared top of the island where the temple was. From his current vantage point, the whole world seemed to fold over him like a vaulted ceiling, and Sam had to tamp down a sudden rush of claustrophobia.

"Marcus? Marcus!"

No one replied. Sam was aware that if the razzie was still alive, which was probable, it wouldn't do to grab its attention. But if Marcus was injured, unconscious, or dead… that was a far worse prospect than getting eaten by an alien feline. Sam couldn't do this on his own.

He started to limp toward the edge of the jungle, his left foot hurting. His ankle had to be strained, but he gritted his teeth and decided to tough it out. An unprecedented act of bravery, Sam might have felt proud of himself if his mind and heart weren't filled with worry.

He kept calling out Marcus's name until he reached the distinct line between the sandy beach and the lush tropical forest. There, buried under decades or perhaps centuries of neglect and overgrown vegetation, he spotted the stone stairs, mostly in ruins but climbable. They had to reach the chamber and the mountaintop.

A flourishing forest teeming with life surrounded him. Sam had to push through the verdant obstacles, using his arms to shove dense growth of ferns and flowers, branches and hanging moss, out of his way. He couldn't see more than a few feet ahead of him.

As he ascended slowly, he kept taking hits from tendrils of bioelectricity off the trees around him. Every time he stepped over an invisible line between two trunks, it was like he had crossed a closed circuit—which resulted in him being struck with shocks. None of them hurt him badly, but he estimated that the compounding effect couldn't be healthy for him.

His feet slipped and stumbled on the cracked and broken stairs. He started to wonder if he'd make it back up to the top of the island without further injuries. Sam didn't stop calling out for Marcus until his voice was hoarse from exertion and breathlessness.

"Shh, bae." Then Marcus was there, standing in front of Sam, a finger over his lips as he shushed Sam silent. "We don't wanna wake that thing up."

About to hug his apparently safe and sound companion, Sam stopped midmotion and frowned. "What?"

Marcus leaned on his knees, blowing out a breath. Blood spatter decorated his cheeks and forehead, and his clothes appeared as torn as Sam's. "As I fell, I bumped into another of those dangerous plants. I rolled past it too fast for the vines to catch me, but it launched a noxious cloud. I managed to grab on to tree roots and stop myself. Then I retraced my path and found that the razzie had been knocked out by the narcotizing vapors. It's out cold a little ways off."

Sam closed his eyes and sighed in relief so deep he almost passed out from the force of it. "Jesus Christ, you scared the shit out of me."

"*I* did? Not that flash-vamp-puss?" Marcus chuckled, but his eyes were round and his skin pale, so he clearly was more shocked by what had happened than he liked to admit. "Listen. If and when that thing wakes up, it's just going to rain on our parade again. I think…. We have only two choices: Trap it somehow or… or kill it."

Sam gulped. Could he murder an alien life-form to save his own life?

"No. I don't want to kill it," Sam replied emphatically. "I just don't want it to kill us either."

Marcus nodded. "That's why my other option was to make a trap, not that we'd trap it only to kill and eat it. Though the meat—"

"Don't even think it. We're not eating an alien animal. No freaking way in hell."

Marcus grinned, seemingly back to his old self. "That's a *no*, then, is it?"

"Shut up."

Marcus glanced over his shoulder and straightened. "I have no idea how long the razzie's gonna stay down, so we should come up with a plan pretty quick. I mean, typically if an enraged animal threatens a person, a cattle prod or a shock stick comes in handy. Here, though, a shock might have a different effect, and we might just get the predators excited and humping our legs while they simultaneously try to eat us."

Sam couldn't help himself; a burst of laughter escaped him. "Can you be serious for a second?"

Marcus shrugged playfully. "Don't know. Haven't often tried that option." He winked and waggled his eyebrows at Sam.

Sam shook his head, chuckling. "You're nuts. Okay. What's your plan?"

Marcus frowned pensively. "We could create some kind of shackles to fasten the thing to a tree or a pillar in the temple."

In Sam's ears that sounded monstrous, capturing an innocent animal that just followed its instincts, a beast that deserved the right to roam free same as any other. "But then the razzie will die of starvation once we leave. It's inhumane and cruel."

"But if the binds are too loose, it'll break free before we get out of here."

Sam merely shook his head more fiercely. "We're supposed to be ambassadors from Earth, so I think we should avoid destroying things. I mean, the UN has a treaty in place about not polluting or owning heavenly bodies. Who knows what our microbes or germs have already done to this moon? For all we know, we could have unwittingly contaminated this whole place. No, I don't like either of those two options. No killing and no shackles. What else?" Sam knew it was probably impossible to hold the creature off without hurting or killing it, but he really wanted them to avoid that if they could.

"Okay." Marcus cocked his head, obviously going over possibilities. "We could build a rudimentary cage to trap the razzie by baiting it with, like, a piece of meat."

Sam pondered the idea. It sounded acceptable—but was it feasible? "What else?"

"There's always the old way, which is to dig a hole deep enough to trap the razzie and then cover it with branches, twigs, leaves, and plants. There are problems with that plan, though, as we don't have adequate tools for digging, a beast that size would demand a huge hole, and the fall might maim it. Or it might simply leap over the hole since its leaps are huge, or it could drop in and jump right out thanks to the lower gravity."

Depression sank in when Sam comprehended the enormity and difficulty of their plan to subdue the razzie. "Damn. Anything else...?" He was almost afraid to ask. Every option seemed to be worse than the last. Realistically, preserving alien life vs. self-protection wasn't an easy feat to accomplish, finding a balance a precarious effort.

Marcus hesitated, and Sam feared the worst. "There's one last option, but it'll be a hell of a Hail Mary." A pregnant pause made Sam cringe in dreadful anticipation. Then Marcus drawled, "We could... harvest buds from the carnivorous plant that creates the sleeping gas, and every time the razzie wakes up, we just... give him a new naptime."

They had little factual knowledge how those noxious fumes worked. Perhaps the fauna on the isle were immune to the effects? The razzie wasn't, that much they could confirm from personal experience, but the rest? No way to know in advance.

But it wasn't like they had options coming out the wazoo.

Sam had been right on the money. One bad option after another. Out of the frying pan and into the fire. *Shit.*

CHAPTER 12

"I HATE to say this, but... knocking that razor beast out with the sleeping gas sounds like our best option if we don't want to do the animal permanent harm." Sam hedged, displaying his concern with a tiny frown and downcast lips.

Marcus smiled. He'd expected Sam would go for the nonviolent alternative. Even if it was a fool's errand. "Then we have to wait for nightfall when the flower sleeps. But we need a plan for how to extract the buds without alarming the plant and getting ourselves either stung or gassed."

Sam rubbed his forehead as if he had a headache. Marcus could relate. He didn't relish the idea of having to extend their stay on the alien moon for the sake of a predator that wanted to eat them.

Then Sam glanced around himself, obviously fretting. "We, um, should go back to the temple. I don't think it's a good idea to be here when the razzie wakes up."

Marcus stopped him with his hand over Sam's arm. "If we use the shackle option, we should try it now that the beast is out cold. That way we could finish taking the measurement for the distance between—"

"No, we're not doing that." Sam's pursed lips and glare warned Marcus not to pursue the notion further. "Besides, we weren't far from the chamber, so I think we can safely assume that we have enough vines."

"That's one thing," Marcus cut in, vexed at Sam for shooting him down. "I just don't want to spend any more time here than absolutely necessary."

"Then we're wasting time arguing," Sam blurted out. He turned his back on Marcus and resumed his climb up the stairs.

The reaction reminded Marcus of all the times before they'd ended up on the exomoon when they'd disagreed about everything, at least on the rare occasions Sam hadn't run away from him. Yet Marcus said nothing. Sam had his prejudices and preconceptions, and Marcus wouldn't be able to disabuse him of them, not when it came to the protection of wildlife.

So he followed Sam, silent as the grave.

"Why have we only seen one single predator? Where's the rest of the pack?" Marcus asked after they'd climbed for a while in eerie quiet.

"You mean pride," Sam corrected him prudishly, then blushed and ducked his head. "They could be highly territorial, I suppose, or the island's not big enough for more than a few of them. Of course, they need a large enough gene pool to avoid inbreeding, but for all we know, maybe they're exceptional swimmers and leave this place for other islands to mate? Maybe each island on this moon is a home to only a couple of them? Many predators are really particular about what's theirs."

Marcus touched Sam's shoulder and turned him to face him. Sam's downcast lashes fluttered as he blinked, but then he met Marcus's gaze. "Listen, bae—"

"No, I'm sorry." Sam sounded miserable. "I shouldn't have talked to you like that, like an asshole—"

"You didn't. You stuck to your guns about not causing harm to an animal. That's not a bad thing. It's commendable."

"Maybe. But you were right too. We shouldn't dawdle but try to get home as soon as possible. God, our folks must be out of their minds with worry."

Marcus pulled Sam into a hug, placing soft kisses on his temple and caressing his back with slow strokes, soothing and grounding them both. "We'll get home, I promise."

"I know." Sam sniffled against Marcus's chest. "When you say it, I believe. Not when I say it to myself." Suddenly he pushed himself off Marcus, blinking his watery eyes. But Marcus could see gears already turning inside Sam's mind. He was onto something. "The razzie's asleep for now, right? And it's daytime."

"Yeah…?"

"I could make a small personal sacrifice in order for us to harvest a couple of those buds."

Marcus sure as shit didn't like what he was hearing. "Come again?"

Sam flashed him a shy smile that tried to be self-confident but failed in its shaky delivery. "The flower reacts to sound. I could use music on my iPhone to distract its vines while we sneak in from another direction. If the plant doesn't destroy the device, we could go back later to collect it, but… it's not necessary. It's just a phone."

That wasn't a bad idea. Heck, it might even work. But they had an extremely small window of opportunity. "Okay. The plant's that way, just a bit more uphill." He pointed upward where the thick wall of vegetation hid the dangerous plant from view.

With swift efficiency born of necessity, they organized their attempt. Sam activated a song on his iPhone, set the volume as high as possible, and then dashed on tiptoe after Marcus who dived into the jungle's lush abundance as though he'd been an adventurer his whole life.

They moved around the flower, careful to avoid the vines everywhere, and approached it from above. The music—Alan Walker's "Sing Me To Sleep"—started out unassumingly sweet, but soon the melody took on an electronic beat that spread out all around them.

The vines and liana crept slowly at first but suddenly shot through the air in the direction where the music came from, beneath the boys' vantage point above the iPhone, which Sam had placed on the stairs.

Marcus and Sam wasted no time. They used Marcus's shirt as a makeshift sack to carry the buds they covered and nipped out. They grabbed three each, praying to whatever gods were in earshot that they wouldn't either be burned by the stinging tongues or knocked out by the gas—and then they ran as fast as they could.

No vines or liana pursued them, so they stopped to rest and recuperate, both panting, Sam with his hurt ankle and Marcus with his bruised ribs, now sore enough to make it hard for him to breathe. No puffs of sleeping gas emerged from underneath the cloth, so Marcus had high hopes of success.

"We could've lost the gas, but I don't think we did," he said cautiously.

"Me neither. But...." Sam sounded hesitant and on edge. "If the gas won't release without the bud being connected to the plant... then we've got a problem."

"Let's not go jumping off any bridges yet," Marcus instructed wisely. "After all, those things could still be triggered by sound or proximity even when disconnected from the plant."

"We should test it," Sam suggested with a shrug, managing to look casual and concerned with a single expression.

They stood at the mountaintop with relatively unobstructed views in all directions. As they watched where they'd hustled from, no razzie emerged. But high in the foliage, the ozzies took to their wings and whizzed from one treetop to the next, mere flickers of colorful feathers.

"I don't want them to get hurt," Sam mumbled broodingly.

"They won't." Marcus resisted the urge to roll his eyes. Instead, he stuck his hand inside the makeshift pouch, grabbed a bud, held the petals closed with his fist, and then tossed it toward the edge of forest.

On impact with the ground, the petals opened. A purple cloud rose high and wide, hissing as it spread, veiling the jungle behind it. After a while the mist evaporated, and only a broken blossom resting on the earth remained.

Marcus harrumphed, pleased. "Wow. Like a gas grenade. Looks like we've got means of self-defense. Moderate, but workable."

"Yes. But we only have a handful, so we can't waste any." Sam's needless advice made Marcus grin. Sometimes Sam thought he was smarter than everyone else. Marcus found that endearing, but also a tad annoying. Still, Sam made sense, so Marcus ignored the irritation. "Do we still need to construct a trap?" Sam asked, turning his attention to his boyfriend.

Marcus shook his head. "I don't think so. If we can keep the razzie at bay long enough to get the vines where they need to be, then building a trap is unnecessary."

Sam closed his eyes and sighed in relief, actually sagging a bit. "Oh, good. I was kind of worried about that."

Marcus chuckled. "You're the sweetest guy, I swear."

Sam bit his bottom lip to suppress a smile, and his cheeks grew ruddy. Marcus wanted to kiss him. Or maybe make out with him. For a couple of hours or the whole night. But time wasn't on their side.

"We don't know how long the razzie will stay under, so let's get those vines in place, okay?" Marcus suggested. Sam agreed with a curt nod, and they went to work.

MARCUS QUICKLY understood that only Sam had the composure to work with the vines. Marcus gritted his teeth the whole time, hating having to sit still and wait for Sam to finish. He did try to help, but the meticulous effort caused him to fidget and shake until Sam finally told him to move off and wait close by.

As much as Marcus hated doing nothing, he admired Sam's ability to focus solely on the work, which required precision, patience, and time. Sam used his pocketknife to cut off sections of the excess vines and then cut them open. These he wrapped around each of the jagged ends of the longer vines and then tied thin strips of cloth he'd sliced from his and Marcus's T-shirts around the liana. This way the fluid wouldn't drip, the cut ends stayed in contact, and the charge they hoped would run in the liquid wouldn't dissipate or get grounded along the way.

"Okay, I'm done." Sam blew out a long breath and wiped beads of fresh sweat from his forehead. "We can attach these to the lightning rod."

"Hopefully we won't get either electrocuted or singed doing so," Marcus murmured as he grabbed the now one really long vine and started hauling it out of their room toward the corner where the lightning rod was.

"Now who's the pessimist?" Sam quipped, flicking his tongue at Marcus.

That single familiar, playful gesture was all Marcus needed to collect himself again. They could do this, and they *would* get home. He laughed because the sound and the emotion both bubbled inside him, and he had to let them out.

They knelt together side by side by the broken glass shielding that housed the lightning rod. The day they'd arrived on the island, the lightning bolts had frightened off the razzie, and the rod had lost its charge. Now, however, the metal spike retained much of the current it had accumulated during the storm the night before, blue cascades of energy flowing around the rod.

The base still glowed blue as well.

"Okay, Mr. Science Man, how do we do this without getting shocked?" Marcus asked.

Sam brought out one end of the vine, which was tied closed with narrow strips of makeshift string they'd torn from the T-shirt. "I guess we... try to wrap this around the rod?"

"You guess?" Marcus wasn't thrilled about the uncertainty of their plan. "Shouldn't we attach the other end first? I mean, the portal has no power, so we're less likely to get zapped and die screaming horribly while we burn beyond recognition."

Sam snorted. "Geesh. Way to stay motivated." Then he smiled and nodded. "Yeah, it's a better plan than mine at the moment."

They uncoiled the vine-made cable as they jumped down from the balcony and made their way outside the temple, mindful of their surroundings, careful of each step. Sam unwound the vine while Marcus kept one fist around a gas-producing bud. The razzie must still be asleep since it didn't appear out of the jungle to hinder their progress. They had no idea how long the effect of the gas lasted, but they kept their fingers *and* toes crossed.

The jungle was unusually silent. *The quiet before the storm?* Marcus scanned the boundaries between wide-open spaces and maze-like greenery. The ozzies flew from one branch to another, but unlike the chirping and singing they'd done earlier, they were now silent. Marcus had a bad feeling, but he kept a tight rein over his nerves.

Sam proceeded to the rundown stairs and headed inside the portal chamber. Once they were both safely inside, they let out simultaneous sighs of relief. The stress of the situation made for a tense atmosphere, as their sweating, heaving bodies proved.

"The chair wouldn't work even if we got it back to an upright position," Marcus noted.

"I figured." Sam laid the vines to the base of the portal, ensuring that the end touched the metal framework. "I'm hoping the point of origin is stored in the database of this doorway, same as the chair."

"We've done lots of makeshift rigging in the past couple of days." Marcus smirked, and Sam gave a ghost of a smile. Despite its lack of enthusiasm, the gesture was genuine.

"Should I untie the end now and hope the solution doesn't flow out? I mean, once we get the other end attached to the lightning rod and a storm comes, we may only have a blink of an eye to get through."

Marcus crouched, grabbed a few big pebbles, and built a small stack, pinning the vine in place against the metal frame. "There. Now all we need to do is untie it. I think that can wait until we make it back here during the storm." Then he frowned, reminding himself that they were dealing with dangerous forces of nature. "Just out of curiosity... how many volts can there be in a lightning bolt?"

Sam shrugged. "Well, the average temperature in a lightning bolt can rise up to fifty thousand degrees Fahrenheit. The temperature in the sun's photosphere, in comparison, is only ten thousand degrees."

"Holy shit." Marcus swallowed hard. "But how many—"

"An average lightning bolt can have anywhere between one hundred million and one billion volts at ten thousand amps." Sam sounded vague again, his attention clearly wandering as he studied the mound of rocks Marcus had erected. "If and when we get here in time and untie the vine before it burns, we must be ready to do it without getting hit. We have to remove all items that might act as conductors. So our iPhones must be stashed inside my backpack beforehand."

"Your phone's still MIA," Marcus reminded Sam. "We should go back and get it."

Sam frowned as if ambivalent. "While I agree we shouldn't leave a trace that we've been here in case the natives return… I don't know if that's smart. The plant might have, you know, devoured it in confusion."

Marcus stifled a laugh. "We won't know that until we check."

Sam let out a long-suffering breath, looking miserable. "I do want it back, but I don't want to put either of us in danger. Not when we can avoid it."

"Let's see what we can do once it's dark again. Who knows? That plant might be off to dreamland, allowing us a window of opportunity."

Though Marcus wasn't sure if the idea of retrieving the device was smart, deep down he agreed with Sam that leaving evidence of advanced technology behind on what at first glance appeared to be a primitive world could go awry. Perhaps one day in the future these lizzies would come to Earth and destroy humanity with the very tech Sam and Marcus had left behind ('cause according to every sci-fi movie he'd ever seen with alien lizards, they tended to be dickwads hell-bent on annihilation).

"Fine. We'll go and get my damn phone back." Sam pouted, clearly still full of doubts, but he sure looked cute doing it.

Marcus would have kissed Sam's reservations away, but Sam was already moving toward the cave entrance with a purposeful stride. Apparently Marcus didn't need to explain his reasoning to his boyfriend, so he quietly followed, smiling.

ON TIPTOE, Marcus and Sam sneaked from the artificial cave down the steep stairs, keeping the gas buds at the ready. No razzies jumped on them from the bushes.

But each time they walked through a gap between two tree trunks, they received a jolt of electricity. The bolts weren't painful per se, but they soon started to get annoying. Marcus figured in time they could and would do serious damage. He couldn't wait to get back to safer ground.

The foliage rustled in the light breeze, a wet heat permeated through their clothes, and the jungle seemed alive with little sounds, small movements, and invisible life they couldn't detect. Pungent odors of both wet and drying earth floated to Marcus's nose, and he felt mildly queasy, the assault on his senses too potent for comfort.

Far too often he'd complained about the mountains. The long harsh winters, the cold winds, the dry air, the frequent power outages, the lack of trendy events, the absence of a personal life in a small town, etcetera, etcetera. So many things to bitch about.

Now all he wished was to make it back there alive so he could fall to his knees, kiss the ground, and thank his lucky stars for home and his old life.

Well, maybe not his *old* life, where he was always restless, on the go, seeking purpose and meaning but never finding it. The idea unnerved Marcus, but he quickly put it aside. His life had purpose and meaning now, now that he had an anchor to stabilize and ground him: Sam, his special bae.

Hot droplets shook loose from the leaves high above, and a couple landed on his neck and trickled down his spine. Marcus shivered and grimaced. Apparently it wasn't enough he was sweating bullets, he had to get a natural shower too? The jungle hated him. No, the jungle didn't really hate him. That line of thinking was irrational, ridiculous, and utterly pointless. Nature did her own thing, regardless of sentient life-forms dabbling within it.

"Shh." Sam crouched and waved Marcus quiet—though he hadn't said a word or made a sound—whispering, "There. See?" Sam pointed, and Marcus followed the gesture.

Under a tall tree, wrapped into a ball, the razzie still slept like a baby, a low rumble emerging from its throat as though it were snoring. The creature hadn't awoken but merely shifted to a better position, big paws under its jaw.

Marcus observed its eyelids moving rapidly. Could the animal be... dreaming? The thought rattled his brain, disturbing his once firm grasp of the universe.

"We're in luck," Sam murmured. "The phone was lower on the steps." He hurried on the balls of his feet, descending the stairs in a muted rush, trying to be swift but not to be noisy. As he stopped virtually midstep, Marcus held his breath, waiting for the worst. But Sam let out a long relieved breath. "I see it."

The iPhone appeared undamaged, but clearly it had been moved from its original spot on the step. The song had changed to "Shatter Me" by Lindsey Stirling, featuring Lzzy Hale, so clearly the device had continued playing music all the time. Even now vines crept around it, every once in a while their tips touching or brushing against it, as dubstep melodies played on a violin and a female vocalist sang with a pure rock edge.

"Can you turn it off without making a commotion?" Marcus asked in a whisper.

Sam nodded frenetically, but he swallowed hard, and his skin had gone pale. If he said a prayer, it was silent. With extra care, Sam sneaked the last few steps until he was within reach of the phone. As he extended his hand, so slowly it seemed not to move at all, Marcus felt like punching a wall in frustration. He wasn't skilled at the waiting game, and his fears grew.

Then Sam tapped on the iPhone's screen. The electronic beat of the music ceased in an instant, and an eerie silence echoed inside Marcus's head, making him cringe in discomfort. Every primitive instinct in him cried out to grab Sam, throw him over his shoulder, and make a run for it. He did his best to resist the caveman urge.

Leisurely, as if taking their time and adding to Marcus's mental strain on purpose, the vines wormed farther away from the cooling device, receding back to the underbrush that hid the carnivorous flower behind a green wall.

Marcus refused to move or even breathe until all the vines had vanished from sight.

Sam closed his eyes and let out a sigh, actually slumping, his fear visibly alleviated. He picked up the phone, tucked it in his pocket, and retreated cautiously, keeping his gaze firmly on the thicket and each flicker of movement, no matter how minute.

When Sam reached him, Marcus pulled him into a fierce bear hug, holding on to his bae until they both stopped shaking. "Next time we fucking leave the phone."

"Yes." Sam chuckled into Marcus's ear, his hot breath brushing Marcus's hair, even tickling him a bit. "Now can we go?"

Marcus said nothing. He gripped Sam by the hand, interlacing their fingers, and started a rapid-fire ascent, hurrying back to the temple complex. He didn't stop once until they stood safely under the entrance archway, both of them panting and leaning on their knees.

"Oh my God…. Can't believe… we fucking… did that," Sam managed to breathe out, supporting himself against the wall, his legs visibly shaking.

Marcus burst out in laughter, bubbling with hope and joy at their success. "Man, you don't know how ridiculously hot you are right now."

Sam snorted as if hearing a joke, but the corners of his mouth lifted. "Yeah, I sure am, if you mean huffing like a beached whale, all red in the face."

Marcus got up in Sam's personal space and pinned him against the wall with his arms. "Fuck, bae, I want you so bad."

Sam blushed, wrapped his arms around Marcus's waist, and rested them over Marcus's hips. He plastered their bodies together tight from head to toes. "Me too. Everything's done, so all we can do is wait for another storm."

"So I'm, what, nothing but time-filler?" Marcus teased softly.

"Shut up." Then Sam shut Marcus up with his mouth. By wordless agreement, they parted their lips simultaneously, letting their tongues out to play.

But then Marcus remembered they still had things to do. He pulled away from Sam, and Sam stopped kissing Marcus abruptly, his lips twisting weirdly from being halted midkiss. The expression on his face was hilarious.

"Wait. Hold up. Shouldn't we connect the other end of the vine to the lightning rod first before we get carried away?" Marcus asked.

"Oh. Uh-huh. You're right." Sam sounded disappointed.

They pushed off each other, as difficult as that was. Marcus noticed the bulge in Sam's pants. He sported a similar boner. But needs must. Marcus took a mental cold shower so he could concentrate on survival and their escape plan. Sam coughed to clear his throat and looked flushed, fidgeting in place for a moment as though he'd forgotten how to walk.

Somehow they made it to the broken pillar that acted as their jumping board and vaulted up to the balcony. They proceeded to the lightning rod in the corner, and as in the chamber underground, Marcus stacked pieces of rubble in a mound and propped the vine between the rocks to keep it firmly in place. Sam attached the end of the vine to the sparkling blue base and untied it.

"Now the saline solution touches the base but doesn't leak out." Sam brushed hair out of his eyes, revealing how nervous he really was by the beads of sweat on his forehead. "I doubt the smaller sparks are enough to activate the portal. I think it needs a bigger boost."

Marcus agreed. "Yeah. Space travel can't be very energy efficient or inexpensive."

"I don't think the lizzies cared about money or even had its equivalent. Nothing in our surroundings suggests they used currency of any kind. If they even created the portals. Which I personally don't think they did."

"We may never know."

Marcus was surprised to find he actually wanted to know the story behind the lizzies, their culture, and their extended absence from the temple. But he had to accept that would never happen—unless they surprised him and dropped out of the sky within the next few hours before he and Sam escaped the exomoon.

"I guess." Sam sounded glum about that. Even without the curiosity of a natural-born scientist, Marcus understood. "Now what?"

"What do you want to do?"

Before Marcus finished his sentence, Sam jumped him and kissed him silly.

How they got back to their room was mostly a mystery. Marcus's memory was hazy at best. All he recalled with crystal clarity was that his hands were full of an eager and willing Sam, who clung to his body as if he were a vine hugging a tree trunk.

Their room was noisy with the whine and howl of the winds as they began to pick up speed. Marcus barely acknowledged their presence—until his skin tingled and grew hot each time a breeze touched him.

"What?" He tore his mouth away from Sam and brushed his skin. There was nothing there—no pollen, no dust, nothing. And yet the draft felt like... fire. More specifically, like sexually hot fire. The sensation seemed to focus precisely in his groin area. His cock ached. "Can you feel that?"

Sam nodded, his fingers dancing on his arms, face, and chest. He was frowning—like most of Sam's expressions, Marcus found it cute and endearing—as he said, "You don't think...." Sam blushed and left his sentence unfinished. Marcus had to prompt him with an impatient wave of hand. "You don't think the winds might carry… pheromones or airborne aphrodisiacs or some such?"

"Uh…." Marcus had no answers. Erotic winds? Was that even a thing?

"We know next to nothing about this moon or how its atmosphere works," Sam said in a hushed tone. "Maybe the winds cause, like… ecstasy or euphoria or arousal. It could be a normal meteorological phenomenon here." Sam's eyes grew glassy as his mind apparently drifted. "That could be another reason the lizzies chose this moon and this island as the base for their lovemaking cult."

Marcus was stumped. All he cared about was that he was hard as rock and hot as molten lava, and they were wasting valuable erection time. So he kissed Sam silent and maneuvered them to the bed. He knelt on the stone surface, laid Sam down on his back, and rested on top of him. Their hands roamed and wandered wherever they could reach, grabbing and fondling shamelessly as their shared need grew exponentially.

Sam wound his limbs around Marcus's body, pressed his heels against the small of Marcus's back, and raked his hands through Marcus's hair, his nails scraping skin. Marcus rubbed his hands along Sam's outer thighs, loving the way Sam's body wrapped around his, and purred in delight. Their lips fused, and their tongues entangled.

As they parted to breathe, Marcus dipped down to place an openmouthed kiss on Sam's neck, sucking on the jugular until the skin was wet, red, and undoubtedly throbbing. Sam moaned, and his hips jerked.

Then Marcus kissed his way farther down Sam's body, tonguing his nipples and biting them till they pulsed hotly against his tongue. Blindly he parted the flaps of Sam's fly to expose his hard cock. There Marcus stopped, hesitating.

Sam rose onto his elbows. "What's wrong? I've never been with anyone but you, so I'm clean, if that's what you're worried about." Marcus opened his mouth to speak, but Sam wasn't done. "Or are you worried about yourself?"

"No, I'm clean. I've been tested."

"You have? When?"

"Two weeks ago, five days after I turned twenty."

Sam's eyes rounded into saucers. "Why? I mean, good." Then he frowned. "If you're clean and I'm clean, what's wrong? Or… is it that you don't want to… you know… blow me? You don't have to do anything you don't—"

"No, it's not that," Marcus hedged, glancing between Sam's eyes and his ruddy dick. "You're seventeen."

Sam groaned. "Oh Jesus, not this again. Are you fucking serious?" He locked gazes with Marcus. "I'm not a naïve virgin, okay? I know what I want. And it's not like I'm in any hurry to shove my ass in your groin and order you to stuff my bare boy hole full with your magnificent member."

"What the fuck? Jesus Christ, Sam!" Marcus shook his head. "Boy hole? Oh my God."

Sam rolled his eyes. "Since when have you become so squeamish? We've had sex before."

"Yeah, but… not like this." Marcus sighed, feeling heat suffuse his cheeks. "I do want to, believe me. But—"

"But nothing," Sam cut in sharply, his eyes flashing. "Physically, chronologically, and biologically we may be two or so years apart. But when it comes to mental stuff, faculties and maturity, we're on the same level, okay? Neither of us is confused about who we are at heart, which is gay guys who want each other."

Marcus closed his eyes, praying for patience. "I get all that, but—"

"We live in Montana, where the age of consent is sixteen years," Sam interjected again, his frustration and vexation clearly rising. "I'm old enough, and I'm fucking consenting. Period." Sam's lips formed a thin line of determination. "Now get down there and suck me off."

At that point Marcus had to concede to the fact that he wasn't going to win this argument. So he pulled Sam's jeans down to midthigh, gripped the base of Sam's prick, and brought the head to his mouth. Sam moaned, dropping back to lie on the stone bed. Marcus sucked on the tip, licked around the mushroom-shaped head, flicked his tongue underneath the cap, and then stuck his tongue into the slit. Sam jolted, bucked his hips, and whimpered, fisting the winter coat under his body.

Marcus grinned around his mouthful. *Green light given.*

CHAPTER 13

IF THEY were going to die, Sam's sole prayer was that their demise wouldn't take place until he'd spilled his seed in Marcus's mouth. That perfect mouth on his cock, hot and wet, sublime suction sending frissons of pleasure through his body.

So this is what guys rave about. Okay, I finally get it. Fucking brilliant.

His senses on overload and his sexual appetite on overdrive, Sam felt like he'd come apart at the seams. His most sensitive organ trapped between Marcus's lips was too much. How could a guy last more than ten seconds? On the receiving end blew his mind. None of his sex fantasies came close to comparing with this heavenly delight.

Marcus sucked and licked around the head, flicking his tongue seemingly everywhere at once. Then he brought his hand into the mix, fisting Sam's dick and pumping almost too hard for him to bear. And even then Marcus wasn't done, for he took Sam's balls in his other hand, rolling them around against his palm, tugging ever so lightly.

Sam moaned. His body trembled and jolted on its own. Cascades of passion flowed in him, pushing him toward the crest of the tidal wave of desire.

Marcus ran the flat of his tongue from base to the tip of Sam's shaft, licking the length like it was his favorite lollipop. Once Sam's prick dripped with saliva, Marcus jerked it with a fierce hold, sucking on the cockhead hard.

Sam lost it. His balls pulled up, his cock felt like it was about to rocket right off, and his body burned within. Crying out, he arched his back and shot come by the bucketloads into Marcus's mouth. Marcus hummed and drank greedily, lewd slurping sounds echoing from the stone walls. He didn't stop until Sam felt like he'd been wrung dry and licked clean.

"Oh… my… God," Sam whispered in a voice that was hoarse from shouting.

Marcus chuckled, wiping his hands on his pants. "How kind of you, bae. Feel free to worship me and my magic cock."

Sam raised himself up on shaky elbows. "S-sorry. Lost myself there for a sec. Come here and I'll—"

"Touch me and you'll get a handful or mouthful of cooling come." Marcus sported a wide grin of satisfaction and a flushed face. He'd obviously pleasured himself while giving Sam a blow job. Did the guy have an invisible magical third hand tucked in there somewhere, or what?

"You…. But I wanted to…." Sam went silent, disappointed at not getting the chance to give Marcus the same sweet delight he'd given Sam. That was definitely an experience he had his heart set on having as soon as humanly possible.

Marcus rested a hand on Sam's exposed thigh, squeezing softly. "I know, my love. But I couldn't wait. Was so thirsty for you. Besides, there's always tomorrow."

Sam was touched by Marcus's optimism. He needed some of that. He inched his way to Marcus, slid into his lap, and embraced him with all of himself. He never wanted to let go. They both reeked of fresh sweat and spunk, but Sam didn't care. It was them, locked together tight in a cocoon of privacy, proof of their love sinking in through their senses.

His perfect boyfriend hugged him back, buried his face in Sam's hair, and whispered sweet nothings in his ear. Except coming from him, they meant everything. Slowly they came down from the heights of climax and relaxed in each other's arms.

"AS MUCH as I love smelling like you, I'm glad we took a shower." Sam stretched and yawned. They'd returned to their quarters after washing up under the waterfall. He got dressed in his dirty, damp jeans since they couldn't afford to waste time if and when another storm brewed.

"Amen, brother."

Marcus packed their winter clothes and their unpacked gear, like the towel, in Sam's backpack so they'd be ready when the time came. Since most of Sam's stuff had never left the bag, the job was quickly done. He tossed a protein bar to Sam and took one for himself.

"Eat up, my brave hero. We're gonna need all our strength when the time comes."

Sam didn't argue. He tore off the wrapping and took a hearty bite, munching slowly, savoring the familiar taste. "These the last ones?"

"Yeah." Marcus sat down next to him on the stone bed. With the winter coats packed, the seating was less than comfortable. But it was stable, and by then they were well acquainted with it. "You think we'll have to wait long?"

Sam shrugged, partially afraid to voice his fears. "I don't know. Last time it was night when the storm came. Maybe they only occur at night. Sun's influence on weather is strong."

Marcus said nothing but continued to chew on his meal, occasionally taking a sip from the refilled water bottle. Sam leaned into him, making the best of his meager nourishment. They ate in silence.

"You know," Sam wondered out loud, gazing up at the ceiling, "it's kind of curious they don't have a hole in the roof or even an open-air structure since rain affected them so. If the point of this place was to get aroused and have sex, why block out the wet element that seemed to give them so much joy and pleasure? Not that I'm complaining or anything."

Marcus shrugged, munched on his small meal, and swallowed before commenting, "It'd be interesting to find out. But I doubt we ever will. Kind of sad."

Through the gaps in the stone wall, they could see the sun going down, the sky turning a burnt orange. They couldn't clearly see if the cloud cover increased as night approached, but Sam dared to hope.

"Will things be different between us if we get back home?" Sam asked quietly.

"*When* we get home," Marcus corrected him. "And yes, they will. You promised that you'd stop running." He planted a kiss over Sam's temple. "I don't know if you plan on coming out, but I do wanna date you. We can do it in secret if you want. Under the radar, you know. But you're my bae, got it?"

Despite their dire circumstances, Sam had never felt happier. Marcus loved him. Sam was his boyfriend. "Yeah. I am yours." He cuddled against Marcus, lifting Marcus's arm over his shoulder so he could get tucked beneath it. "As for coming out... I don't know yet. Haven't had much time to think about that kind of stuff. Even before we came here."

"I understand." Marcus leaned into Sam too, resting his head on Sam's. "I just said it 'cause sometimes it's easier to come out if you're not doing it alone, you know. If you've got someone special at your side."

"Thanks." Sam was grateful. Marcus's support meant the world to him. Here, in their own island paradise of sorts, it was easy to grow closer, physically and emotionally. No one here to interrupt them or invade their privacy. Back home was another matter entirely.

"Just giving you food for thought," Marcus added. "Reminding you you're not alone."

Sam smiled, though Marcus couldn't see it. "You think Simon's gonna freak out when you start dating me?"

His big brother's reaction worried Sam more than he cared to admit out loud. What if Simon forced Marcus to choose between them? Or what if he broke with Marcus for good and ended their friendship altogether? It would be Sam's fault, and he wasn't sure if he could handle it.

What if Simon couldn't handle his baby brother's sexuality at all?

Marcus let out a sigh, a touch of sadness in his tone. "To be honest, I don't really care what he thinks. I'm not giving you up. I love the big guy, don't get me wrong, but… I love you more. Way more. You're the one I've been dreaming of for years. You're my bae."

Ridiculously happy, Sam couldn't have stopped his grin to save his life. Although to be fair, the feeling was a confused mix of joy and relief. Perhaps Marcus was onto something, that it really was easier to take those baby steps out of the closet with someone who loved you the way you truly were at heart.

That, however, meant Sam should love Marcus the same way, care for the person he was inside. Despite their stay in close quarters of late, Sam had a lot of questions.

"Don't take this the wrong way, okay?" Sam took a breath to calm himself. "Why do you pretend to be dumber than you are?"

Much to Sam's surprise, Marcus chuckled. "People see things in terms of roles and stereotypes. I'm a jock. All brawn, no brains."

"I get that. College. Blending in. But that's not an answer. Like, I know you read."

"Yeah, I do. There's even books I really like. But I'm mildly dyslexic, so it's never an easy task for me to undertake."

Sam pulled away to stare at his boyfriend in shock. How could he not have known this before now? "You're dyslexic? Does Simon know?"

"Yeah, he does. Apart from him, my parents, my English teacher, and now you, no one else knows. It's not something I like to talk about."

"Why? Do you think it makes you look weak?" Sam immediately regretted asking the question. Shame overwhelmed him. Was he this shallow?

"No. I'm not embarrassed. I was born this way. Just like I was born being attracted to both sexes. It's normal for me. I can't say why I don't wanna talk about it. 'Cause it's private? It's not like I'd hate or dread people finding out." He shrugged. "Just one of those things, I guess."

"Yeah." Sam didn't know what else to say. "I'm not judging you or anything. I'm into books and reading, but—"

"I know, chipmunk. I know." Marcus smiled at him, drew him closer, and kissed him on the lips, his touch warm and soft, less erotic and more comforting. "We're a dating couple, bae, not doppelgangers. If we were the same in every aspect, I sure as fuck wouldn't be making out with you."

Sam laughed and returned to his previous position, snuggled under Marcus's arm. "For sure." He sighed then. "I'm just... worried we're too different."

"How? And more importantly, does it matter we're not the same?"

"We have comics and music in common. But what else?"

Marcus leaned in and whispered in Sam's ear, "Hot naked gay sex?"

Sam blushed. "A-apart from that. Dirty dawg."

"Well, thanks to an awesome source of information—Simon—I happen to know we're both into finger foods. You like veggie pizza and my fave is BBQ pizza."

Sam didn't have to say anything. He already knew that. He'd kept a close eye on his crush whenever Marcus was at their house. Which was often because Marcus and Simon were best buddies. Not that Sam had been spying or anything. He'd just... watched him surreptitiously. That wasn't stalking. That was admiring a perfect specimen of masculinity.

"Your silence speaks volumes," Marcus said, laughing. "But seriously, Sammy, what do our differences matter if we love, care for, and trust each other?"

That reply stumped Sam. Marcus could be wise when he wanted to. He was right too. Sam was clutching at straws due to his doubts about whether they could continue like this when they got back home. He hoped for the best but prepared for the worst. His cynicism talking.

"I'm *not* leaving you, Sammy." Marcus tilted Sam's face up with a hand under his jaw. "Now that I finally have you, you're mine, and I'm keeping you. So stop listening to whatever those voices inside your head are telling you. 'Cause I can practically hear them. I know you so well, and I know you're scared. But the way I feel about you and the way I want to be with you… those are things you *never* need to worry about."

Sam turned around and straddled Marcus's thighs, sitting on his lap. "Thank you. You always know exactly what to say." He kissed his first real boyfriend even though neither of them had cleaned their teeth with anything other than water during their shower. If Marcus didn't mind Sam's bad breath, he wouldn't either.

When Marcus's hand dipped under the waistband of Sam's jeans and felt up his buttcheeks, a boom of distant thunder echoed over the ocean into their private perch. Startled, they separated, looked around. This was it.

They scrambled to their feet in a rush, yanked on their T-shirts—Marcus's barely reaching his waist after they'd used most of the tail on the vines—and grabbed their gear, including one of the spears. Then they took one last look at the room they had shared for the length of their stay. Though small, the space was intimate, not because of images of sex on the walls, but thanks to the memories they'd created there. The place had been a shelter to them. Without speaking a word, they said their silent thanks and goodbyes to the room.

"We're never coming back here, are we?" Sam had expected to feel relief. Instead, a bewildering ruefulness assailed his heart.

Instead of a rude joke, Marcus touched Sam's shoulder. "Never say never. After all, if things don't work out, this'll be our home sweet home for the rest of our lives."

Sam snorted, smiling. "You're nuts."

Marcus winked at him. "You're on fleek about that."

Sam grimaced. "Not really into slang."

Shaking his head in amusement, Marcus merely laughed in response.

They hurried to the balcony then, and together they jumped down from the ragged edge onto the stone altar. Marcus stretched out his hand, indicating without words that he would carry Sam's backpack. At first Sam thought to argue that he was no weakling. But Marcus was built for strength and speed and could therefore better ensure their stuff would make the journey home, so he handed over his bag without protest.

Once they stepped under the entrance archway, Sam snapped his last pictures of the ruined Temple of Love with his iPhone, even though he had full albums of everything already. His battery was about to die anyway.

Marcus balanced the metal lance in his hand, as if testing the weight and handling. He studied the hostile jungle spreading beyond the flat, cleared mountaintop. In the coming decades and centuries, it would probably grow over too.

"Green's my favorite color, and I love the idea of sunshine and gold sandy beaches, but, man, I'm so done with this place."

He fanned himself, pulling his undershirt away from his undoubtedly hot and sweaty chest. Humid heat got in everywhere.

"I like all the colors of the rainbow equally," Sam commented off-handedly as he took a last few shots and then stowed away his iPhone. "And yes, I mean that in every sense of the word."

Diversity of sexual orientations was one of his interests, not because he was gay but because some straights preferred to pretend nothing else existed beyond their narrow view of sexuality. The world needed to learn in order to be more understanding and accepting. Not quite a social crusade, but important to Sam nonetheless.

Marcus grinned. "I figured. C'mon. We're wasting time."

They abandoned the safety of their temple sanctuary and jogged down the ceremonial path, their gait swift, their gazes aimed at the jungle around them. Every second Sam expected the worst, a vine slithering to tether them, a razzie jumping out to attack them, or an unknown danger falling on them from an alien sky.

The sky was turning dark, ominous clouds gathering to form puffy promises of rain, thunder, and lightning. Soon the clouds blocked out the stars and the stunning view of the alien ring planet, the gas giant shining green and its rings glimmering in the darkness, looking close enough to reach out and touch.

Rain pelted Sam and Marcus in an instant, raging hotly over their clothes and skin, in part blinding them. Thunder shook the ground and lightning flashed, turning night briefly into day. Drenched, they increased their pace toward the artificial cavern.

But the trek became more arduous due to the growing harsh winds that blew against them, pushing them back, until each step forward felt like a huge accomplishment. What should have been a few minutes mad dash turned into a battle of wills as nature put up a fight.

And their battle wasn't made any easier as the winds gave them untimely boners. Excitement built within them, each caress from a new breeze sending flashes of heat through them. Sam wanted to forget running and rip Marcus's clothes off and fuck him then and there.

Suddenly the winds ceased, and lightning halted in an instant. The sky grew brighter from the light of the luminescent gas giant. The eye of the storm opened a chasm amid the clouds.

And an enormous splash heralded the majestic flight of another mazzie.

The massive sea creature glided through the air, its movements as fluid as the waves in the ocean, undulating. High-frequency songs floated through the opening amid the menacing storm clouds, as if the mazzie were giving a heavenly performance of sound and movement just for their benefit. Lightning bolts struck the flying beast's body repeatedly from the clouds surrounding it but the creature seemed to suffer no ill effects.

"You think it does this sky dance during every storm?" Sam asked in awe.

"That's not the same mazzie," Marcus threw in, surprising the heck out of Sam.

"What?"

"This one's got silver on its sides. The last one didn't."

"You sure?"

"Positive. This ain't the same beast we saw earlier."

"Maybe they're, um, gender or age differences? The silver sides, I mean."

The mazzie floated in the eye of the storm, as if it owned the wild, erratic space. Spark showers from its fins and flippers spread around it, cocooning it in a blue blanket of electricity. The sky was ablaze with a natural light show born from an animal that at first glance seemed far too big to even break the waves.

"Maybe." Marcus shrugged and stared upward same as Sam, halting their escape midstep. "Why do you think they're doing that?"

"No clue. Perhaps they're guided by... oh, what's it called? A magnetoreception."

"Uh, magnet... what?"

"It's a sense some animals have for navigation where they use magnetic fields to find the right direction, altitude, or destination."

Marcus harrumphed, not sounding particularly impressed. "Wow. Far out."

Sam laughed. Marcus's company lifted his spirits. They really should have done this long ago, tried being together. And they could have, if Sam hadn't been so busy being afraid and running away like a scared bunny from a hungry wolf.

"C'mon, bae. We need to get a move on."

Marcus resumed heading for the portal cavern, and Sam followed. He snapped one last picture of the mazzie singing and flying before stuffing his phone inside the backpack Marcus carried. As they hurried toward the stairs, heated drizzle started, followed quickly by rolling thunder and lightning flashes.

They'd reached the top of the broken steps—when a low growl came from the bushes.

Sam and Marcus froze, dread making their hearts skip a beat. They knew what would follow.

At least until another purr emerged from a different thicket behind them.

Sam whipped around, his back to Marcus's.

A tiny head poked out of the greenery. The three-colored stripes, round butterfly ears, and gray horn on its forehead were familiar features. This creature must be the cub Marcus had seen earlier, attacking the sole squizzie in sight.

The bigger razzie stalked them in a circle, snarling. The cub, however, zipped closer to them and retreated immediately, as if taunting them or playing with them. It didn't take Sam long to figure out what was going on.

"The mother's teaching its cub how to chase and toy with its food," Sam murmured to Marcus, trying not to move his lips a lot in case that prompted an assault. "It develops a cat's hunting instinct while ensuring they don't get injured in the process. But… if it's like Earth cats, if it gets the chance, it'll deliver a lethal neck bite to any prey larger than itself."

"'Kay. Quick safety tip. Thanks." Marcus sounded agitated, and his hunched position confirmed his readiness to do battle. He held the spear in front of him, waving it in sweeping arcs to test how close the predators would dare to venture. "Can you back up toward the stairs?"

"No. The cub's in the way."

"Shit." Marcus glanced over his shoulder at the smaller feline. "What will the mother do if we manage to hurt or kill the cub?"

"Kill us instantly most likely." Sam was scared out of his mind. "You planning on that anytime soon?"

"We could change places. But then the mother might attack you since you don't have a weapon. And without mine, I can't get rid of the cub."

"So what's the plan?"

"Thinking."

"Think faster!" Sam urged with a rising pitch.

"That's incredibly helpful, thanks." Marcus swung the spear in front of him, but both of the felines were out of weapons range. "Got one of the blossom grenades? Throw one."

Sam dug into his pocket, fished out one of the closed buds, and tossed it without a great deal of preparation. He was too freaked out to keep his hands from shaking, so he didn't aim.

The purple bud landed on the ground close to the big razzie. The petals popped open, and purple vapors spread all around, fast and noxious. The razzie jumped out of range, growling.

Without waiting for an attack, Sam delved deeper in his pockets, pulled out more gas buds, and hurled them in the general direction of the big razzie. A couple bounded against the huge feline and a few landed on its feet, but with little effect. The feline seemed more than capable of avoiding the sleep-inducing fumes.

Then Sam had no more to spare. "I'm out. No more gas grenades. Sorry."

"Damn. Shit. Fuck. Hell." Marcus's angry growl sounded almost the same as those of the alien cats.

Sam shifted positions from one foot to another, preparing to quickly dash in any direction to steer clear of the cub. Purring, the little creature waved its paws in the air, as if trying to reach for them, but it was too far away. It was still just a game. The second that stopped, they'd get eaten.

They had faced the razor beast before. But being double-teamed was a new and frightening experience. Sam could barely hear anything past the drumming of blood in his ears. He feared his damn heart would burst through his chest any minute now.

The rain wasn't making things any easier. Winds had started up again, throwing water in their eyes, soaking them to the bone. But the cats seemed utterly indifferent to getting drenched. Their coats dripped, quickly followed by waves of bioelectricity moving along their raised hackles.

Sam began to doubt if a lightning bolt could even damage these creatures, let alone kill them. The lightning rods in the temple must have produced a charge greater than that of lightning if the razzies feared them.

That seemed paradoxical, but Sam didn't have time to ponder the issue to his satisfaction. All he could do was act and react according to the primal fight-or-flight instinct and try not to die.

"Just in case... if...." Sam swallowed hard. "I love you, Marcus."

"I love you too, chipmunk. Forever and ever."

Marcus's strained voice spoke volumes. He was nervous, perhaps even afraid, the same as Sam. They were up shit creek without a paddle. How could things possibly get any worse?

Then Sam had his answer.

The cub leaped through the air. Sam screamed.

Marcus shoved him out of the way into the dirt and swung the spear in a wide arc. The cub cried out, its jump interrupted but not its forward momentum. It rolled into a ball and continued to bounce till it reached its mother's feet.

The razor beast sent out a roar that shook the ground and assaulted Sam's ears till they bled.

Then it crouched and vaulted toward Marcus. The spear didn't work. With one paw, the razzie batted the lance aside like it was a toothpick, while with another it swatted at Marcus, who yelled in pain and was struck back a few feet. In horror, Sam watched as red lines opened on Marcus's side, blood oozing out of what looked like deep gashes.

Sam didn't stop to think. He fumbled for the lance, jumped to his feet, and yelled, "Get back! Go away!" He kept swinging the spear in front of him as he stepped between the razzie and his boyfriend.

The beast growled, its fangs bared, its coat aflame with blue sparks, and it kept trying to slap the offending weapon aside with its big paws. The animal was gigantic, and Sam knew he'd lose soon.

Was this the end of their off-world adventure?

CHAPTER 14

A HIGH-PITCH chirp startled both Sam and the razzie, and they stopped midmotion.

Having seen the pictures on Marcus's iPhone, Sam recognized the squizzie right away. It really was supercute with its floppy ears, big white eyes, bushy tail, kangaroo-like legs, and gray-and-white striped thick fur with a collar resembling quills.

The small critter stood nearby, inching toward the moaning cub, tilting its head this way and that as though it couldn't see clearly. Sam assumed it was blind or had poor eyesight, just as Marcus had indicated. Those eyes as pure white as driven snow suggested as much.

It bounced closer and stopped by the cub.

The mother razzie growled, ignored Sam, and skulked toward her cub and the squizzie.

Then, out of the blue, the squizzie spread its bushy tail into a fluffy fan that emanated blinding white light. Even the razzie ducked its head, though it didn't stop its approach. A moment before the brilliance became too much, Sam could have sworn the tail appeared torn.

Sam had a feeling there was going to be some kind of smackdown. He tossed aside the lance, grabbed Marcus by the arms, lifted him from the ground, and supported him as they hurried toward the stairs. Groaning, Marcus stumbled and swayed, and the swinging backpack didn't help matters. But Sam kept a firm hold of him, part urging and part dragging him down the steps and into the portal chamber.

There Sam laid Marcus down on the ground. "Stay awake, Marcus, please. Just a few more minutes. Then we can rest, I swear."

Marcus pressed a hand on his side, blood wetting his fingers. He was pale, sweaty, and shaking, but he managed a curt nod, his face in tight lines as he apparently fought to control the pain.

Sam rushed to the portal and to the pile of rocks where the vine was lodged. He untied the end of the liana and made sure the thick liquid was in direct contact with the portal's frame. He then hustled back to Marcus and helped him stand, though wavering. The low gravity helped take some of his weight off Sam, so for once he appreciated the moon they were on.

"Now we wait," Sam murmured, out of breath, watching the liana and the portal with intense focus. If their plan didn't work, this would be a short trip when they ran right into a solid rock face. "Listen. If the liana bursts apart or burns up... crouch, keep your head against your chest, your eyes closed, and your mouth open. If the lightning hits us... be a low target, don't let the bolts blow up your eyeballs, and let the hit have an exit point through your mouth, okay?"

Marcus muttered something unintelligible. He was fading fast, and Sam was losing his shit. The advice he'd just given might save them, at least until the razzies found them and ate them. Maybe none of their preparations mattered. Only the way they'd die seemed to change.

Thunder boomed outside. Trees swayed violently in the grasp of rough winds, casting lively shadows on the chamber floor. Sam couldn't see the bright light from the squizzie anymore, but he dared to hope the poor thing wouldn't get devoured.

"Th-that squizzie... it was the one... I met in the forest," Marcus muttered faintly, his eyes closed, his body trembling. "Saw the... wounded tail.... It tried to... help me?"

Sam was flummoxed. Animals with memory or sentience? Then again, didn't that sort of describe humans too? "No clue," he replied, starting to feel the tension in his muscles from holding up Marcus, who was heavier than him.

"If it did... that was nice of him," Marcus whispered, his voice hoarse. He must have been in agony, Sam thought. His fears were mounting. It seemed like a new cause to be afraid rose every few minutes. He wasn't sure how much more stress he could take.

Lightning flashed outside, illuminating the chamber. A knell of thunder followed on its heels a second or two later. The storm was right above them. Somewhere in the distance, another splash drowned out the sounds of the tempest, suggesting another mazzie had either risen or fallen.

The artificial cavern functioned like an echo chamber, the sounds of the furor outside intensifying. Sam shuddered. Or perhaps he merely felt Marcus shivering. He couldn't say for sure anymore.

A rattling accompanied by the din of static briefly grew louder than the gale.

Electricity bolted out of the liana's end and climbed the framework of the portal like a vine creeping around a tree trunk. A low hum buzzed in the air. All the hairs on Sam's body stood on end.

Then the blue light above the doorway lit up, the glow at once ominous and soothing.

"It worked." Sam almost couldn't believe his eyes. "C'mon."

He all but dragged Marcus to the portal, the opening now so immensely black that no light seemed to escape its impenetrable surface. Was this what a black hole looked like? Sam didn't think so, since a black hole's name didn't mean it was actually black the way this portal seemed to be.

A fierce roar came from the stairs to the chamber. Frozen in fear, Sam turned toward the sound.

The big razzie sneaked down the crumbling steps, its eyes burning with vengeance.

"God, please, no."

Sam was almost at his wit's end. But he acted on instinct.

He released his hold of Marcus and shoved him into the swirling blackness of the portal.

At the exact same moment the razzie growled and leaped.

Fortunately for Sam, Marcus also apparently acted on instinct. He gripped Sam by the arm as he stumbled forward through the portal, in essence yanking Sam with him till they fell into the blackness in a heap of limbs.

The last thing Sam felt was a sharp sting on the back of his leg from the beast's claws.

"HEY, BAE. Still with me?"

Sam awoke with a start. Marcus had roused him from unconsciousness or sleep; Sam couldn't tell which. Every part of his body, inside and out, hurt like a motherfucker.

"Marcus? You okay?"

With a sarcastic harrumph, he answered, "Super. You? Heard you scream when we…."

Wincing, Sam pulled himself up into a sitting position. The back of his leg hurt and his jeans were torn. His fingertips came away red-smeared with drying blood when he touched his leg through the tear. The razzie's slap hadn't ripped his whole leg off, thankfully, merely left three gashes that looked and felt superficial.

"I'll live. A quick bandage job and a tetanus shot will probably do the trick. How's your side?"

"The bleeding's stopped. So I guess I'll be fine too." Marcus looked around. His smile was genuine and relieved. "Ah, home sweet home."

Sam scanned his surroundings and recognized the ruined chamber they had left behind a mere few days ago. "Oh my God. I never thought I'd be this happy to see this place again." With a deep, gratified sigh, he took stock of their situation. "Can you walk? We need to get out of here."

Marcus pushed himself up with one hand until he stood, rocking in place as though he were about to collapse at any time. "Well, I ain't fucking staying here for another minute, if that's what you mean." He glanced at the chamber. "Man, whoever built this hellhole should really mark those fucking exits."

Sam burst into hysterical laughter that went on till his stomach hurt. When the buzz of adrenaline faded, he noted that though the chamber was warm, it wasn't in the tropics. And the broken edge of the floor above had snow and ice buildup, with flimsy flakes falling in slow motion, like a dream made manifest.

"We're really back home." He opened the backpack Marcus had placed on the floor, dug out their winter coats, handed Marcus his, and put on his own. "How long have we been gone? Best guess."

Marcus frowned, seemingly lost in calculations. "Can't say for certain how much time has passed, but since that moon's days and nights lasted roughly six hours, then… thirty hours or so? If we're lucky, it's not long enough to get our folks all worked up and—"

"Fat chance," Sam cut in sarcastically. "My parents have absolutely called the cops by now. I've never not slept in my own bed."

"What? No sexy sleepovers or sultry slumber parties?" Marcus teased as he made his way to the platform, likely to assess the possibility of climbing up.

Sam snorted. "Yeah right, 'cause guys do that *all* the time."

A faint rattling sound gave them a second's warning before a spark shower lit up the dim room.

By the metal chair, a distorted electric blue image began to form. Due to the warp of the projection, it was hard to discern what sort of being was displayed. Calling it vaguely humanoid wasn't a huge stretch, but describing it as human certainly was.

Sam had seen enough videos of three-dimensional holographic images to tell what it was. After all, that was the technology of the future, coming to life before his very eyes.

A voice began to speak but the words made no sense to Sam. It sounded like gibberish or a broken recording, static affecting the quality.

"It sounds… feminine," Sam murmured. "But the message's all garbled and messed up. Maybe it has cracked over time?"

Marcus gave him an odd look. "I understand it just fine. It sounds like English."

"Not to me." So the effects of the metal chair still worked on Marcus even after they had returned from their trek to an alien world. "What's it saying?" he asked, still curious in spite of everything that had happened to them.

Marcus listened, his head tilted, his gaze focused. "The message repeats in a loop. She says…, 'Welcome back to the auxiliary hub of Inter-Dimensional Expeditions. IDX is a full-service provider to all galactic travelers and planes walkers. IDX allows exploration of countless worlds in countless universes with the aid of our unique safety features and—'"

"What freaking safety features?" Sam interjected in vexation. "The first, last, and only place we visited had a broken portal and no repair instructions. That blows." He harrumphed to get his feelings sorted. "Is that the whole message?"

"No, there's more." Marcus waited briefly, his head cocked as he focused hard. "She goes on to say…, 'IDX, your safe port of call, catering to all your interplanetary, intergalactic, and interdimensional needs. IDX, experience firsthand our revolutionary portal technology and discover for yourself a multiverse of endless wonder. IDX, to take you where you want to go.'"

Sam wasn't sure whether to laugh or cry. "So… it's an alien infomercial."

Marcus chuckled but then winced and pressed a hand over his wounded side. "Sure sounds like it."

Sam frowned. "She did say 'welcome back,' so the system at least partially recognizes that we're the same people who left a few days ago and have now returned. An automated welcome-home note. Charming."

"I detect sarcasm." Marcus's grin was irreverent and catching, and Sam smiled back. "In any case, now the loop's started again. Let's find a way out of here, shall we?"

Last time they'd been in the dimly lit chamber, there had been no exit signs or alternate entrances, and the raised platform that had crumbled beneath them was out of reach. That situation hadn't changed—until the hologram spoke again. This time Marcus stopped dead in his tracks and stared at the projection wide-eyed.

"What?" Sam asked, the old black magic of fear raising its head again.

"The message has changed." Marcus frowned, but soon his furrowed forehead smoothed. "She's asking us if we wish to travel again or if we want to take a break and leave IDX."

Sam almost broke his ankles jumping up and down in excitement at the possibility that they might soon be free from their ordeal. "Oh my God. Can we reply?"

Marcus shrugged. Then he said out loud, "We want to leave IDX, please."

The hologram stuttered and contorted until it finally flashed and disappeared. Silence reigned in the dark chamber again.

"Was that a yes or a no?" Sam asked in alarm.

A deep grinding sound echoed in the room, like giant stones rubbing against each other, but the sound soon ceased.

A doorway opened before them, having blended into the wall so seamlessly that it had been virtually invisible. The door slid open with a soft *shush* that seemed loud after the noise within the walls ended. Above the oval opening, a red button blinked on.

"It doesn't have arrows or say Exit, but it's as good as, right?" Sam commented.

Marcus nodded. "At this point I'm ready to take a leap of faith."

He stepped through the arched doorway. Above, bluish lights flickered on, revealing a winding staircase of metallic steps going up.

Marcus whooped. "Yeah, I think we've got it. C'mon."

He took Sam's hand in his own and started up the stairs. Their footsteps came off loud and clunky as the metal structure compounded the sounds, giving the place an unpleasant haunted-house vibe neither of them felt comfortable with after everything they'd been through.

The spiral staircase wasn't long, perhaps one or two floors. When they reached a new doorway, they realized it had taken them to the uppermost level where Marcus had fallen. They could see the round hatch over their heads, falling snow and a darkening sky above.

Cold air breezed through the opening, and the boys shivered. Their jeans and boots were wet from the storm on the island in a galaxy or universe far, far away, so they were both aware they needed to get home to dry warmth as soon as possible.

"I'm gonna climb out first and then pull you out, okay?" Marcus suggested.

Sam was down with that plan. Marcus was stronger, but he was also badly hurt, so Sam could give him a push from below. "'Kay. Hurry up. I'm freezing my nuts off."

Marcus chuckled even as he pressed his side and winced. "Better not. I've got big plans for them in the near future."

Sam blushed, more than pleased Marcus wanted him so much. He prayed that situation wouldn't change just because they weren't all alone in the world anymore.

Marcus stepped on tree roots to get a decent footing, with Sam holding him by the hips so he wouldn't fall. They both trembled from the winter weather and staggered a bit, but Marcus managed to stay upright long enough to reach the top of the hole, with Sam sort of desperately jostling his backside from below.

With a pained groan, Marcus caught the rim of the hatch and slowly dragged himself up and out until he vanished from sight. Sam waited with bated breath, balancing on the same sturdy tree root and wanting more than anything to go home.

"Marcus?" he hollered tentatively.

"Right here, chipmunk. Haven't gone anywhere." Marcus's face appeared framed by the hole, a mere silhouette against the blackening sky. "Gimme your hands, bae, and jump if you can."

Sam hesitated, worried the sudden strain might reopen their wounds. But he obeyed Marcus's order nonetheless. He raised his arms and reached for his companion's strong hands. Pushing off the root, he gave himself a minor boost, gripped Marcus firmly, and let himself be hoisted to the surface until he could clamber out on his own and drop face-first into a snowbank.

Relief flooding him like a drug, Sam wanted to lie there in the familiar wet cold of ice and snow. But Marcus roused him with a hard grip and tugged Sam onto his feet.

"We can't stay there, numbnuts, or we'll freeze to death. Come on. We'll be home in no time." Marcus scanned his surroundings and let out a muffled curse. "My backpack's not here. Someone must've found it. Fuck, I hope it was the authorities and not some douchebag thief. I had a perfectly good tablet in there."

"I'm sure the sheriff's office has got it," Sam said wearily. Exhausted, he trudged back to the path, which was already snowed in. No plows out there. "What about the hatch? If we leave it like that, someone else might—"

"Good call." But when Marcus leaned over the hatch, it closed in front of him, a holographic image of a solid tree trunk appearing over the metal trapdoor. "Guess the creators of that place have thought of everything."

The dark clouds above sent a soft snowfall onto them as they made their way back to their families, who undoubtedly were worried sick. Sam estimated the time of day at late afternoon or early evening since it was already dusky. That seemed to confirm Marcus's guess about exactly how long they'd been away, which was roughly thirty hours or so. It had been afternoon when they had fallen down the rabbit hole.

Sam's house was closest, so they reached it first.

"What are we going to tell them?" Sam asked, slowing his steps as the building came into view. "If we tell them the truth...."

"Yeah, I figured that'd be a problem." Marcus sighed. "You know my dad's got that cabin up on the mountain, right?"

"His hunting lodge?"

"Yeah. Let's say we were there."

"All this time, and we didn't so much as call to check in with our folks?"

Marcus waved vaguely at their disheveled, bloody forms. "We got into an accident, of course, and we couldn't get a signal, but we managed to make our way back nonetheless. Both of us have our phones with their batteries dead, so... yeah, I think they'll buy that."

"Unless your dad stopped by the cabin with the police."

"Nah. I don't go there with him. Not into hunting. So he thinks I hate the place, and he wouldn't have suggested looking for me there. Makes it a perfect getaway, then, to take a break from school, the stress and tests, you know? An impromptu idea that just went really horribly awry."

Sam admitted that was as good a plan as any. It wasn't like they could tell the truth to either their families or the authorities. They'd get locked up forever in a lunatic asylum. "Fine. Let's just get this over with. I'm cold and hungry and practically dead on my feet."

They supported each other as they walked up the driveway to the front door. A knock and a ring later, Sam's parents opened the door, pulled them both into fierce hugs, and refused to let go. Sam didn't mind. Soon they were all crying and trying to speak at once, with Marcus providing the fake story of their mountainous ordeal.

Sam was flooded with familiar sensations he didn't even realize he'd longed for. His mother's warm plumpness that carried the scent of apples from her shampoo; his father's cardigan that smelled of books and paper and ink; his home's foyer with coat racks and a soft light hanging above, casting a loving glow over Sam and his family; the sounds of lively, joyful chatter ringing all around him from the people who meant the world to him, and the distant static of TV.

The next couple of hours were a blur. Later he recalled only flashes. Sam and Marcus hopping into (separate) hot showers, and Sam getting his wounds bandaged while an ambulance was called for Marcus, whose injuries, though sanitized, demanded further treatment in the hospital; both of them dressing in dry, warm clothes, and being unceremoniously dumped onto the couch with cups of hot chocolate and marshmallows; the police and the sheriff's office stopping by for statements and congratulations on their escape from the elements (ha! Sam couldn't even say how close to the truth that comment came), with Sam delivering them the details of their fake tale of survival horror; Marcus reuniting with his mother, who proceeded to hug him till he was breathless and blushing, her arrival coinciding with the ambulance coming to take Marcus to the ER.

The feeling of having been missed so much and having missed them back just as much made both boys teary-eyed, grateful, and happy.

The police and the sheriff left while the paramedics readied Marcus for transport, and things started to settle down. Sam's parents quickly prepared a hot, hearty meal for Sam and packed a doggy bag for Marcus's mom to take with her to the hospital, because Marcus said he was starving and everyone knew how wretched hospital food was. As the smell of home-cooked food wafted through the air, Sam thought there really was no place like home.

When Marcus was set to leave, Sam embraced him, shaking from the emotions churning uncontrollably within him. Marcus hugged him back with equal fervor, and without words, all was understood between them.

Then Marcus kissed Sam goodbye, in full view of everyone, and Sam's heart leaped, and his life clicked into place. Thankfully no one broke out in hushed, reproachful murmurs or outright hate speech. Not that Sam had expected that.

"We'll talk tomorrow, yeah?" Marcus whispered in his ear, and Sam nodded eagerly. "Sleep well, chipmunk. Love you."

"Love you too." Sam's voice cracked, his throat tight, but his heart light.

With a rueful smile and glistening eyes, Marcus waved goodbye and left with the paramedics, with his mom following in their car. Sam stayed in the doorway until he couldn't see the ambulance anymore, not even the red taillights' beam in the night. Snow came down calmly, as if washing the slate clean, ending their thrilling adventure in a peaceful mood.

Sam's parents fussed over him, for the first time in years sitting by his bed, petting his hair and cheeks until he faked falling asleep. Even Simon, who could under normal circumstances be a dick to his little brother, was unusually affectionate, hugging Sam several times over the course of the evening until everyone finally went to sleep in their own beds.

After everything that had happened, Sam had expected to nod off in a blink of an eye. Instead, he stayed awake for a long time, staring up at the familiar ceiling, where lively shadows were cast from the streetlights below.

Years ago, after he'd gotten into stargazing and space, he'd had the ceiling painted to depict the northern night sky in autumn and winter. The constellations and stars everyone should recognize twinkled above him: Orion the Hunter with its canine companions, Canis Major and Canis Minor, and its brightest star, Sirius, the dog star. The V-shaped Andromeda and to the right, the Andromeda Galaxy, bright as a star but mysterious like a nebula. And Aquarius, named after a handsome boy whom the king of the gods wanted....

Sam frowned as he pondered where in the visible night sky they might have been. Had they been near Orion or Ursa Major? Had that moon even been in this galaxy, or had they perhaps been in Andromeda, or farther still? Had they even been in the known universe?

Sam had to accept he would most likely never know. Even if they returned to that dim portal chamber, they still might not get any real answers. It seemed to be an automated system created by a people long gone. Or could they still be out there somewhere, traveling the universe, alternate dimensions, or strange planes of existence with the aid of the portals? And what were those magical doorways anyway? Wormholes or space folds or hyperspace conduits? Who knew?

Sam and Marcus had narrowly fled from the hostile jungle. They had almost become permanent fixtures of that alien moon. If tonight had shown Sam anything, it was that his home and family were a solid foundation for him. He'd never felt more cherished, not even when in Marcus's arms.

Sam sniffed and wiped his wet cheeks and eyes with the backs of hands. He was superemotional, but that was understandable, wasn't it? He and Marcus could have died, many times over. But they had persevered in spite of almost insurmountable odds. And that meant something.

It meant everything.

CHAPTER 15

NEXT MORNING, a Saturday thankfully, Sam awoke from a deep sleep that left him groggy to find Simon sitting in a chair by the desk. He said nothing, just smiled. And though Sam was admittedly still bleary-eyed, that gesture didn't seem nervous or off.

"Hey," Sam murmured in a hoarse voice, rising enough to lean against the headboard, blinking in the bright sunlight through the shutters. "What's up?"

Simon was a finer version of the same genes Sam had. His short hair was golden blond and his eyes emerald green, his physique that of an athlete, and his manners those of a gentleman—most of the time anyway. At the moment, though, he looked… at peace.

"Sorry if I woke you. Didn't mean to." Simon actually sounded bashful, and that tipped Sam off that something had changed.

Sam blinked and glanced at the alarm clock on the bedside table. It was past noon. "I don't mind. Don't wanna sleep all day."

"You're entitled to sleep in for a couple of days. If Mom gets her wish, it'll be closer to a week or two."

"God, I hope not. I'd miss school."

"You're such a weirdo."

"Weird and proud of it."

"And don't worry. I brought you your homework. The teachers miss you too, their star pupil."

Sam blushed and ducked his head. He was proud of his straight A's, perfect attendance, and extracurriculars. He had cause to be, and he was one of those people who actually liked college and learning new things. If that made him an outcast from the young adult populace, so be it.

"Thanks. I appreciate that. So…." Sam glanced at his big brother under his brow. "You didn't think I was dead or something?"

Simon shrugged, but the tightening line of his mouth showed he was not indifferent. "I… I thought it was best to stay positive. Mom was freaking out, and Dad was fretting over every minute that passed. Someone had to keep a cool head."

"I'm glad they had you to support them." Simon shrugged again, looking away. He seemed anxious about something. Sam had a pretty good idea what it was. "Ask me what you want, or tell me what's on your mind."

Simon locked gazes with Sam. "You and Marcus, then, huh?"

Sam swallowed hard but lifted his chin in defiance. "Yeah."

"How long's that been a thing?"

"Not long. For the duration of our trip, if you must know."

"Ah. Whose idea was this trip?"

Sam hesitated. "It was sort of a… an impromptu thing. By accident, you know."

Simon stared at Sam so long without speaking that Sam started to sweat. "Huh. Well, considering how long the guy's been carrying a torch for you, I'm surprised he finally acted on it."

Sam's eyes widened in shock. "You knew? This whole time?"

Simon chuckled. "About what? That Marcus swings both ways or that the first time he saw you years ago his eyes lit up like a Christmas tree? Yeah, kinda hard to miss."

"Oh." Sam was fresh out of words. "Why didn't you ever say? I mean, I…." He didn't know if he should come clean about how long he'd had feelings for Marcus too.

Simon got there first. "Look, Sam, I've seen how you look at him too when he's not looking. But, you know, your sex life's none of my business. You two had to figure things out on your own."

Sam worried his bottom lip. "So… you're not upset we're having sex?"

Simon's eyes narrowed. "What kind of sex? And don't worry about embarrassing me. This falls under the big brother purview. Unless of course you want to discuss possibly taking it up the ass with Mom and Dad."

"God, no!" Sam's heart almost stopped then and there, the thought of having the sex talk with his parents now that he was actually doing it, and with a guy no less, bothering him more than he cared to admit. Besides, they'd had that damn awkward discussion years ago, when Sam was nine and started to notice he wasn't like other boys.

Simon smirked, crossing his arms over his chest. "Well, then. Gimme specifics. 'Cause you're still seventeen, and there's stuff—"

"Geesh, Simon, stop." Sam grimaced. "Look, I know all that, okay? And for your information, big brother, we're not doing…." He held his breath, his cheeks flaming, hardly able to believe he was actually going to say it. "Anal," he finally whispered, mortified out of his mind.

Simon quirked a knowing eyebrow. "Yet." Then he shrugged. "Okay, cool. You've decided to wait." He snorted. "That won't last. Not when you two are alone in a room and there's a bed within easy reach."

Sam cringed. "Please, stop. I'm humiliated enough."

Simon laughed. "Not nearly enough in my honest opinion, baby bro. But fine, I'll let you off the hook. For now. And... I'll be having an equally awkward discussion with my boy Marcus too."

"Go easy on him, please."

"Of course. What do you think I am? An ogre? Still, if the guy plans on spending time with you in the future, he's gonna adhere to some rules." Simon's eyes held a dark glint. "And next time... no trips to desolate places without telling me, Mom, and Dad first, got it?"

"Check. What about... Mom and Dad?"

"They're cool with you dating Marcus, and you being gay. It's not like you've been hiding your crush very well. We've all known for quite a while. We're all fine, believe me."

Sam smiled. A huge weight lifted from his shoulders. He'd been nervous about his big brother's reaction to him and Marcus. Since that didn't seem to be a problem, Sam felt relieved and vindicated. His family was okay with him being gay *and* being in a relationship with Marcus. That surprised Sam pleasantly, especially since they had to suspect the two of them were getting it on.

Now all that was left was coming out to the rest of the world. Though people probably didn't care who he slept with, nor should they. It was no one's business.

Sam wasn't going to hide or cower anymore. That was a life lesson Marcus had taught him on the island, and Sam decided to heed the call of courage and be honest with the world.

The next day, Sam dyed his hair turquoise like his favorite K-pop artists.

"Do you still think about girls too?" Sam asked while lying on top of Marcus, both of them naked on Sam's bed, on a lazy Sunday afternoon a week later.

Marcus had been right. It was easier coming out with a boyfriend. Now they were both out, at home and in college. No one had batted an eye about them holding hands in the hallways. They'd been way more interested in the bruises and wounds. Sam was grateful that these days most kids were enlightened enough to understand that straight wasn't the only orientation in town. Plus, there were other out kids at Whitefish Lake College, so it wasn't like the two of them were some sort of gay and bi pioneers.

Despite them being out as gay and as a couple, Sam nonetheless wondered if his beloved might still have a hankering for the fairer sex.

Marcus had his eyes closed and was smiling leisurely as he drew lazy circles over Sam's back with his fingers. "Well, chipmunk… if Ariana Grande stood in front of me in her black latex Playboy bunny costume and asked to sleep with me right here, right now… hell yeah, I'd drop your ass in a heartbeat."

Sam chuckled but tickled Marcus till he squirmed. "You're such a boy slut."

"You mean… a butt?"

"Shut up."

"Hey, that rhymes."

"I'm a poet and didn't know it."

"Oh!" they said at the exact same time. They snapped their fingers and laughed as one. The movie reference from *The Adventures of Ford Fairlane* was old, like from 1990, but it was a flick they'd just seen on TV, so it was fresh on their minds. They didn't have the energy or patience to watch anything more than reruns of B movies amid their bouts of vigorous sex.

"So…?" Sam gently encouraged Marcus to spill more of his secrets.

"Being bi and with a a guy is great. Especially with you. I might occasionally think of a pretty girl or a hot woman. But… I still wanna sink to my knees in front of you and suck your dick for hours, even at the risk of lockjaw. I still get a boner every damn time I see you, whether you're doing something insanely hot, like smiling at me, or something stupid and ordinary, like brushing your teeth or doing homework or… or drawing your dirty pictures of me. Yeah, I know what you've been doing, my perverted little artist."

Sam blushed. Instead of the BL comics he usually liked to draw, he'd been doing a lot of so-called boudoir drawings of his hot boyfriend in the buff. He'd just assumed Marcus wasn't aware of Sam's guilty pleasure.

Marcus's seductive chuckle sent chills and hot flashes chasing each other up and down Sam's spine. He couldn't take the torment anymore.

Sam kissed Marcus slowly, then slipped his tongue past Marcus's full lips to slide against his. As time passed, their hands wandered and their bodies shimmied together. Sam traced the patterns on his lover's skin, the once red welts that had turned white, the ones he shared. Not to mention the slashing wounds from the razzie. Now the marks were a part of them, visual proof of their off-world sojourn.

When they parted, Sam let out a sigh. "Ariana, huh? Well, at least you've got good taste."

Marcus grinned. "Duh. I'm with *you*, aren't I? Pure genius, that."

He rolled them both around so that he was on top. Sam giggled and spread his legs to accommodate Marcus between them. Their bodies and cocks aligned, and their hips began to rock and sway on their own. Marcus kissed Sam, nibbled on his bottom lip, licked away the sting, then plunged his tongue into Sam's mouth, where it intertwined with Sam's.

Sam wrapped his arms and legs around Marcus as Marcus kissed his way down Sam's jaw to his neck, softly sucked up a mark or two, and then nibbled on Sam's earlobe. Sam moaned, his body jolting from a surge of pure physical need. His hips pumped involuntarily, and his dick leaked precome.

"Mmm, love how you respond to me, bae," Marcus purred.

He kissed Sam's clavicle, dipped down to lick around Sam's left nipple, then sucked on the hardening peak. Sam felt his nipple throb like mad from the delicious torment Marcus inflicted upon him. With his beloved boyfriend, he'd entered a whole new world of sensuality he'd only dared to dream about before.

And Sam had fantasies up the wazoo, all inspired by Marcus. He was in a constant rut around his boyfriend, and lately all his dreams had focused on one thing: Marcus inside Sam in a most intimate way.

Yet he knew Marcus wasn't about to do that just because Sam asked. For a rogue and rebel, Marcus could sometimes be an annoying stickler for the rules. While Sam appreciated acknowledgment of age in matters of sex—some people sure as shit weren't ready at sixteen, eighteen, or even twenty-one—*he* was ready right the F now.

Or so he thought….

"God, Sam. I can hear your brain spinning again." Marcus kissed under Sam's ear, a little ticklish, a lot hot. "I know what you're thinking. And the answer's still no fucking way."

"But—"

"Look, bae, I checked, okay? The legal age of consent in Montana is sixteen, as you said, and you're already seventeen. But I'm twenty, and Montana doesn't have a close-in-age exemption—"

"We're both over sixteen, so it's legal. And I'll be eighteen next week. But if you're worried… no one has to know." Sam knew he was treading on thin ice even as he spoke.

Marcus gave him a knowing look that left Sam wilted and red in the face. "I love you, Sam, but—"

"We're having sex already," Sam argued. "What does one more position matter?"

Marcus opened his mouth, but surprisingly, nothing came out. He blinked and snapped his mouth shut. Frowning deeply, he seemed to ponder both sides of the argument. At least that was what Sam hoped Marcus was doing. With neither of them under the age of consent, they couldn't go to jail or be registered as sex offenders. Sam really didn't see what the problem was.

Then Marcus's glassy gaze lit up again and refocused on Sam. "You sure you want to do this? Now? With me?"

Sam nodded firmly. "Hell yeah."

"Fine." Marcus didn't seem too pleased, though, not if his scrunched brow was any indication. Sam began to doubt the wisdom of pressuring his boyfriend into doing anal. Then Marcus's expression softened, and he smiled shortly. "I don't want to hurt you."

Sam kissed the top of his nose. "You won't, I promise. C'mon, Marcus. When have you ever known me to stay silent about anything? Why would I say nothing if I thought you did something wrong?"

"Hmm." Marcus didn't seem entirely convinced but he nodded and his cock hardened again. Guess they were back on track. Wherever that path led.

Marcus pulled up and unceremoniously flipped Sam onto his stomach. Sam's lungs emptied with a whoosh at the rough treatment, and his belly knotted with nerves. The pillow and sheets were soft, warm, and rumpled against his skin. His hips refused to stay still, pumping till he practically humped the mattress. Marcus chuckled evilly and stopped his movements with a hand on the small of Sam's back.

"Nuh-uh. Bad boy." Marcus's playful scolding almost had Sam creaming himself.

Marcus rested his body over Sam's, his front fitting against Sam's back perfectly, his dick nestled between Sam's buttcheeks. They both moved their hips on instinct, too horny to think rationally.

"Like this?" Marcus murmured in Sam's ear. His breath fanned over the sensitive skin, giving Sam goose bumps. "Like how I touch you? Love how close we are? Wanna go further?"

His cock slid over Sam's most intimate place, driving him mad with the continuous motions, the touch fleeting but ever-present. Marcus's dick was hot and heavy and smooth, and Sam pictured Marcus shoving his dick inside Sam in his mind's eye, that plump piece of meat pushing into his ass, deeper and deeper, until Sam was stuffed full.

"Can you feel me, bae? Feel my cock pushing into you, hard and deep?"

It was so much like the numerous hours of gay porn and yaoi porn Sam had watched since they got back. He groaned loud enough to wake the neighbors. Hopefully they were all napping or shopping at the mall. In his head, every dirty word Marcus uttered came to life, every picture Marcus painted with his seductive utterings heightening Sam's anticipation.

"Come on already," Sam whispered, his voice raw and hoarse.

"Not yet." Marcus could be such a cocktease, dammit.

Sam was drunk on desire. Yet he wasn't sure how comfortable he was with what was about to take place when he had no prior experience. Sure, there had to be a first time for everything and everyone. But... how could he trust his senses and his body? Would they demand to be filled before he was relaxed enough to feel pleasure rather than pain? His heart and head weren't quite waging war over it, but it wasn't a stretch either. His feelings for Marcus cried out for more, more, more, while his rational mind warned him to be careful and cautious.

Marcus moved off. He kneaded Sam's bunched back muscles, unwinding all the kinks. Sam sighed and relaxed in an instant. This was Marcus, the man who loved him and whom he loved. Sam could trust him.

Marcus massaged Sam's back, inching slowly lower until he was rubbing his hands along Sam's plump buttocks. Sam stifled a moan by biting into his bottom lip. His mind was mush. Marcus's touch felt so good, familiar yet new, strong yet soft. Marcus parted Sam's asscheeks and licked over Sam's hole.

"Oh God, oh God, oh *God*," Sam moaned repeatedly, clutching the pillow, his dick so hard it hurt as it throbbed along with his heartbeat.

Each sweep of Marcus's hands sent Sam flying higher. It was sensual, the pure pleasure of being close to the person you loved and wanted. Then Marcus stuck his tongue inside Sam, a wet warmth probing his already fluttering hole and spasming channel.

"Holy shit!" Sam's exclamation was muffled thanks to the pillow, for which he was grateful.

He was also grateful Marcus kept his hips from jerking, or he might have ended their lovemaking by unintentionally breaking his lover's nose.

When Marcus pushed his tongue into Sam's hole, wiggling it past the resistance, Sam thought he couldn't possibly continue to be so undone. But he was, every damn time. His need and pleasure all centered there, in that hidden place Sam had never himself seen, his own, that was.

Marcus clearly knew what he was doing. He was basically fucking Sam with his tongue instead of his cock. And it was perfect. Sam wanted more. And he was afraid of more. Stupid contradictory body and brain.

Then a moist thumb pressed on Sam's vulnerable opening.

Sam's belly developed a storm of butterflies. And his body clamped up tight.

"I… I'm so sorry," he murmured, embarrassed at how quickly he'd closed up. "I… I can't. I thought I could but… I'm not ready. I'm sorry."

Marcus kissed the curve of his backside and chuckled. "It's okay. And as it looks like this ain't happening, that's okay too. I'm not going anywhere. We can try this later."

Sam closed his eyes and let out a breath. Sam had lost that thrill of pure excitement and unadulterated need. His dick wilted in seconds. What happened to his groove? He'd dreamed of this, fantasized, anticipated, and assumed he'd treasure the experience. His body had betrayed him. Why? Hadn't he been imagining doing exactly this for months, if not years? More than anything he wanted to be with his beloved in every sense. And he wanted Marcus to be his first, last, and only one. This should've been the best day of his sex life, the culmination of all his expectations. Why was his butt disagreeing with him? Not fair.

"Hey, bae. I promise we're good." Marcus left a trail of openmouthed smooches over Sam's back as he moved up to kiss his nape. "There's no rush."

A tender kiss on Sam's shoulder was followed by a sudden sharp bite that sent Sam's body reeling—and into sensual overdrive. His dick swelled again, hot and heavy and ready to play.

"Oh yeah…," Sam moaned, delighted that they hadn't lost the moment.

"Mm-hmm" came Marcus's articulate response.

Marcus scooted down again, this time rolling Sam onto his back, and then he swallowed Sam's dick whole. Sam cried out, thrashing about on the bed while Marcus worked to hold him still with his palms on Sam's hips. Marcus traced the shape of Sam's hipbones with his lips and teeth, and then did the same with Sam's shaft, licking up and down the length, taking his time.

Sam shoved him off. "Stop. No. Too fucking close."

Marcus merely chuckled, that mischievous streak back in full force. He dipped lower to lick over Sam's balls and then softly sucked them into his mouth. Sam sobbed and almost popped then and there.

But Marcus moved up to kiss Sam's shivering stomach, his palms hot over Sam's cool skin, his fingers digging into soft flesh. Marcus licked around Sam's bellybutton and sucked up a few marks on his trembling belly.

Sam couldn't take it anymore. He knew now they weren't going to do anal today. But he'd be damned if he wasn't going to give Marcus the next best thing.

He grabbed Marcus by the arms, took a firm hold, and flipped them around once more. Straddling Marcus's hips, Sam almost made both of them fall off the bed.

"Whoa. Easy there, chipmunk." Marcus chuckled, hands on Sam's waist, eyes dancing with mirth.

"Shut up." Sam hoped his growly words would stop the infuriating guy from making fun of him while he was trying to be assertive and shit.

When Sam smeared his fingers with lube from a half-used tube and then wiggled his hand under his butt and fisted Marcus's cock, Marcus finally did shut up—briefly—until he arched his back, threw his head back, and groaned. Sam pumped his dick a few times for emphasis to show Marcus he could play too.

"Mm-mmm, Sam, I love your fucking hands on me," Marcus murmured, his face melting into a stunning portrait of ecstasy. Sam tried not to get a big head. His little head sure was getting bigger.

"We ain't stopping now," Sam muttered back, restless for some physical contact and sexual intimacy. The kind he'd hoped for wasn't on the table today, but that didn't mean all was lost.

He sat astride Marcus, just below his balls so that Marcus's hard cock protruded between Sam's legs. Sam fumbled to stroke along his lover's smoldering, swelling member from root to tip, taking his time. But he had a different plan, and he was about to execute it. He wasn't 100 percent sure of his plan's success, but he prayed some coordination, a touch of lube, and an ample amount of rutting heat were enough.

Sam's legs trembled as he let go of Marcus's dick, slid forward until he had Marcus's cock nestled between his asscheeks, and started to rock back and forth.

Marcus's eyes flew open and widened in shock. Then his parted lips went as slack as the rest of his expression, and his hooded gaze glimmered with dark lust. "Mmm, yeah…."

Sam prayed his weight wouldn't put too much pressure on Marcus's cock as it lay on his lower abdomen, hot and wet, trapped between Sam's quivering buttocks and against his perineum as he rode his lover's body like a cowboy on a horse. It was the ride of a lifetime.

Marcus gripped Sam's hips hard enough to bruise, partially controlling Sam's pace, his gaze so intense Sam all but burned under that enormous heat. Sam placed his hands on Marcus's chest, over his pecs, for leverage and increased his speed. Marcus moaned hoarsely, but his eyes never left Sam's. They stared at each other, unable to look away, sharing a bond of dark desire that forced them to move on instinct, primal and demanding.

The bed creaked, and the headboard banged against the wall. That was new for them. Sam swallowed hard, his mouth drier than a desert, his body burning with a fervor he'd never before known. The sensations and emotions within and without mixed, and he was lost on a sea of passion.

"Oh God, Marcus, please…."

Marcus actually growled then, a possessive grimace giving him the appearance of an animal. A predator like the razor beast. "Mine. Mine. Mine."

Sam gasped. Marcus had never behaved in such a way. But he understood.

"Yes. Yes. I'm yours. Yours forever."

"Touch yourself, bae," Marcus grunted. "Wanna see you do it. Do it, Sam."

The command shouldn't have turned Sam on, but it did. It pushed buttons inside him he hadn't known he had. He gripped his own dick and started a fierce stroke, jerking himself off to the beat of his heart. All he could hear was the drumming of his pulse, the gush of blood in his ears. And all he could see was Marcus; he was blind to the rest of a world that might as well not have existed at all.

Sam's nails dug into Marcus's chest, and Marcus's did the same to Sam's hips. They couldn't stop moving. They were no longer in control. Their coupling was primitive, two bodies in heat, locked together to rut until they'd reach climax. It was a mad dash toward a frenzied peak and a headlong dive into the depths of pleasure.

Marcus stiffened and held his breath. Warm wetness coated Sam's ass; he could almost taste it. His hand flew on his dick. Marcus's low snarl shoved him over the edge of delight. Sam cried out and came, spurting ropes of come over Marcus, showering him with creamy, sticky droplets like a Pollock painting. He continued to jack off until he'd wrung himself dry.

With a sigh, he collapsed over Marcus, who took him in his arms, cradling him and whispering sweet nothings in his ear. Sam shook like a leaf, clasping his lover as though he were a lifeline to a drowning man.

"Love you...." It didn't matter who spoke.

They stayed that way for a while. Finally Sam released his death grip on Marcus, slid off him, and rested on the bed, floating in the soft mellowness of afterglow and love made manifest.

Once Sam's breathing had slowed and he could hear again, he grew aware of Marcus beside him, still panting like an overheated dog. He'd expected the jock to have better recovery skills. Then again, they had really exerted themselves this time.

Sam stared up at the ceiling, his mind a million miles away. Or more to the point, a gazillion light years away on an alien moon where it was hot and humid all the time, where storms were frequent, and where he'd learned who he was.

He frowned. He'd just experienced bliss, but his mind remained restless. Even a climax couldn't wipe his memory of their shared adventures. What did that mean in the long run? For him, for Marcus, or for them as a couple? Had Sam evolved into an adrenaline junkie? Seemed unlikely considering his serene temperament.

Yet in both his dreams and his waking thoughts, he continued to return to that faraway alien world. In his mind's eye, he watched the heavenly display of a green, ringed gas giant and constellations he knew nothing about but longed to become familiar with. Every night and each time his attention wandered, those same stars, planets, and moons came to him—unbidden but not unwelcome.

Sam wanted to ask Marcus if he thought about that place too. But he was afraid to hear the answer. What if Marcus just wanted to put the past behind them, focus on them in the here and now, and look forward to a future without weird portals and mysterious planets? Perhaps Sam was alone in his inability to let go.

His attention veered back to his bedroom when he heard a tiny rustling noise from his backpack. Or behind it to be precise.

Sam cursed inwardly. It had to be the neighbor's damn cat again. It had an annoying habit of sneaking into other people's houses through open windows. Sam must have thrown the critter out four times already this past week.

He sat up and reached for his backpack, shifting it aside, expecting to find a lousy little ball of fur crammed inside his slipper again.

Instead he came face-to-face with a smiling creature the size of a mouse. Like a small piece of wood, it appeared to be covered in bark and mushrooms and moss, with petite pink paws and a lightly furred tail winding upward like a corkscrew. Big, round, amber-hued eyes blinked up at him, innocent and adorable.

"Oh… my…. God…." Sam's whisper roused Marcus to peek over his shoulder. They both gasped in shock at the sight. How could that little thing have been hiding in his room all this time? Seemed impossible, but the evidence was irrefutable. "It's a… a barkzie." Sam glanced up at Marcus, serious and solemn. "We must take it back home."

CHAPTER 16

"WE ARE doing the right thing, aren't we?" Sam asked.

Marcus heard the tremor in his voice. "Second thoughts? I wouldn't have believed that possible. You'd never doubt the need to help someone out. Or in this case, a helpless little alien that needs us to get back home."

Sam shook his head, frowning, working with the straps of his backpack, his motions nervous and fidgety. Clearly the straps were fine. "All we have to do basically is to open the portal and send the barkzie through."

"Yeah?"

Sam worried his lower lip, avoiding eye contact. Then he shrugged and slumped, as if he'd decided to not speak after all. "Nothing."

Marcus gripped Sam's jaw and gently raised his face till their gazes locked. "Talk to me, bae. Don't make me spank you. We'll just get distracted, then."

Sam's tense shoulders relaxed, and he smiled. "Yeah. Definitely."

"So… what's bugging you?"

"Well… I've been thinking."

"I'd be shocked if you ever stopped."

"Shut up." But Sam brushed a kiss on Marcus's lips, so he wasn't really angry. "That tiny animal being in our charge just confirmed everything that's been on my mind lately."

Marcus snorted. "Let me guess. The island?"

Sam's eyes widened and his mouth gaped. "You too?"

"Uh-huh. Not an easy thing to forget. Although, to be fair, I haven't tried extra hard. I mean, why should I? I have a lot to thank that place for. You, for one."

Sam blushed, making Marcus want to kiss him and not stop. "Love you too. You're the best thing that's ever happened to me. Hands down."

"So apparently we've both been thinking about what happened to us." Marcus studied Sam carefully. They might not have developed a couple's weird love telepathy yet, but he figured he knew what was going on. "You're feeling as restless as I am, or am I wrong?"

Sam let out a relieved sigh. "No, you're right. I keep thinking about everything we saw and did… and what else is out there."

"Me too." Marcus looked around Sam's bedroom, which had become so familiar to him in the past week and a half. Although their parents had kept anxious eyes on them since their recent misadventure, they had relative privacy in Sam's room in the afternoons. They had used it to discuss returning the barkzie to the island, among other things, though Sam had seemed reluctant to do it immediately.

Marcus thought he had finally figured out why.

For the past two, three days, Sam had concentrated on his things, gathering supplies in his backpack. At first Marcus had assumed he feared getting trapped on the other side of the portal again. But now Marcus realized Sam was making preparations for a trip.

A planned journey to another planet.

"You want to go back to that exomoon, or—"

"A part of me did want to find out what happened to the lizzies. But no, I don't. I want to see someplace new." Sam shuddered, looking forlorn. "But… I won't go anywhere without you. I can't."

Marcus embraced Sam, wrapping his arms around his beautiful boy. "Funny, but I was thinking the exact same thing. Guess we're on the same wavelength already."

Sam hugged him back, his breath warm and his cheeks moist against Marcus's neck. "You mean that? You wanna come with me?"

"Since we came back, I thought being with you was enough to make me happy. And it's been great."

"But?" Sam pulled off, but he was smiling, his tone encouraging.

"For a few days, coming out with you was awesome, and I didn't feel the need to seek thrills. But when that faded—'cause no one cares these days about one more gay couple—I realized something was missing. I mean, that island was hell at times, and I'm glad we're out of there."

"But?" Sam asked again, his smile widening, his eyes beaming.

"That place taught us a lot about each other *and* ourselves."

Sam nodded firmly. "Yes. I learned to view the world from your perspective, through your eyes, and stop being afraid all the time of what *might* happen or what might *never* happen. You taught me courage and how to stand up for myself and what I want. And that place showed me I can manage in a crisis much better than I ever imagined."

Marcus rubbed Sam's nose with his own. "Yeah, it sure did. We were screwed, but we worked together like a well-oiled machine, made the best of a bad situation, and lived to tell the tale. That's saying something."

Sam chuckled. "What, you want a medal?"

Marcus snorted. "Anyway, you taught me that sometimes having second thoughts and reservations isn't fear but common sense. That at times it's better to think before you leap."

"Looks like even though we nearly died there, we're insane enough to go right back for more." Sam laughed, but he sounded a bit unsure again.

"I'm ready to jump in the deep end... but only if you are too. Like you, I don't want to do this alone. What the heck would I do out there on my own? I'd die within an hour."

Sam slapped Marcus on the arm, the sting sudden but gone quickly. "That's bullshit. You'd do great." Then he fisted Marcus's shirt, bunching and wrinkling it. "Let's go together... or not at all."

A hushed chirp sounded from the windowsill where Sam's mom had placed a potted plant to brighten the room. Marcus glanced toward the bright red flower he didn't recognize. On the dirt beside the stem stood the barkzie, smiling at them, its amber eyes mesmerizing and kind.

Both boys returned the gesture, though they had no idea if the barkzie even knew what a smile was.

"YOU KNOW, we have to thank this little critter for serving as a catalyst for us to decide what we really want out of life." Marcus chuckled at his own comment because, admittedly, a significant part of it was experiencing the glories of gay sex with his dream bae.

Sam smirked at him, continuing to stuff things into his backpack. "I saw what you did there. Dirty dawg. But yeah, you're right. About all of it." He winked suggestively at Marcus.

As usual, Marcus felt a buzz in his chest, under his rib cage where his heart was. A similar hum of contentment seemed to come from his dick, which loved Sam a lot too.

It was Friday. School was over for the day. Sam and Marcus had told Simon and their parents they were seeing a movie and afterward going up to the cabin again for the weekend. Predictably, their families argued against the plan. Marcus made a relevant counterargument about getting back on a horse after it threw you off, or one might never ride again. They lived in the shadow of the mountains every day of their lives, so they couldn't fear them. After what seemed like an endless tug-of-war, their parents finally acceded, probably more worn down by Sam's relentless nagging than seeing the error of their ways.

They'd written delayed emails to their parents and Simon in case of emergency, such as if their trip lasted longer than the span of a weekend. Finally they were good to go. They'd get additional healthy snacks and water bottles at the store, pretend to go to the movies, and then sneak out and head to the woods and the hatch that opened to the portal chamber and… who knew where else?

"Got everything you need?" Marcus asked, surveying the piles of things Sam had been busy all week gathering. Sam was an organizer, so he'd made a comprehensive list (naturally) and then assembled enough supplies to last a family of five over a week.

Sam checked and rechecked his list, frowning as he did so, and slowly nodded. "We have enough provisions to sustain us on a longer trip, the jumper cables you modified in shop class—"

Marcus grinned, proud of himself. He'd not realized just how important it was to know and understand how things worked until they'd needed that information on an alien world. Now he had taken to studying electrical engineering to ensure he got the gist of things. He wasn't about to be caught with his pants down again.

"—and the portable rechargeable battery to jumpstart the portal in case it doesn't work wherever it is we go. And we have solar-powered cell phone chargers if we need to take pictures or video or if we need another distraction. We also have matches, lighters and lighter fluid, a tent and sleeping bags, multipurpose tools, pocket knives, leather gloves, a small lantern, two flashlights, nylon rope, canteens—"

"We can get a few extra bottles from the store," Marcus cut in, examining all the gear they'd be carrying. The load wouldn't be light but these were the bare essentials. "Plus, like, snack bars and granola bars, dried vegetables and fruit, beef jerky, ramen noodles—"

"Yes, yes, food we got." Sam frowned, clearly vexed. Marcus smiled. His boy was in full tactical mode and didn't abide interruptions. "As for clothing, we'll be wearing long pants and long-sleeved undershirts, so we won't need to carry those. We've got socks, underwear, makeshift raincoats, sunglasses, sunscreen, toothbrushes and toothpaste, shaving cream, straight razors—"

"God, bae, please tell me you've got toilet paper in there."

Sam snorted and rolled his eyes. "Duh. Biodegradable too. Last but not least, antiseptic wipes, antibiotic ointments, bandages, gauze, scissors, tweezers, pens, paper, whistles, pins, a sewing kit—"

"You know how to sew?" Marcus was more than mildly impressed, and he expressed his awe with a low whistle.

Sam blushed and ducked his head bashfully. "I learned. Okay, fine. I watched a couple YouTube videos, okay? How hard can it be?" He huffed out a breath while pouting cutely. Marcus wanted to kiss those perfect lips and suck on them for, like, a month. "What else? Oh yes, painkillers, a first aid guide, latex gloves, hydrocortisone, antihistamines, an epipen—"

"Where'd you get that?"

"I'm allergic to mold." Sam gave him an odd look. "I was under the impression Simon told you all about me and then some. He didn't tell you that?"

Marcus shrugged. "Nope. Must've missed it. Good to know, though." Then he puzzled over their experiences. "That island temple was really old and in ruins. There had to be mold. How come that didn't affect you?"

Sam opened his mouth, but nothing came out immediately. Then he shrugged. "Don't know. Alien mold not like Earth mold?"

"You asking me or telling me?"

"Shut up. In any case, the epipen's there if we need it. Anaphylactic shock is nothing to sneer about." Marcus raised his hands in a surrendering gesture, and Sam smiled. "There's also some medical charcoal and ipecac if we're, like, poisoned or something and we need to vomit."

"You gave pretty good advice back on the island," Marcus reminded him, reminiscing about the poison berries. "The skin irritation test, or whatever."

Sam nodded. "Yes, that works. We've established as much. Hmm, what else?" With a cocked head, he went over the list again.

"You didn't forget the essentials, did you?" In answer to Marcus's question, Sam gave him a baffled look. Marcus grinned. "Lube and condoms? Lots of them?"

Sam blushed from head to toe, going beet-red. He ducked his head but nodded quietly. Marcus smiled. So they were well stocked after all.

Strange alien planet or not, they were going to have anal sex, and any other kind of sex, whenever they damn well pleased.

Then Marcus hesitated. "You, uh... should we... bring some weapons with us?"

Sam's gaze snapped up in an instant. "What? Please tell me I misheard just now."

Marcus coughed to clear his throat. "I'm mostly worried about a whole new batch of dangerous animals we might encounter...."

"I get your concern." Sam's lips thinned, but his jaw trembled too, so he clearly was of two minds. "I... I realize we'll need protection. How about, like, pepper spray, tear gas, Tasers, or something? Nonlethal weapons. I mean, what's the likelihood we'll come across another planet or moon where the animals are some kind of bioelectric supervillains?"

Marcus smiled. "Fair enough. Taser it is. Dad has one fully charged for emergencies." Then he grew serious. "You're really antigun. Or are you just anti-NRA?"

Sam growled, baring his teeth, righteous fury flashing in his eyes. "What? Haven't we seen enough fucking school shootings already? Those NRA enthusiasts are psychos anyway. They put their points of view above the lives of innocent kids. That's just all kinds of wrong. The right to bear arms was written in a different time and no longer applies. I bet those guys don't give a flying fuck about all those dead kids. They forget their names and faces on purpose. As long as their rights exist, they don't care who dies because of them. Bunch of selfish, violent assholes."

Marcus smiled, liking this strong side of his boyfriend's character. "Gee, tell me how you really feel."

Sam's jaw dropped. "What? You disagree?"

Marcus shook his head. "Not at all. I'm on board. I admire your zeal, your passionate conviction. Placing a human life over your constitutional right to bear arms is admirable."

Sam grunted. "If even one person needlessly dies because of your rights, then your rights are wrong."

Marcus raised his eyebrows to his hairline in awe. He loved this ferocious aspect of his beautiful boy. "Well said. Apt."

Sam smiled shortly, but Marcus sensed the sorrow in him over seeing too much death in his young life, same as most kids in America. Then Sam took a deep breath. "Okay, I think we're all packed." Sam sounded pleased with himself and his mood had lifted.

"Um, any room in there for our little guest?" Marcus asked, studying the two stuffed-to-capacity backpacks with a doubtful eye. They already had a lot to carry between the two of them, and the barkzie was a living being, so they couldn't simply shove it anywhere.

"Oh." Sam's brow cleared as he glanced at the small wooden creature that seemed to like close proximity with the potted plant, its little feet digging into the dirt. Gosh, but the thing was super-fucking-cute. Marcus almost aww'ed out loud, quite out of character for him.

"What's it doing there?" Marcus leaned closer to inspect the barkzie, which immediately turned toward him and... waved? "D-did you... did you see that?"

"Yes. It's been waving at me too." Sam came next to him. "It makes the oddest sound at night. A kind of humming. And you wanna know what's really weird? I think the flower loves it. It's bigger and more... well, everything after the barkzie started sharing its pot with it."

Marcus shook his head in bafflement, chuckling. "Wow. An alien gardener of sorts. Man, it's so cute."

"You think that's cute? Watch this." Sam scratched softly on the barkzie's belly where the bark appeared to be the softest. "It likes belly scratches."

Marcus laughed, his worldview once again tilted in Sam's company. "Just when I'm sure I've seen it all. Let me try."

With his fingertip, Marcus gently rubbed the barkzie's front. The tiny creature's eyes closed and it... purred, a soothing small sound that reverberated through Marcus's awareness. And he kept getting tiny static shocks, so mild they tickled more than anything.

"Amazing. Fucking amazing. I almost wanna keep it."

Sam kissed him on the cheek. "I hear you. But we can't."

Marcus frowned. "You think the heavier gravity's hurting him?"

"At the moment? Hard to say. Long-term, sure." Sam sounded hesitant, but Marcus had good cause to believe him. And neither of them wanted to harm the barkzie. Not just because it was so adorable, but because it was a new life-form that deserved a peaceful existence on its native soil.

"Okay, bae. Let's get him home—and us on an adventure."

EVADING THEIR families had been an exercise in futility over the past two weeks. Now they had freedom again, so they took advantage and made their way to the woods. The sun had set, and night had fallen. Soft snowflakes came down from the dark skies slow and steady, a hushed white blanket that made everything dreamlike and magical.

Marcus felt guilty for betraying his parents' trust in him so soon after his last stunt, but if all went well, he and Sam wouldn't be out there for more than a few days, just over the weekend. Nothing would go wrong. This time they were prepared for every conceivable contingency.

The tree stump hiding the hatch was still in place, though covered in snow. Sam wiped the top clean with his mittens and revealed the stub. The hologram stuttered briefly and then disappeared, revealing the rusted brown metal hatch.

"Why did it go away?" Sam asked, shoving the last pieces of snow and ice aside.

"Maybe the system recognized us because we've been here before?" Marcus shrugged. "Let's just get down there before someone comes along or it starts to snow again."

As Marcus's voice faded into the night, the hatch slid open, a grating sound piercing the darkness. Taking a quick, wary look around, Marcus saw no one. Then again, this path through the woods was deserted a lot of the time since it only went to certain houses and mostly school kids used it.

Marcus dropped down first, wiggling through the hatch. The familiar floor hadn't gone anywhere. Sam handed him the backpacks, one at a time, and then followed Marcus's lead. Above them, the hatch closed with a jarring grind. Then the underground was quiet once again.

By then they knew the way, and soon they stood in the rotund chamber that resembled the inside of a donut. Familiar flickering lights, shimmering metal walls, and an upright metal chair were all still in place. None of the blue lights over the oval doorways were lit, indicating none of the portals were active. Their pitch-black state attested to as much.

"You should sit this time." Marcus waved in the general direction of the metallic chair. "You'll need to know alien languages same as me if we mean to make sense of the worlds we visit, just in case they were... or *are* inhabited."

Sam agreed with a curt nod. He took off his winter coat, exposed his arms, and with a nervous look sat down. A blue beam of light landed on him from the round lamp above. Then Sam let out a yelp and whisked his hand up from the armrest.

"Jesus, that hurt." He rubbed on the spot where the machine had injected him, but the circular wound had already closed, leaving nothing but a tiny speck of blood that quickly dried. "It doesn't sting anymore. I'm fine."

Marcus smiled in relief. "Okay, bae. Last time I chose a place. It's your turn. After we return the barkzie, of course."

"Yes." Sam remained sitting, seemingly waiting for the system to come online.

With great care, Marcus brought the tiny tree-like creature out of his breast pocket where he'd made sure it was safe and warm. "Hi, baby barkzie. You're going home." He caressed the belly, and a soft chirp and a purr followed. "Gosh, but I'm actually gonna miss you."

From his position, Sam giggled. "You're such a big softie behind that cool exterior."

Marcus had no argument, not when the barkzie's innocent eyes gazed into his, that sweet smile unchanging. Whatever this alien being was, it was unique and alive. The universe wasn't empty. For some reason, despite their trials and tribulations with hostile animals, it lifted Marcus's spirits, the knowledge they weren't all alone in boundless space and time.

The round light above the chair brightened, the blue glow mixing with pure, brilliant white. Behind the walls a low hum rose steadily. It was soon replaced by the drum of machines grinding and working out of sight, the ground beneath their feet shaking ever so slightly.

A sharp flash of light brought to life the tilted, panoramic holographic screen, sparkling bluish like the lights, and the IDX hologram they'd seen in the chamber before their last departure appeared.

An image burst into being on the monitor, the picture vivid and alive, motion detectable in plants and grass, as if the images were live videos. The familiar shape of a tropical island with a ruined temple on top and a green-ringed gas giant behind it came up. Marcus saw the text appear: Isle of Suryan.

"Can you read that?"

Sam's sigh and smile spoke volumes. "Yes. Yes, I can. Isle of Suryan."

"Guess the shots we got work. The new shot on you *and* the old in me." He pointed at the lush green-blue image. "Press your hand on it. The portal should open then. Just resist the call to walk through. Only the barkzie goes, got it?"

Sam nodded, swallowing, his skin pale under the bleak lighting. His hand trembled as he laid it against the hologram. The screen flashed intently. A blue lamp lit up above the portal they had used.

"Good work." Marcus raised the tiny creature on his palm closer to Sam. "Say goodbye to our first interplanetary visitor on Earth. At least the first we brought here. Unintentionally."

Sam tickled the barkzie's belly, causing it to chirp and purr. "Bye, little one. Be safe."

Marcus walked over to the oval opening, refusing to stare into the swirling abyss with the knowledge he might not be able to ward off temptation again. He put the barkzie on the floor and gently urged it to move through the doorway with a gentle shove to its behind.

The scent of earth came off the creature, reminding Marcus of sunshine in gardens and wet soil in warm greenhouses. Its bark grazed against his fingertips, and he wondered with longing if he'd ever feel that sensation again.

The barkzie purred and waved, then hurried across the threshold on its tiny feet—and the sound and smells vanished in an instant. Marcus swallowed down an emotional lump in his throat, swiped his wet eyes with his hand, and stood slowly.

The portal's black surface shimmered briefly. Then the blue light above diminished till it was extinguished entirely. Through the oval alcove Marcus saw only a rugged rock face, proving that the portal was turned off.

"Guess it's just us now," he said ruefully, already missing those beautiful amber eyes and that smile so mysterious it exceeded Mona Lisa's.

Sam nodded with that understanding he often displayed and gave Marcus a come-hither chin lift. "Where should we go?"

Marcus came to stand behind Sam and the chair and leaned over his shoulder to see better. "At the risk of sounding like Goldilocks, no place too hot or too cold."

Sam snickered. "Cool. Just right it is, then."

Images ran in an endless stream, amazing places too fantastical for Marcus to believe could be real—if he hadn't seen one of them with his own eyes and touched it with his own hands. They awakened his curiosity and sense of adventure.

Distant mountain ranges with binary or trinary suns above; coral clouds hanging over peculiar azure oceans coruscating like a sea of stars;

rains of amber flower petals over giant golden flowers overshadowing abodes resembling gourds and onions; colossal bones of long-dead beasts covered in moss and vines arching high over rivers and valleys; remnants of monstrous machines and clockwork engines buried under millennia of rocks and waste; familiar, soothing otherworldly landscapes—with crumbling pale moons high above; strange metallic gas giants with complex twinkling space stations and uncanny spaceships orbiting them like beacons of civilization; glass spirals and metal towers rising high toward silvery clouds, standing in advanced alien cities or amid swarms of butterflies; large crystal caverns shining in all the colors of the rainbow; ancient cities growing on giant seashells on vermilion seas; planets with large floating transparent bubbles where bewildering flora and fauna grew independently; worlds with tiny sandy islands wafting about with the winds; scorched red-and-black lava fields dotted with massive stone henges of worship; thick woods where roots and branches grew like impenetrable mazes both above and below; high-tech structures that spiraled upward toward the heavens like the double helix; strong stone pillars rising from the earth, from a desert—with gray cubes twirling above them around their own axes; lakes on which grew frozen trees; and so on. Visions of incredible places he longed to see firsthand.

"So many choices," Marcus whispered in awe. All the stupendous options were endless and mindboggling. Marcus was so excited about the possibilities his heart nearly beat out of his chest. This was going to be awesome.

Then he heard Sam draw in a breath. "There."

Marcus stared at the holoscreen with anticipation.

The vivid image depicted a lush green valley tucked away between snow-topped hills. A winding river flowed across the steppe where tall grass swayed in the wind. The sight spoke of serenity, a flourishing undiscovered country that hinted of adventure and exploration.

By a lazy bend in the river stood an obelisk, its surface as white as the clouds, with a strange red stone shining in the center. A sign of civilization?

"Valley of Keidash," Marcus read from the screen. "Beautiful. Why that one?"

Sam smiled dreamily, never taking his eyes off the inviting image. "It seems familiar, like a wilderness on Earth, but also new and mysterious, like a puzzle to solve."

Marcus chuckled. "You excel at puzzle solving."

"And you at problem-solving. What a pair we make."

Marcus's smile faded as he grew serious. "Listen, Sam…. Are you sure you really want to do this?" Sam gave him a bewildered look, a frown on his brow. "Don't get offended or anything but you're seventeen. For two more days at least. The question is, I suppose, if you're… heck, if either of us is old enough to make an informed decision about traveling to another world—"

"No, that's not what this is about." Sam pleaded with his eyes. "This isn't about age. This is about intelligence, analytical skills, resourcefulness, street smarts, stuff like that. Plus drive, motivation, curiosity, passion. When it comes to all those… I'm good. I know myself, and recently I've learned more about myself. I'm pretty good in unknown situations, as are you. I've got this. So… I'm good. Marcus? I'm going. I'd rather go with you than without you."

"You'd do that?" Marcus's mood and heart both sank.

But his spirits were soon lifted as Sam smiled shyly and shook his head. "No. I want to be with you, Marcus. In every way, on Earth and… wherever." His expression shifted to sadness. "Don't you want to see what else is out there? I thought you—"

"I do." Marcus took Sam's hand in his. "I guess I was just… playing devil's advocate. I still wanna do this—and with you." He nodded toward the shimmering screen. "So… ready?"

Sam grinned, practically bouncing on his seat. "I wasn't born ready, but I am now."

He pressed his palm over the live feed from an alien world. A hum filled the room, a flash briefly blinded them, and then a blue lamp lit up over a different portal.

A vortex, black as coal, spun in the oval opening. Where it lead… a mystery.

Marcus took Sam's hand in his. Together, side by side, they stepped into a new world.

EPILOGUE

TEMPORARY BLINDNESS and brief nauseating dizziness swept over them. Whatever it was they walked through played havoc on their senses, especially their equilibrium.

They stepped onto the other side. A familiar circular chamber gleamed metallic, polished, and clean, not a creeping vine or pile of dry leaves in sight. A functional control chair stood in place in the center of the room, with a lit bluish-white lamp above it as proof that this chamber had power.

"Oh, thank goodness." Sam blew out a breath, relieved that they wouldn't need to work out any kinks in the system during this trip.

"Amen, brother." Marcus's grin widened. "I'm so proud of you, my brave bae."

Sam's heart jumped at the compliment, spoken freely with love.

"You too." Sam took a deep, shaky breath and swallowed hard.

Wide, round double doors opened as they approached, sliding without a sound. Metal stairs appeared before them. Tiny white lanterns lit up as they moved along. A new set of oval doors parted, and without hesitation they walked up ahead. A hologram of a rock face blocked the view of the closing double doors, hiding the entrance to the underground chamber.

A landscape both Sam and Marcus recognized, thanks to the computer in the portal chamber, revealed itself.

Rugged gray hills rose around them, with snowy tops high enough to reach the puffy white clouds. The winds carried the taste of dirt and rocks to them, dry and familiar. They could easily have been at home. Far below them a verdant valley unfolded, grass-covered plains spreading farther than the eye could see, a blue river flowing leisurely through the lowlands. Sweet scents from the steppes floated all around like a natural perfume, hinting at unseen beauty.

"We're really here," Marcus whispered, his gaze aimed at the distant white obelisk.

Sam had no words. He was too stunned to speak. The view was breathtaking.

And beyond the valley, on the far horizon… giant trees were walking.

SUSAN LAINE, an award-winning, multipublished author of LGBTQ erotic romance and a Finnish native, was raised by the best mother in the world, who told her daughter time and again that she could be whatever she wanted to be. The spark for serious writing and publishing kindled when Susan discovered the gay erotic romance genre. One of her books, *Monsters Under the Bed*, won the 2014 Rainbow Award for Best Gay Paranormal Romance.

Anthropology is Susan's formal education, but she has set her long-term sights on becoming a full-time writer. Susan enjoys hanging out with her sister, two nieces, and friends in movie theaters, bookstores, and parks. Her favorite pastimes include pop music, action flicks, and doing the dishes, while a few of her dislikes are sweating hot summer days, tobacco smoke, and purposeful prejudice.

Website: www.susan-laine-author.fi
E-mail: susan.laine@hotmail.com

FLUSHED

SUSAN LAINE

To prove to his annoying older brother that he's a man, well-to-do sculptor Rupert Pemberton tries to repair his broken toilet. But he has no knack for practical tools and no know-how. After a flood of biblical proportions, he has no choice but to call for help.

A gorgeous hunk of a plumber named Paul Cooper shows up at Rupert's doorstep with a ready toolbox and a sexy smile. With Paul at his side, Rupert realizes he wants more than a quick fix. After a couple of cozy dates and a few bouts of steamy sex, Rupert wonders how he can keep Paul around for good.

www.dreamspinnerpress.com

after the romance novel

Susan Laine

A Before… and After Story

Romance novels always end with a happy ever after. Right?

Evan and Adam are best friends, but they don't know everything about each other. For one thing, Adam doesn't know Evan writes and publishes gay romance novels until he discovers one while snooping on Evan's laptop.

This revelation changes their relationship in ways neither could've imagined. Adam's reaction to reading Evan's stories is not what he expected, nor is the new way he's looking at his lifelong pal. After all, Adam is straight, or so he's always thought, and that is what Evan believes about Adam as well.

When Evan admits he might be bisexual, Adam suggests he try dating girls to find out for sure, but when Evan follows his advice, Adam is caught off guard by his feelings of jealousy. And when the date proves Evan isn't bisexual, but gay, Evan's request that Adam find him a guy might be the last straw.

How can Adam admit he wants that guy to be him? His epiphany will either end their relationship—or change it into something wonderful in their very own friends-to-lovers romance.

www.dreamspinnerpress.com

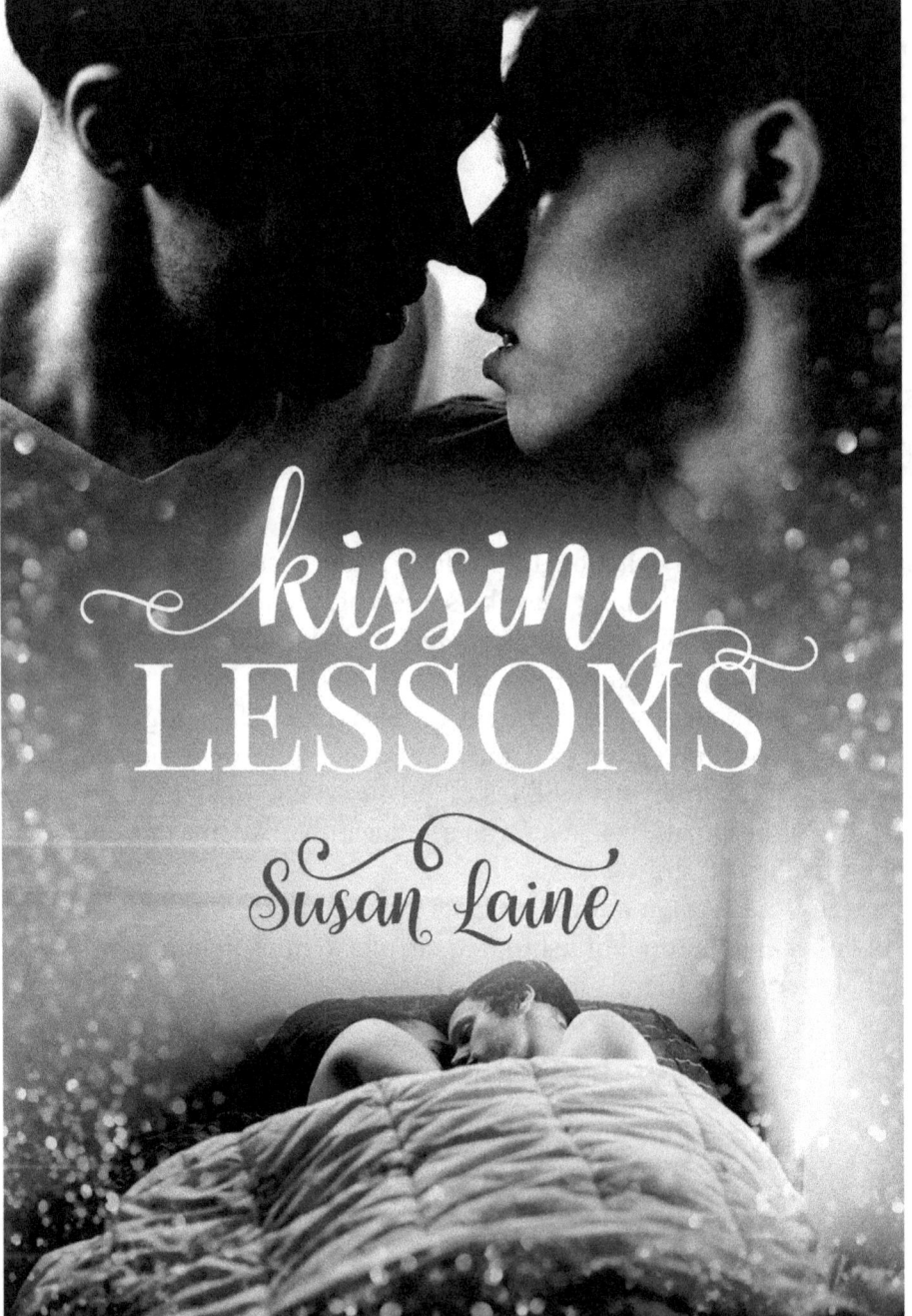

kissing
LESSONS

Susan Laine

A Before… and After Story

A kiss is just a kiss. It doesn't have to mean anything. Does it?

At seventeen, Merry's never been kissed. Since he doesn't want to disappoint his prom date, he asks his more experienced best friend, Boone, for some pointers. Surprisingly, Boone agrees to give him a hands-on lesson.

But they have no idea what they're getting into.

They explore hundreds of ways to make out, but somehow it isn't enough. A week later, they're back together for another session. This time things go further than either of them planned, and their relationship becomes awkward and uncomfortable.

Have they learned enough to salvage their friendship *and* help it evolve? Their lessons have come to an end. They can either part ways forever… or share a true love's kiss.

www.dreamspinnerpress.com

SUSAN LAINE

SPARKS & DROPS

The Wheel Mysteries: Book One

Magic is in the air when Gus Goodwin, a pagan shopkeeper and owner of the Four Corners' occult shop, meets a Niall Valentine, a mysterious PI investigating the disappearance of a local witch named Joy. What starts out as harmless flirting and information gathering soon turns into a partnership, with both men determined to solve the case.

Then bodies begin to pile up. Someone is using fire and water to kill witches associated with Joy, and it is up to Niall and Gus to find out what's going on. But when their friendship blossoms into something else, the unknown dangers looming ahead become even more frightening. If they can't solve the murders soon, they're going to get themselves killed.

www.dreamspinnerpress.com

SUSAN LAINE

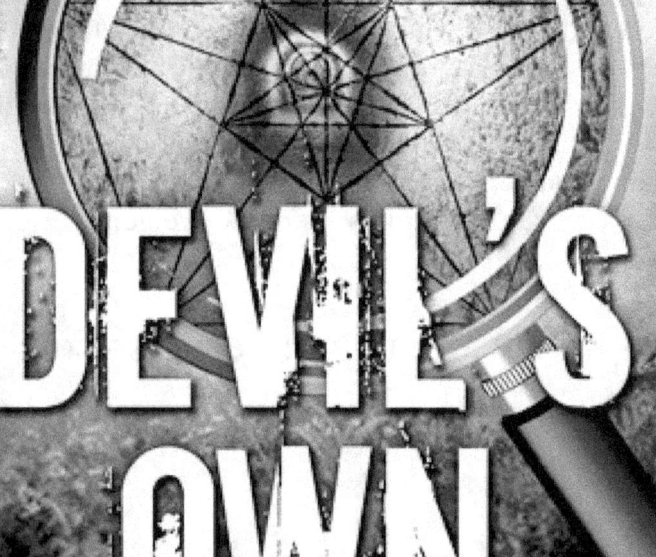

DEVIL'S OWN

Sequel to *Sparks & Drops*
The Wheel Mysteries: Book Two

A month and a half into their relationship, PI Niall Valentine and his occult shopkeeper boyfriend, Gus Goodwin, are hoping for a little time alone, but they're thrown into another murder mystery.

Niall's client, Angelina Talbot, is certain her new husband attempted to kill her, ambushing her in their bedroom, half-naked and covered in blood. Scared out of her mind, Angelina hit him with a lamp and ran away. Florian Talbot lies dead in the bedroom, his head smashed in with a lamp—but the door is locked from the inside. Is Angelina truly an unwitting murderer, or are more sinister forces at play?

With a family of eccentrics, borderline criminals, and Satanists, the real killer could be any number of people wandering the mansion that night under the cover of darkness. The entire Talbot clan thrives in secrecy. Still unfulfilled and utterly perplexed, Niall and Gus are tasked with shedding some much-needed light on the shadowy case.

www.dreamspinnerpress.com

www.ingramcontent.com/pod-product-compliance
Lightning Source LLC
Chambersburg PA
CBHW070121260626
47160CB00004B/1573